HOUSE
OF THE
WOLF

HOUSE
OF THE
WOLF

Ezzat El Kamhawi

Translated by
Nancy Roberts

The American University in Cairo Press
Cairo   New York

First published in 2013 by
The American University in Cairo Press
113 Sharia Kasr el Aini, Cairo, Egypt
420 Fifth Avenue, New York, NY 10018
www.aucpress.com

Exclusive distribution outside Egypt and North America by I.B.Tauris & Co Ltd., 6 Salem Road, London, W2 4BU

Dar el Kutub No. 1843/13
ISBN 978 977 416 620 4

Dar el Kutub Cataloging-in-Publication Data

El Kamhawi, Ezzat.
        House of the Wolf / Ezzat El Kamhawi; translated by Nancy Roberts.—Cairo:
The American University in Cairo Press, 2013
        p.   cm.
        ISBN 978 977 416 620 4
        1.   English fiction
        2.   Title
        823

1 2 3 4 5   17 16 15 14 13

Designed by Fatiha Bouzidi
Printed in Egypt

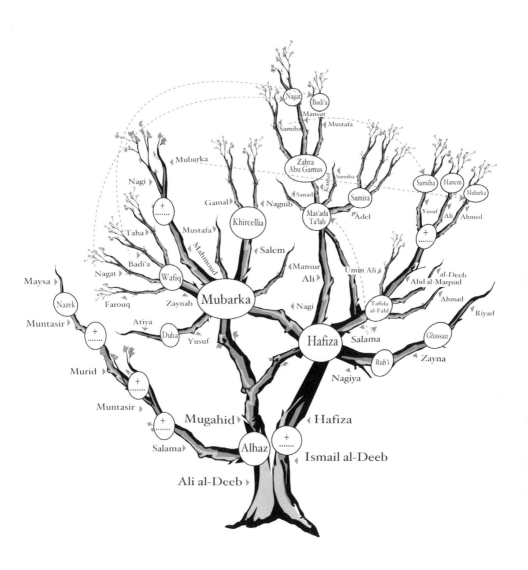

The al-Deeb Family Tree

Mubarka al-Fouli, who lived to see her grandchildren talking to friends from parts of the globe they'd never seen, started asking them to send messages to God.

"A little note, just to remind Him of me," she said to the young boy seated in front of the computer who, with serious mien, prepared a new page and asked her to dictate the note. She began composing a flowery preamble, and the writer of the complaint followed along with her until he burst out laughing over her difficulty in choosing the words. He stopped typing and asked mischievously why she was in such a hurry to die.

"For starters, it's not nice. It's really not nice at all," she replied.

She was afraid of seeming disrespectful by having lived to such a ripe old age, and she spoke with the anguish of someone trying to relieve herself of the discomfort of being found in an unseemly situation through no choice of her own. Feeling as though she'd overstepped her bounds, she softened her tone:

"It's just a gentle reprimand. I mean, He has an excuse. He'll think, who is this, after all?"

They laughed, since they knew she would be willing to withdraw her complaint the minute anybody reminded her of Muntasir, whose scent wafted powerfully across her nostrils, numbing her and causing her to think twice about the whole idea of complaining or reproaching death.

"His manly smell," she replied tersely when she was asked what it was that had kept a man alive all those years in an otherwise failing memory. She didn't know how to describe the way Muntasir's scent had surrounded her one day during a summer from hell. It was the summer that had witnessed the outbreak of fires on the threshing floors, the likes of which al-Ish had never seen before.

The villagers had worn themselves out speculating over who might be setting the fires, which broke out at the same time every day. They'd jailed a crazy man they suspected of trying to get even with them because their children had thrown bricks at him. But the fires didn't stop. Everyone who had suffered damages from the fires started combing their memories in search of old enmities that might have been reawakened for any reason. Some of them sought assistance from elderly folks in neighboring villages, and the trade in memory-enhancing potions was booming.

Since stirring up the past is like digging around in a pile of dung, every one of them found at least one feud in his or her family history. Some of them had led to nothing more than an argument, mowing down somebody's crop, or poisoning some livestock. Some had left people dead on both sides and the case had ended in a settlement, while others had left someone dead on one side only, in which case the person's spirit might have gathered itself together in pursuit of forgotten vengeance and come back through these mysterious conflagrations. After all, they only broke out after people had retreated to their houses when the day was at its hottest, leaving the fields and threshing floors to wandering spirits.

The fires in the wheat would have ignited a war among the families had it not been for the efforts of a group of young men. They were dedicated to restoring the state of peace the village had enjoyed for centuries thanks to the complete equality established by its founders. They set up watches around the threshing floors in hopes of catching the arsonist. However, the guards saw the straw catching fire all by itself at the same time every day: at high noon, when the sun was directly overhead and the temperature was peaking.

This discovery prompted them to organize firefighting teams. Two young men would be stationed beside each threshing floor, ready to announce when the fire started, while the others were divided into groups prepared to put it out. A group was also stationed at the edge of the large irrigation canal, where they would fill jars for the women and girls, who had formed a long line that was ready to take off in whichever direction the call for help came from.

The earth's glow was visible beneath Mubarka's bare feet as she balanced the earthenware water jug on her head, and it was such a sweltering day, she could almost hear steam rising from the path as she listened to Muntasir al-Deeb's hurried, restive steps behind her. He greeted her in a tremulous voice, then moved three steps ahead of her. He was wearing a white tunic that came down to his thighs. She felt the tingle of the amorous glances coming from eyes in the back of his head as he walked uncertainly in front of her. He nearly stumbled, then righted himself again, deliberately demonstrating his ability to endure the earth's fiery lashes.

Some time earlier Muntasir had begun paying frequent visits to his paternal aunt Nabiha at the far end of the neighborhood, without daring to speak to Mubarka, the mysterious girl who rarely said a word. However, he was sure she'd begun to notice him. She would wait for him with the door ajar. When he glimpsed her, his steps would falter and he would turn in her direction, on his lips the shadow of a hesitant smile. When he didn't see her shadow, he would make a point of raising his voice in song or calling out to some imaginary person as his eyes penetrated the narrow interstices between her window's wooden slats, and he would see her there, pressing her face against the trembling shutter.

Then at last he dared. That brief meeting of the eyes and the tremulous, "How are you, Mubarka?" had the effect of magic on her body. She made no reply. But the sweetness of the raw manliness in his voice went straight through her, flooding her with a delectable tremor that resembled the ache of a fever. She broke into a cold sweat that mingled with the water trickling out of the

3

jug. It came rolling down over her face, neck, and chest, then made its way between two tomato-like protuberances before reaching her batiste waistband, which absorbed it before it got to the fuzz in her navel.

After the discovery of the heat's conspiracy to set the threshing floors on fire, the daylight hours were devoted to firefighting, and the nights to threshing the grain. The work took place in an atmosphere of solidarity the likes of which the village hadn't witnessed since the generation of its founders, who had drained the swamp, then joined hands to build houses and prepare the land for sowing. They'd been so taken up with their tasks at first that they hadn't even found time to choose a name for their harmonious assemblage. Then, after years of stork attacks on the village, they decided to name it al-Ish—the Nest. It was as though the name was a protective incantation that would bring an end to the stork raids that had been launched in revenge for the thousands of young birds lost and eggs destroyed when they removed the swamp's reeds and cut down its small trees.

The solidarity generated by their confrontation with the sun buried the unwanted memories that had been unearthed during the days of suspicion, and al-Ish became like one big happy family. It no longer surprised anyone to see a man, young or old, in some neighborhood other than his own. They would collapse from exhaustion, then eat and sleep in the first house they came to. Consequently, Muntasir no longer had to put up a pretense of going to visit his aunt in order to see Mubarka. However, he stopped approaching her.

So, although peace now reigned in al-Ish, Mubarka had lost her inner peace. She wasn't herself any more, and she began feeling timid and fearful of her father because of the ruin that seemed to befall everything she laid her hands on.

"Maybe you grabbed a cat's tail!" he would shout at in her in consternation. Little did he know that she herself was the cat, and that someone had set her tail on fire, then abandoned her. She began to spend her days distracted. She would hover near the door, waiting for him to come, and invent reasons to go out so that she could see him. When she got into bed at night she would lie there with her eyes wide open, listening to the crackling of her limbs like a handful of popcorn exploding over the fire before it grows still in the form of delicate balls of fluff. She'd almost begun to believe she'd been afflicted by some sort of madness that frightened men away. She waited from one afternoon to the next to get close to him, and every time he walked awkwardly past her, their eyes met. Then at last he got up his nerve again.

"Behind your house after supper."

He said it less uneasily than he had the first time, but in such a low voice that she wasn't sure whether he'd really spoken or whether she was imagining things. And if he had spoken, she wondered if he had been speaking to her. She found no reassurance in recalling his words, whose undulations would steadily die away until they were transformed in her head into a mere puff of air that was like a moan or a sigh. Even so, she went out behind the house at the time he'd specified and found him there.

He was trembling, and she also began shuddering violently, though they knew there was no one in the houses at that hour but elderly folks with failing eyesight, and young children who didn't understand a thing.

As he drew her into his arms, each of them could hear the other's heart pounding wildly like a drum. His fragrance made her dizzy. It wasn't pleasant or unpleasant. It was simply the fragrance of a man who was squeezing her, causing her skin to contract and expand in a delicious shudder.

She felt his thing convulsing wildly in her navel. For a few moments she lost consciousness. Then she screamed as she loosed herself from his grip and went running back into the house. Meanwhile, he stood there frozen in place until the wet feeling between his thighs brought him back again to the fear that had preceded the shudder of pleasure. He thrust his hand into the opening of his gilbab, running his fingers over the viscous liquid and making sure it wouldn't hinder him from making it to one of the threshing floors, if not to take part in the work, then at least to pass the time among people, since no house could have contained what he was feeling that night.

Mubarka didn't sleep that night either. She was afraid someone might have seen them. But she was also happy.

She began recalling what had happened over and over again, distilling the fragrance from the warmth of the frenzied breathing, running her hands over her breasts and rubbing the nipples that stood erect beneath her touches, trying to recover the way it had felt when his powerful hands pinched her, and feeling her womb throb with desire amid the racing of her heart.

Now that her unnamed longings had taken on a feel and a smell, she carried on with her life, both unsettled and happy. Prior to this she'd sensed the changes happening in her body and the pains associated with her budding breasts. She was enveloped by a nebulous sense of enjoyment, the way a shaded plant intuits the direction of the sun. And as the plant continues its frenzied upward movement, she palpated herself in search of the pleasure that lay concealed in a body no man had approached, not because she was ugly, but because her beauty was so disquieting.

Muntasir wasn't the first to have noticed her. However, he was the first to have gotten up the nerve to do anything about it. She'd seen passion in young men's looks, but the moment their eyes met hers they would freeze, looking like dead men who had no one to close their eyes for them. She didn't know whether what she felt toward Muntasir was love, or gratitude and admiration for his audacity. She began doing her chores fretfully, scurrying to the window when she heard his voice and nearly inviting him in, then drowning in her fear and leaving the window in a panic. As for him, he kept making the rounds of her house with or without reason. He would find any excuse he could to head for his aunt's house, but sometimes he would turn around in front of his aunt's door because he didn't have anything to say to her. Glimpsing Mubarka on the roof, or in the yard feeding her birds, he would mumble a new place and time to meet. Then she would spend the day laying plans to go out. When she got tired, she would decide she wasn't going and feel a kind of sad relief. Before long, however, she would go back on her decision. And so it went, hundreds of times a day, until at last she found herself in his arms at the agreed-upon time. As she took in his scent and he licked her, they would roll around on a hay-covered threshing floor whose golden straws clung to their bodies, or atop a pile of wheat that would pull them under, forcing them to hold on to each other for dear life until they struggled to the surface again.

As their encounters continued, she stopped falling into the deathlike swoon that had come over her in the beginning whenever Muntasir placed his hand under her ear. Her fingernails found their way to his skin and she learned how to move and caress the various parts of his body as she sniffed his armpits, and her insides trembled as he massaged the place between her thighs. After their frenzy had abated, he would whisper to her about their prospective wedding night, and when he got too graphic in his description of the encounter, she would bop him on the chest. He would tell her about their future house and how many children they would have. And so went his solo rantings every time they met.

She didn't lack the ability to speak. However, after having lived for so long in silence with her father, she didn't risk the use of words. She didn't hate her father, but saw no need to converse with him and had nothing to converse with him about. As for Muntasir, he saw nothing strange about her silence. On the contrary, in it he found a game of suspense that piqued his curiosity and prompted him to go on talking in hopes of hearing a declaration of love, although he never managed to get her to utter more than one or two words without any particular meaning. As a matter of fact, he didn't have any urgent need to hear the word "love," since he figured that the stripes her fingernails had left on his chest and back were her special way of talking.

By the time the summer of the fires was over, Muntasir had asked his uncle to request Mubarka's hand in marriage on his behalf.

"That crazy girl, Badr al-Fouli's daughter? Everybody in al-Ish says she's possessed!" retorted Mugahid al-Deeb, surprised that his foster son would ask for the hand of this girl in particular. He figured Muntasir just sympathized with her because she was an orphan like him.

"She's not crazy, and she's not possessed," Muntasir declared, insistent on his request.

So, not having any other reason to refuse, Mugahid broached the subject with Badr after the final evening prayer.

"I'd like to come by for a cup of tea," he said.

Badr welcomed the suggestion, and when he asked Mubarka to get ready to receive a visitor, her face lit up and she energetically set about polishing the copper teapot and glasses with ashes and straw. After all, they would be the first sign of the kind of housewife she promised to be. After making certain that the tea service was clean, she placed the utensils on the red copper tray in front of the stove in the sitting room. Then she began sweeping the house and court-yard and sprinkling them with water.

After the final evening prayer, her father took his place in front of the stove and Mubarka ascended the mud staircase that led to the roof of the house. Then she hid at the bend in the staircase in such a way that she could see whoever came in without being seen. When she heard the knock on the door and her father's voice wel-coming the person who had arrived, she peeked down and found that it was Mugahid al-Deeb.

"O God, send down blessings on the Prophet," he said, as if to apologize for the look he had planted on her body. As for her, she felt such a mixture of excitement and embarrassment that she jumped down from where she stood and disappeared hurriedly into the farthest room of the house.

After her breathing had quieted, she crept closer, and gluing her ear to the door of the sitting room, stood there listening intently.

"My goodness! We'd even send her along as a maid if you asked! After all, could we find anybody better than you?" said her father.

"We'll proceed with God's blessing, then," Mugahid replied. "Let's recite the Fatiha."

The agreement didn't bring her the joy she had expected. In fact, it stabbed her like a knife. And what she had sensed vaguely in her heart, her father confirmed after the guest was gone.

"Mugahid asked for your hand, and I agreed," her father said. She didn't reply. Her features registered no feelings of any sort. Badr realized that his daughter no longer just resembled her mother in looks; she also resembled her in her ability to close the windows to her spirit so tightly that he couldn't see anything of her. And she realized how cruel it was to be a bride without a mother. All night long she lay staring up at the baking room's tar-daubed wooden rafters. As she lay there her ears rang with the last thing her father had said: "Could we find anybody better than you?"

Mugahid told Muntasir he'd spoken clearly, but that her father, who had indicated it would be an honor to be related to him by marriage, had insisted on marrying her to him personally. This was because his daughter was young and an orphan and needed a man to protect her, not somebody who was just a child like her.

Badr hadn't said this, of course, since he knew that Mugahid was a burden to his wife and children and that he couldn't have protected a chicken. At the same time, he hadn't known that Mugahid was requesting her hand on behalf of his nephew, and he knew the bewitchment that had befallen his daughter, whose suitors had been late in coming around, confident that Mugahid wouldn't be able to harm her no matter how irresponsible he happened to be. What mattered was that he was the head of his family and the person who controlled them, and that Mubarka would derive her status from his.

Muntasir swore to get revenge. He left the farmhouse he'd grown up in as though he were Mugahid's eldest son, and went to stay with his aunt Nabiha. Hafiza, Mugahid's wife and paternal cousin, was no less distressed.

"He'll see," Muntasir fumed.

Swearing to avenge both himself and his uncle's wife Hafiza, to whom he referred affectionately as "sister," Muntasir asked for his share of the land so that he could settle down on his own. Mugahid's response was to tell him that before he died, his grandfather had registered all the land in his name as if he'd bought it from him. Then, as if that weren't enough, he began raking Muntasir over the coals, saying he'd done more for him than he had for his own sons since the time he took him in, and that he expected Muntasir to revere him as a father.

The attempts at mediation made by the people Muntasir sought out for help failed to persuade Mugahid to go back on his decision, and all his aunt Nabiha did was keep Muntasir at her house so as to keep the two men away from each other. She advised him not to lose his uncle over the matter. After all, she said, even if Mugahid was the one who had asked for her hand, her father had agreed, and it wouldn't be proper for him to go after a girl who was engaged to his uncle. It would be better for him to look for somebody other than that bewitched girl, and not to imagine that she had something he wouldn't be able to find in some other woman.

"It's nothing but piss and poop down there," said the old woman, reducing Mubarka to her private parts with a dismissive tone that froze the tear in his eye.

"I wouldn't be Salama's son if I didn't demand what's mine," he retorted.

When, after his night out, Mugahid headed for his sister Nabiha's house shortly before dawn, Muntasir refused to go back to the farmhouse with him. He hadn't expected the slap that descended on his cheek, and he reached up and stopped Mugahid's hand before it fell on his other cheek as well. Trembling with rage, Mugahid tried to loose himself from the grip of a man he had, until that moment, considered nothing but a boy. Muntasir released him with a fling of the hand and marched outside. Mugahid grabbed him by his muffler. It tore off in his hand, so Muntasir left him half the muffler and kept on walking. His aunt Nabiha followed, wailing at the top of her lungs, and people came out on either side of the street to see what was going on. Hafiza and his cousins blocked the door to keep him from leaving, but he bade them farewell and continued on his way with nothing but the gilbab on his back and half a muffler around his neck. Not knowing where he could go, he was choked by the conflicting emotions that had paralyzed his hand and prevented him not only from returning the blow he had received from his uncle, but even from carrying out the plans he had laid, then abandoned over the course of the previous sleepless nights.

Mugahid's act of depriving Muntasir of the girl he loved wasn't his last theft from him. However, it was the cruelest. The man who upbraided him for not appreciating the fact that he had raised him since he was a child had never shown him an iota of tenderness or affection. Hafiza was the one who had fed him, covered him up on cold nights, washed his clothes, and given him baths on holidays. And it was Hafiza whose tears had fallen on his feet as she sloughed layers of dried skin off them with a stone. Her children's feet, including those of hunchbacked Nagiya, were no smoother than his. But she felt that, even though they hadn't had an attentive father, they hadn't been deprived of a mother's tender loving care the way Muntasir had. Muntasir had never known his mother; nor had he ever seen his father, the strongman who had given the family, and the entire village of al-Ish for that matter, a reason to hold their heads high.

It hadn't disturbed her when Mugahid kicked one of his own sons, as long as she could wrap her arms around Muntasir to shield him from his blows. After striking her too, Mugahid would leave the two of them in tears and not come back till nearly dawn.

By the time Muntasir was ten years old, the solidarity that had grown up between him and Hafiza had become a reciprocal thing, and the two of them began managing affairs in both the house and the fields. Before long they were joined by her eldest son Salama, who was two years younger than Muntasir, followed by Nagi and

Ali. As the years passed they managed to revive the fields and the livestock, which began flourishing again after being left to share-croppers who hadn't taken good care of them. The buffaloes got fat, started producing several times more milk than before, and had babies right and left. It became difficult to find foot room between the ducks, geese, and rabbits in the inner farmyard, while the small windows in the farmhouse walls and the earthenware jars that hung from its ceiling were filled with pairs of doves. The two young men would finish mowing the clover for the livestock, then begin helping the boys Nagi and Ali to chop up a generous amount to take to Hafiza's birds. She would slaughter some of the birds and sell enough of the rest to provide clothing for the family, since Mugahid didn't give the family a thought. He knew nothing about the household, in fact, except for the times he needed cash for opium and hashish.

He made them plant one out of their three remaining feddans in barley to feed his filly, which he was constantly bathing, decorating, and teaching to dance so that he could use her to escort brides to their new homes or take her to the mulid celebrations for racing or showing.

Mugahid wouldn't wake up until it was nearly time for the midafternoon call to prayer. Then he would go to the mosque and pray the noon and midafternoon prayers together. When he returned, the roast rooster would have to be ready, after which he would have some black tea with a joint of opium. When he heard the filly's neigh summoning him, he would saddle her and bring her out, tie her to the iron grate on the sitting-room window, come back in to put on a clean gilbab, and ride her to exercise her legs until sundown. After the final evening prayer the shisha wouldn't go out, since he spent his evenings smoking, either alone or with a group of friends. His family members considered him not to exist. They were ashamed of his way of life, which was less like that of a genuine peasant than that of a gypsy, and of the hashish parties he held with hooligans young enough to be his sons. Yet, in spite of it all, he was keen to assert his authority. He would tug on the filly's reins, turn off the village's main street where he was accustomed to training her, and head all of a sudden to the field to watch the boys as they did the work he knew nothing about. Then, without reason, he would start hurling insults at them.

"What is this? Are you a bunch of weaklings?"

He would jump off the filly's back, grab a hoe out of one of their hands, and proceed to show them how the work was supposed to be done. When they were young, their tender little arms weren't strong enough to lift the hoe as well as he could. Even so, he didn't have their stamina. He would end his experiment panting and out of breath, then vent his rage by treating each of them to a couple of swipes with a thin bamboo rod that would leave its marks on their backs.

The murder plans Muntasir had drawn up over the course of the previous nights, he had thought about thousands of times before. The difference was simply that now he would be capable of carrying them out. When he was a young boy, the plans he'd made had been the reaction of a helpless person. Mugahid would lose his temper at them for no reason, and deprive them of chances to increase their land holdings because of all the money he spent on his whims and on his filly Aziza. One time Muntasir had asked Mugahid to sell the filly so he could buy a feddan next to their field.

"Well, well, well. So now you have some say-so in these matters?" Mugahid had screeched. Then he slapped him. Muntasir didn't flinch, and didn't make a move to return the blow. He considered that if he reacted in such a way, it would be directed at the same time against his sister Hafiza and his paternal cousins, whom he called his brothers. This, he thought, would destroy the family image that Salama, his father whom he had never seen and whom he loved based on others' descriptions of him, had worked so hard to build.

Every time he passed through the crisis he would feel pleased with himself, considering his well-mannered behavior toward his uncle to have been a show of wisdom on his part. This time, however, as he trudged ahead in hopes of getting somewhere before nightfall, he reproached himself for the ease with which he had given up his right to Mubarka and his inheritance.

He was like a drowning man whose survival instinct has reduced all his feelings and thoughts to a single question: how to make it out alive. He felt the loss of his father in a way he never had before, and he was overwhelmed by a sense of shame for being alone, wronged, and pathetic. He proceeded cautiously at that early hour over the dew-moistened soil, fragile as ashes beneath his feet, and when al-Ish disappeared beyond the mist, he remembered that he'd left Mubarka behind. He felt an iron grip constricting his breathing and a fire consuming his heart. But he had to keep going.

He'd known there were cities and countries outside of al-Ish. However, he had always treated their news as though they were something out of a fairy tale. Since he'd never expected to need them, he'd never tried to imagine where they were. Now, however, he suddenly found himself cast outside the womb. The aunt in whose home he'd sought refuge hadn't made her brother give him the fair treatment he deserved, nor could he have gone on living as her guest. Instead, he would have to find a home for himself and begin the life of a day laborer—he who, until just the day before, had behaved like one of the village's wealthy and privileged, overlooking the actions of an uncle whose neglect and nights out with people he considered to be beneath the al-Deeb family's dignity were a cause of such shame. If only his uncle had contented himself with these transgressions! Instead, though, he'd suddenly unmasked the face of an enemy.

Muntasir thought of going to either Bilbeis or Zagazig, both of which people reached mounted on riding animals. He didn't know which to choose, or how to get to them. Consequently, he decided to stick to the path that ran between the fields of clover and wheat, whose ears had turned golden and ripe. He was led along by the traces of the mounts' dung and the scent of their urine, and whenever he grew weary he would lie down for a while under a mulberry tree and alleviate the bitter taste in his mouth with some of its fruit.

As he trudged along beneath a sun that was moving heavily in the opposite direction, he was overshadowed by a flock of storks. No one had seen these birds for hundreds of years, although they survived in memory on account of the village's name—"the Nest"—which always called to mind the story of its founding and kept it alive from one generation to the next. Some people who saw Muntasir plodding along under the black cloud warned that the birds would go back to attacking al-Ish for not being able to protect a young man from his own uncle's excesses and injustices, while others insisted that they weren't birds at all, but rather a cloud that had been sent to shade the orphan.

∫

The people of al-Ish lived for centuries in the bliss of forgetfulness, until one day a sudden cloud of dust blew up. It cleared to reveal seven men on horseback with rifles slung over their shoulders and big ledgers in their hands. They were bewildered by the architecture and layout of the village, which had no main square, and every point of which seemed like its center. There were no neighborhoods that were closed off at one end. Instead, every street opened onto another, and every one of them led to the fields. Nor were there any distinctive structures that would have indicated where its most prominent residents lived, since all the houses consisted of a single story of unbaked brick, and all were the same size and shape.

The strangers asked about the village leader in a cryptic language, which they completed with gestures. Those who gathered around them had no idea who should speak on their behalf.

"We all speak for the village," they said.

Up until that time the people of al-Ish had been devoted to preserving the state of complete equality that had been established by their forefathers. It had encompassed everything: the shapes and sizes of the houses, the areas covered by their fields, and the families' successive generations. The founding fathers, originally from different villages, had gathered on some swampland, seeking to avoid exorbitant taxes. Then they'd proceeded to drain the swamp and establish their village on its unpromising briny soil. In order to ensure that none of them would abandon the others and go back to his own village, they pledged to leave all their memories behind. They even replaced their old names with names taken from the new lives they had staked out in this stubborn spot.

They began with the name of their village. Then came their own names: The person who first succeeded in growing wheat they called al-Qamhawi (the wheat-grower). The person whose land produced the highest yield of foul, or broad beans, became al-Fouli (the broad-bean grower). The family of the person whose buffalo cow gave birth to the first male offspring was dubbed al-Fahl (the stud). Someone who was in the habit of licking his fingers after a meal they called al-Lahis (the licker), someone who bit his refractory camel's ear was called al-Addad (the biter), someone who walked in front of his donkey instead of riding it was called al-Gahsh (the little donkey), and someone who went into the mat-making trade they called al-Husari (the mat-maker).

As the centuries passed, new villages sprang up near al-Ish. However, it continued to be self-sufficient, and thus had no need for contact with other villages. If someone in al-Ish had an unexpected surplus of corn or wheat, he wouldn't know what to do with it, so he would keep it until it was requested by a neighbor whose land hadn't produced as it should have, and if anyone had a buffalo cow that gave birth to twins, he would make a vow to serve one of them at a banquet.

The village remained forgotten until there came from Europe a new adventurer who dreamed of making Egypt a jewel in his crown. Before long he had translated his dream into ships fitted out with cannons the likes of which Egypt's slave rulers, so skilled at wielding swords in combat, had never imagined. However, the routing of the Mamluks didn't mean that the country had fallen like a ripe fruit into the lap of Napoleon, who forthwith brought his scholars with him to examine the jewel. The Egyptians fought valiantly in defense of their country, and when the Ottoman sultan saw how they had managed to send the emperor fleeing crestfallen back to Paris, he came to share their contempt for the Mamluks, and fulfilled the Egyptians' demand to appoint the Albanian lieutenant Muhammad Ali as governor.

No one had imagined that Umar Makram's uprising, which had succeeded in liberating Egypt from Mamluk rule, would lead to the occupation of al-Ish. After the ambitious officer Muhammad Ali had slaughtered his dangerous Mamluk rivals at a banquet in the Citadel, he stood before a detailed map of Egypt and its neighboring countries to decide which he would occupy first. He passed his hand over the headwaters of the Nile, then looked eastward toward Anatolia and westward toward the sands of Libya. He drew a circle that encompassed Egypt, Burqa, Sudan, the Hijaz, and the Levant. His lips formed a triumphant smile. Then he bowed his head at length, noting an infinitesimal point, the color of which was somewhere between the greenness of a valley and the yellowness of a desert. He pressed with his finger, but felt no moisture. The finger didn't sink into the presumed softness of a bog that had yet to dry up. He shook his head in amazement at his aspiration to invade other countries while there were still pockets within Egypt itself about which he knew nothing and where the fleeing Mamluks might seek refuge, especially in view of the fact that the most skillful of them had managed to jump with their horses over the Citadel walls.

The lieutenant, who would later bear the title of pasha, ordered preparations to be made for the campaign, which was smaller than those to be led later by his son Ibrahim to the Hijaz, the Levant, and Sudan. But, small though it was, it was sufficient to change life in al-Ish forever.

For weeks on end the strangers enjoyed generous hospitality. They counted up the people and the animals, computed the land areas in the village, and apprised themselves of how much grain each household had stored up in its silos. They took stock of the old cheese in jars buried under the firewood on the roofs, as well as the ghee and the fat from slaughtered animals in the casks and jugs suspended from the ceiling to keep them away from insects. The men doing the inventory didn't notice any of the individuals they had questioned concealing any of their property or misleading them when reporting information. The problem was that they were receiving the information more than once. This was because they would get disoriented and go down the same street a second time only moments after having left it, and the villagers would answer their questions without complaining about having to restate information they had already provided. The census-takers had to spend their nights hunched over the dim light of an oil lamp deleting the redundant information they had collected as a result of the similarities among the village streets and overlapping family trees. And when they completed their task, they left in such a state of confusion that more than once they were stopped along the way by people calling them to come back and get things they had forgotten.

That visit was nearly lost to oblivion. But then a new storm blew up. This storm yielded a Turk on horseback who pressed his red fez all the way down to his ears with the result that, what with the drooping flesh under his chin, he looked like a turkey guarded by seven armed soldiers mounted on seven donkeys.

Matin Agha produced a decree appointing him mayor of al-Ish and a detailed plan of the village with colored markings on it. He pointed to a red circle in the center of the map and instructed the owners of the houses located inside it to vacate their homes so that the mayor's mansion could be built in a spot that was equidistant from everyone in the village. He said they would receive compensation for their homes at the start of the new year. He then pointed to stars that had been drawn at the ends of some of the streets, stressing the need to close them off and make them into dead ends so as to reduce the number of entrances lest al-Ish be vulnerable to thieves.

The house owners didn't know how much compensation they were to receive, and even when they did know, they never received it. Rather, they waited for it generation after generation, and were bound to go on waiting till Judgment Day. However, they had obeyed the command, since refusal was something they weren't familiar with yet, and up to that moment, they didn't know the difference between the interests of those who make demands and the interests of those who carry them out.

They began mixing mud with straw to mold bricks. Then they began building houses outside the village for the people whose homes were gone. They also erected walls to close off the streets indicated by the stars.

Mule-drawn carts laden with white stones and other building materials began pouring into al-Ish. The builders set about constructing the mansion and surrounding it with a wall. Inside the wall they planted mango, orange, and lemon seedlings, none of which the people of al-Ish had ever seen before, along with roses and palm trees for decoration. In front of the mansion a structure of unbaked brick was built to house the soldiers, while weapons were to be stored in a room that opened onto the street, from which the soldiers would keep watch over the mansion's walls at night.

When everything was complete, the furniture arrived on carts led by seven soldiers, who had gone out to receive the procession before its arrival in al-Ish. The mayor arrived in a horse-drawn carriage with his wife, two sons, and daughter. The carriages came to a halt and Matin Agha went scurrying into the mansion as a security precaution that was lost on those who had lined up to see this family that was as white as china dolls. No one went near the mansion for a long time, and no one saw the family outside the wall. All that concerned the people of al-Ish was whether they knew how to talk and in which language they communicated. Even when some of the women began going into the mansion to help with the cleaning, they were amazed at the peculiar magical-sounding twitters and chirps exchanged by the family, and wondered how such mysterious combinations of sounds could mean anything.

The soldiers went on guarding the mansion for several months, and didn't leave until they'd trained sentinels recruited from among the men of al-Ish in how to use, clean, and maintain weapons. In choosing the sentinels, Matin Agha made certain that each of them was from a different family in order to ensure the loyalty of the largest possible number of families. For the first time there were men in al-Ish who did something other than till the land. They received wages for a night watch in which they could see no point. However, it afforded a good deal of entertainment for their families, who would satisfy their curiosity by watching their sons-turned-sentinels engrossed in the game of disassembling and reassembling the shotguns whose barrels never once grew hot, either in that generation or the one that succeeded it.

Matin Agha's orders, and those of his son Orhan after him, were obeyed without question. The word "refuse" only made it into the villagers' vocabulary when the mayor's grandson Ismet started burdening them with taxes and humiliating orders. He doubled the tax his grandfather had levied on newborns, circumcisions, weddings, and the sales and purchase agreements that had become commonplace. The state of equality that had once existed among the families of the village came to an end, while orders to work without compensation in the fields and on poultry and livestock farms owned by Matin Agha and his son and grandson multiplied over the course of the three successive generations. And as if that weren't enough, anyone riding an animal was required to dismount when passing in front of the mayor's residence.

One evening Mugahid's father, Ali al-Deeb, was coming home from the field with a buffalo cow, the only animal that remained to him after his livestock had been depleted through sales and starvation. The buffalo cow relieved herself in front of the mansion while Ismet was sitting there enjoying the sunset as he did every evening. He ordered the sentinels to stop Ali and force him to pick up the cow's dung and carry it in the hem of his gilbab.

When he got home, Ali hurled the dung into the cattle pen, picked up a heavy stick and began beating the cow furiously until he'd bloodied her back and his hands were swollen. It didn't look as though he intended to stop. His son Salama got him away from the cow before he killed her. Then Salama brought out a billy club and headed to the mansion. The sentinels kept him from attacking Ismet, who ordered them to arrest Salama and throw him into a cell he'd added to the security building.

The next morning they found the cell door open, and no sign of Salama. The mayor lined his sentinels up and asked them how Salama had managed to get away while they were standing watch in front of the prison door. He slapped them one by one, ordering them into the cell and closing the door behind them.

"You stay in his place, you cows, until you say where Farmer Dog went!" he shouted in broken Arabic.

When the sun rose a few days later over Ismet's land, his cotton plants were a blanket of solid green. Not a single stalk on his fifty feddans remained standing. Neither the sentinels, whom he released, nor the security reinforcements that came from the provincial governor succeeded in protecting his property. Over the course of the following three years, not a single plant on his land reached maturity, and not a single animal of his remained in its stable. Ismet had lost his former prestige, and he saw malicious glee in people's eyes. Even the sentinels began exchanging winks and whispers in his presence, and grew lax in carrying out his orders. It had become impossible for him to stay, so he began offering his land for sale one plot at a time. He found no buyer for the mansion, so he boarded it up, loaded as much furniture as he could onto carts, and left al-Ish with his family in the same way his grandfather Matin had come eighty years before.

After this, al-Ish went back to the state of equality it had enjoyed during the first centuries of its existence. No one in the village was willing to hold the position of mayor, and the authorities, who were busy pursuing Salama, saw no need to send a new one.

There were now ongoing thefts of the livestock belonging to the region's mayors and wealthy residents, and if a mayor in the Governorate of Sharqiya crossed someone related to a member of the gang Salama had formed with his friends in the region's villages, the mildest penalty he could expect to receive was to have his crops mowed down or set on fire.

No one saw Salama in al-Ish any more. But everybody knew he slept in his bed every night. He would come home in the dead of night and leave again before daybreak—that is, until the ill-fated night when he stole the khedive's livestock from his corrals in Inshas. He'd delegated the necessary tasks to the members of his group and kept guard for them from the rooftop, and when the operation was over, he jumped down to join them. However, the butt of his rifle had sunk into his side.

He hadn't felt any pain at first. In fact, he had gone on exchanging gunfire with the khedive's corral guards until he was sure his men had gotten away with the herd of buffaloes and cattle. He'd also managed to oversee the slaughter of the calves and the distribution of their meat on that same night. He hadn't returned to al-Ish until all the participants had returned to their villages with their shares of cattle and fertile buffaloes.

Three days later, the black-and-blue bruise on his side had become a frightful swelling, and he began suffering unbearable pain in his kidneys. None of the poultices succeeded in halting the swelling, and on the seventh day Salama died, without having sought out a physician. Those who came to offer their condolences at the guesthouse were surrounded by security forces. Half the members of his gang were arrested during the funeral procession, and the rest fled.

This operation was the bite on which Salama's gang finally choked. However, it would be a long time before Khedive Abbas Hilmi II—who lived out the years between the two wars in exile, despite the Egyptians' demand that he return—would recover from the pain it had caused him. Throughout his thirty years in exile in Italy, he kept telling his entourage that what pained him most was the thought of dying without seeing the British ousted from Egypt, or seeing those who had robbed his country estate behind bars. When he died, they found among his papers a list of the names of his enemies. Salama occupied second place, between British consul general Lord Cromer, who was first on the list, and the young hit man Mahmoud Mazhar, who shot the khedive in Turkey during his visit to the Topkapi Palace.

Muntasir was still in his mother's womb when his father died, and the young widow remained in her husband's house until she gave birth. She had been expecting Mugahid to ask for her hand so that he could raise his brother's son. To her surprise, however, she learned that he had asked for the hand of his paternal cousin Hafiza. Consequently, she left Muntasir in their care, saying that she also wanted to marry, and that she had no intention of living alone as a widow in order to raise their offspring for them.

Hafiza was hurriedly married to Mugahid, who was a conscript at the time, so that she could begin taking care of the orphaned Muntasir. On her gloomy wedding night, Mugahid stumbled and fell with her as he helped her off the horse's back. His uncle slapped him angrily, and when they were alone behind closed doors, Mugahid deflowered his bride with a finger into which he poured all his rage over the public insult he'd received from her father. Then he turned his back to her and sobbed himself to sleep.

At midnight, Hafiza's mother-in-law Alhaz knocked on the door and asked her to come out and change Muntasir's soiled diaper. He was only nine months old, and she found herself obliged to learn how to deal with a newborn before she herself had experienced pregnancy or childbirth. She would milk the goat for him and give him goat's milk to drink until he was satisfied. Then she would lie down beside him and bring out her breast for him. After a couple of attempts to nurse that failed to wet his lips, he would spit out her nipple, but continue scratching it with his fingers until she fell asleep, and she would spend the rest of the night holding him in her arms. Sometimes after he fell asleep, she would leave him in the care of his grandmother and go back to her room with Mugahid, where she would doze off while listening for her mother-in-law's shout, which might come at any moment.

Moved by a hard-to-explain affection for his deceased father, she wished Muntasir were her own son. It had nothing to do with a woman's love for a man. Rather, she loved the revered status of her paternal cousin, the mere mention of whose name struck terror in people's hearts, and who had earned prestige for the family not only in al-Ish, but in the entire region.

Hafiza's only contact with Mugahid consisted of tepid copulation during his brief furloughs. As soon as he arrived in al-Ish he would go out to join his friends for hashish-smoking sessions that lasted till nearly dawn, after which he would come home to mount her in a groggy haze.

She persevered in her life with his parents for six years, like a widow whose widowhood was interrupted during brief vacations. Yet even during the vacations she hardly saw him. She worked in the house and in the field with a torn-off piece of linen around her waist, and grasped the hoe like a man. When they brought in hired help, she would give the worker a loaf of plain bread to eat with some greens that were in season: radishes or watercress in the summer, and sow thistle or dandelion that grew up by itself with the clover in the winter. If the worker asked for another loaf, she would retort, "One's plenty! Just take smaller bites and eat more sow thistle with it!"

When Mugahid was released from military service, he came back to al-Ish with a passion for horses, which he had learned about during his military tour, so he bought himself a little foal and began training it. He was completely distracted by the foal, and Hafiza saw in him what she hadn't been able to see during his brief furloughs. He took her work in the field for granted and lived a life of self-absorption. He would stay out at night, and seclude himself with the filly during the day. He didn't even notice the children, as though they belonged to Hafiza alone.

Nagiya, Hafiza's first taste of motherhood, was a piece of wrinkled flesh that began to grow. As the days passed she grew limbs, while the wrinkles were concentrated in the girl's face and in a large

25

hump that caused her to move about like an old woman. After her the males began to come in succession: Salama, Nagi, and Ali, who, with Muntasir, became Hafiza's source of support and sustenance and her world of bliss.

Mugahid only ate at the same table with them on holidays and other special occasions. Alhaz, a scrawny woman who was hard as nails, had a three-tiered arrangement for the food in the household. A couple of pigeons or roosters were reserved for Mugahid and his father, and some blackstrap molasses, cheese, and possibly a bit of cream for the male children, including Muntasir, who joined the ranks of the men from the time he reached puberty, thereby reclaiming his father's place at the short-legged table around which they gathered for meals. And last came the food for the females, that is, for Alhaz herself, Hafiza, and Nagiya: pieces of rock-hard leftover bread with whey or pickled bitter orange. From time to time they might also have a bowl of mulukhiya or okra when they were available in the field, cooked with the broth from the birds the men were eating.

One time when Hafiza came back from the field, her mother-in-law had brought an earthen casserole dish filled with meat out of the oven and placed it before her. Despite her astonishment, she ate with gusto, and when she'd had her fill, her mother-in-law informed her that what she had taken for rabbit meat had actually been a cat, and that this was to teach her not to make eyes at the men's food ever again. Alhaz always said that women don't need the nourishment that men do, and this belief of hers had become a law that Hafiza dared not break, even after her mother-in-law had passed away.

She didn't feel fully human until after Muntasir and Salama had grown up, followed by Nagi and Ali, and relieved her of having to work in the field. She then found herself the queen of a beehive founded on love, and among whose residents Mugahid was not included. Despite his growing ferocity and his squandering of their hard-earned sustenance, he stayed away from them. He no longer sat with them, nor shared a bed with her. However, feelings of jealousy weren't instinctive to her, despite what she'd heard about his relation-ships with the gypsy women who came to the mulid celebrations.

When Mugahid stole Mubarka from his nephew, what had con-cerned her wasn't the fact that he would be taking another wife, since, as far as she was concerned, his disgusting habits were best spread out among fifty different women. Rather, what had pained her was to see Muntasir—Ibn al-Ghali ("son of the beloved"), as everyone in al-Ish referred to him—move away.

"Ah, if the dead could speak!" Hafiza said sorrowfully as she recalled the way Muntasir had kissed her hand and forehead, then gently moved her and his brothers aside on his way out. Choking on her tears, she had spat on the world, where death takes the best of us and leaves the wicked in peace.

Mugahid had now moved his evenings out to the new bride's house. When he arrived after the final evening prayer, the stove would be ready in front of Badr, along with the shisha and the tea-making paraphernalia. He would take a package of honeyed tobacco and a piece of hashish out of his pocket. Then he would cut the hashish into tiny pieces the size of grains of wheat and bury them in the handful of tobacco in the bowl of the shisha as an awed Badr looked on.

Mugahid began to make himself completely at home. He would take off his turban and set it beside him on the straw mat so that it looked like a third man who'd been swallowed up by the ground. As for Badr, who had no previous experience with anything stronger than a cup of tea, he began joining in with the eagerness of a little boy who's just discovering life. This gave Mugahid a heady feeling of superiority, something he lacked when he spent his evenings with professional potheads. It gave him the pleasure of finding himself the object of someone's admiration as opposed to the disrespect he endured at home, even if it only took the form of piercing, wordless glances. Yet none of this prevented him from being constantly curious to see Mubarka, who only showed herself when her father asked her to bring some corncobs for fuel or to change the water in the shisha. She would enter silently, dogged by Mugahid's eyes, which dwelt on her body and stole furtive glances at her cleavage when she bent down. His pupils would dilate as they devoured her breasts. Feeling herself pelted by his gaze, she would quietly conceal the area around her neck with her hand. However, his eyes would remain glued to the prominent nipples that blazed beneath her gilbab.

Day after day she slipped further into the abyss of her sorrows behind the mask of indifference that she donned in her dealings with the two men. Now and then she would daydream, and her heart would flutter for a few moments as she imagined Muntasir coming up behind her. She would close her eyes and conjure up his voice: "How are you, Mubarka?"

But before long she would revert to her state of despair and envelop Muntasir in her wrath as she thought about how he'd up and left al-Ish just like that! Why hadn't he fought for her? Why hadn't he forced his uncle to let an arbitration council look into their dispute and decide between them? Had he forgotten her? Would he come back to exact revenge for her and for himself?

But her anger would quickly give way to pity as she imagined the difficulties he was facing so far from al-Ish, stripped of everything. His desire-quickened eyes would glisten, then multiply until they turned to stars that dotted the sky above her, and out of their depths would be born an image of her mother that began pressing itself upon her. She remembered the comment her mother had made when a neighbor lady asked her which of two suitors would be better for her daughter. She said, "A handsome man is like a pendant around a girl's neck."

She didn't recall which neighbor had requested the advice. However, that moment had become one of those rare instants when she was able to conjure her mother's image with perfect clarity: the roundness of her dark, bronze-like face, the soft black hair from which a couple of lovelocks dangled, the honey-colored eyes gracefully outlined with kohl brought straight from the Hijaz, and the green tattoo on her lovely chin.

It was the only moment when she was able to conjure her mother complete with the sweetest voice in the world. She hadn't hesitated for an instant in her choice. Rather, her voice had emerged confident and authoritative.

"Did she sense what was going to happen to me?" Mubarka wondered aloud. It saddened her to think of the finality of that response, which in hindsight seemed to have been made in her defense. At the time of her misfortune, all she'd received were commiserating looks, pursed lips, and prayers calling down mercy upon her deceased mother from women who knew what it meant for a newly budding rose to be buried alive with a man old enough to be her father.

Mugahid agreed with Badr that the wedding would take place after the cotton harvest, and he swore to buy her a bed fit for the wife of the Governorate's commanding officer. When her father informed her that they would be going the next morning to Bilbeis to buy her trousseau, her only response was a gesture to indicate that she'd heard him. She seemed neither frightened nor happy nor angry. All one could discern was a hint of curiosity to see the city. When Badr came home from the dawn prayer, he woke her up to fit out the donkey with the packsaddle with colorful wool padding that was reserved for special occasions. Mugahid came out on his filly, and brought a donkey for her father to ride. Before long she found herself heading out with the two men, their three mounts' hooves leaving imprints on the road's dew-moistened soil.

When Bilbeis appeared beneath the morning sun's first gentle rays, Mubarka was gripped with a mixture of elation and turmoil. Her first impression as they approached the city gates was one of opulence and splendor. She felt she was in a world of fairy tales, as though it were Paradise, with its stone houses and broad verandas overlooking small gardens. When she opened her eyes, she saw they were greeted by the sight of a fair-skinned woman whose hair hung down beneath a wide-brimmed hat and who wore a dress that revealed the curves of her upper thighs and bosom. She was walking arm in arm with an equally fair-skinned man clad in tight-fitting trousers that revealed the contours of his buttocks.

30

They dismounted in front of a large building where riding animals were kept. At its entrance stood a guard, to whom they handed over their mounts. Then Mubarka took off walking behind the two men, who were busy talking about what they would buy for her. With every step, the basalt beneath her feet became more fragile, and she felt increasingly giddy at the sight of the immaculate shops and the fragrance of grilled meat wafting out of the restaurants.

Suddenly, she was gripped by the thought that Muntasir might appear on some street corner. How would she act? What would the two men do? The thought grew more vivid as she scanned the horizon, and for the first time since her father had informed her of Mugahid's intention to marry her, she sensed from the look of astonishment he cast her that he knew what she was thinking. For a moment she was in turmoil. Then she regained her composure and continued to follow them, turning the matter over in her mind: What if he appeared and asked her to elope with him? What if a fight broke out between him and the two men? She hoped he would appear and that she could run away with him like a fairy-tale heroine.

They went to the bazaar, which was roofed with wrought wood. She looked deep inside the shops in hopes of seeing him. Her eyes were blinded by the play of light and shadow over the baskets of hibiscus, carob beans, black pepper, and cumin as the strands of light filtered in through the openings in the market roof, and she breathed in the mélange of fragrances. She followed the two men among the fabric shops, where enormous rolls of every color imaginable reached from floor to ceiling. The two men ran their hands over the cloth, making their choices and bargaining in front of her as though she were in a dream. She was startled out of her trance by an argument that had broken out between them in front of the brassiere shop. Mugahid had stopped there unexpectedly, without knowing what to call the objects that had so animated his features.

"We want some of those!" he said.

Trying to get him away from the place, Badr said imperiously, "Come on, let's get going. Now's not the time to be thinking about boobs!"

The garish colors of the domed, breast-shaped brassieres and Badr's exasperated tone created an awkwardness among the three of them, as though something disgraceful were happening in public. In the end, Badr had no choice but to shut his mouth and leave the matter to Mugahid in hopes of getting them out of the situation as quickly as possible. Little did he know that this event would be the source of greatest fascination among the people of al-Ish when news of his daughter's trousseau started to get around.

At sundown they headed home on their mounts, with Mugahid and Badr riding abreast along the dusty path, and Mubarka behind them, her bosom now adorned with a massive gold necklace which, reflecting the autumn sun's weary rays, put a glow in her face, and her ankles encircled by a pair of huge silver anklets.

The threesome looked like an advance honor guard for the mule-drawn cart, which bore a bride's trousseau the likes of which al-Ish had never laid eyes on before. It was headed by a wardrobe with gold-colored handles and a mirror on one of its four doors. Behind the wardrobe were three wooden sofas, on top of which lay a wrought copper bed with round mirrors and stained glass between the rails. Atop the bed lay the copperware: cooking pots and basins of all sizes, plates, and a pitcher with a gooseneck spout. All these, together with a number of straw mats, were topped by sections of coarse calico and cloth figured with plant designs to be used for mattress covers, and turquoise satin for coverlet cases. Wrapped in a bundle of coarse calico was a white silk dress with a wedding veil and three lace-embroidered silk nightgowns. And, wonder of wonders, nestled inside the nightgowns lay three brassieres—one red, one black, and one white.

Mubarka started preparing for the wedding: embroidering pillowcases and bedsheets, going to the mill to prepare flour for the wedding cakes, crushing antimony to make kohl, and making vermicelli noodles that she would spread in the sun to dry atop large flat sieves, then toast in the oven to take with her to her new house.

Those who noticed Mubarka's lack of interest in her sumptuous trousseau and the indifference with which she carried on with her wedding preparations concluded anew that she was a mystery, and went back to whispering among themselves about her marriage to a jinni that had scared young men away and caused her to feel no grief over Muntasir. Such people were of the belief that the degradation and unhappiness Hafiza had endured with Mugahid would be thrown back in his face by this young girl. She went about her tasks all day long as though the occasion she was getting ready for was something that concerned her alone and had nothing to do with the two men who came back every night after the final evening prayer and sat together until the wee hours of the morning.

Before going to bed, Mubarka would make sure her father and her fiancé had whatever they needed by way of tea, sugar, corncobs, or wood for the fire. But as the wedding date approached, she also began making requests for the things she wanted in her new home. She would voice the requests briefly to her father as they occurred to her at odd times of the day: when she was serving him his lunch, when he asked her for a clean shirt, or as he was on his way out to the field. He would pass the requests on to Mugahid.

"The girl wants a house of her own," said Badr, pleading with him to agree to the request, since she wasn't willing to share a house with his first wife. With no choice but to comply, Mugahid bought her a three-room house. However, she wasn't satisfied with it.

"Mubarka wants the farmhouse," said Badr as he poured the tea one evening. Mugahid remained silent for a long time before voicing his agreement. He didn't know how he was going to fulfill this demand against his sons' will. After all, they'd opposed him ever since his engagement, which had deprived them of Muntasir—their cousin, their brother, and their friend. And what he expected came to pass.

When Hafiza conveyed the father's demand to her sons, Salama lost his temper and threw his father's clothes into the middle of the street. Then he closed the farmhouse door and stood guard with a club in his hand, determined to kill him if he tried to break down the door or move them by force.

"It's shameful enough that he spends his evenings with the scum of the earth, and now he up and marries another woman and makes us a laughingstock!" he said.

He didn't back down until his mother knelt before him and kissed his feet, saying, "Please, son. We've had enough scandals, and your father's a hardheaded man."

She asked Mugahid for a chance to placate his sons and move with them to the new house. But no sooner had he managed to do this than he was faced with Mubarka's newest demand: that he repaint the farmhouse. After all, it wouldn't do for a new bride to live in a house whose paint was peeling. So he had it painted with white lime in keeping with her wishes. In fact, he would have been willing to fulfill any demand she made—any, that is, but the newest one: that she have a proper wedding celebration and be conducted to her new home on the back of his filly.

"Anything but that!" fumed Mugahid. Badr felt as though he shouldn't have conveyed this request in particular, since time had apparently not succeeded in erasing the bad memory Mugahid still harbored from the night Hafiza was escorted to his house as a new bride. To this day Mugahid didn't know for certain whether the slap he had received from his uncle on that night had been the reason for the lack of warmth and enthusiasm he had experienced with Hafiza, or whether there were other reasons for it.

"That would be disgraceful," he objected. "I'm too old to be escorting a bride on horseback!" Muttering to himself, he jumped to his feet and headed for the door, waving Badr's hand away when the latter attempted to calm him down. However, the following night they came back from prayers together the way they always did and began exchanging whispers, and in the end Badr managed to persuade Mugahid to grant the wish of the orphan girl, whom he couldn't deprive of the right to enjoy her wedding day. Besides, she was entitled to be escorted to her new husband's home since she was marrying for the first time.

On the day of the wedding, thick clouds gathered, an event people viewed as a good omen so early in the winter. Late in the afternoon, the guests gathered to accompany the bride's dinner procession, which was preceded by women carrying cooking pots filled with stuffed pigeon and oven-browned rice with milk. They were followed by a camel bearing the household furnishings and the cart that held the bed, wardrobe, and kitchenware. That evening Mugahid, clad in a new woolen gilbab and a snow-white turban and looking discomfited and jaundiced, was mounted on his filly. Behind him rode his bride with her white silk dress and gold necklace, which covered the entire area above the neckline of her dress. It glistened in the light of the torches over youthful breasts whose cleavage peeked out of a black brassiere that had been touched by every hand in the village when the clothing in her trousseau made the rounds of the houses.

The dress wasn't new. The merchant had informed them that it had belonged to the daughter of a bey who had sold it. However, it was the first of its kind in al-Ish, where, after having her feet washed and donning her first pair of leather shoes, a bride was generally escorted to her new home wearing an ordinary gilbab, though on rare occasions she might wear a satin dress whose color and modest neckline made it suitable for use after the wedding. Hence, clad in a gown that billowed out from the waist down, Mubarka became the first expression of the notion of the female form as an object of pleasure, and a primordial spark flowed through the procession as it moved to the rhythmic beating of the drums.

Then the good omen of the late-afternoon clouds was transmuted without warning into a violent downpour that lashed the wedding procession. The torches went out and the streets turned rapidly into churning streams in which many were unable to keep their balance. The drummers and pipers, who had broken into a run, quickened their tempo as though there were a certain amount of drumming and piping that had to be accomplished before they could stop, and their music took on the rhythm of a war chant that receded into the distance as Mugahid attempted to calm the filly for fear that she would slip and fall.

When they reached the farmhouse, he dismounted gingerly and held his hands out to his bride. She jumped down, avoiding his outstretched hand, and followed him into the farmhouse, whose courtyard was filled with wedding guests. The door to the room that had received her bed only hours earlier opened, and she entered behind him with the same wordless impassivity with which she had comported herself since the day of their engagement. Two elderly women entered with them, and he closed the door behind them. The women took off her dress and shoved her onto the bed, where one steadied her waist while the other pulled down her bloomers. Their task accomplished, they gestured to Mugahid, who was standing beside the bed, to come forward.

The raucous merrymakers listened for the scream from just outside the door, then rowdily passed around the blood-soiled sheet the two elderly women brought out. Mugahid shook hands with his new father-in-law and the male guests, who began withdrawing to their houses. He closed the farmhouse door and went back to the bedroom, where Mubarka lay curled up in a fetal position, her tears falling without a sound. He undressed and slipped into bed beside her. When he began running his hands over her hips, she instinctively smacked his head so hard that she herself screamed from the pain. Furious, he clung to her brassiere. She kicked him between the thighs and he writhed in agony, gritting his teeth as she leapt out of bed and tried to open the door. He followed on his knees, gripping his testicles, and promised imploringly not to bother her for the rest of the night. So she came back to bed, but instead of lying back down, she sat up, eyeing the cringing figure who reclined next to her. As she sat there she stared at the ceiling, which had sprung a leak as the rain continued to pour down, while the storm winds nearly tore the farmhouse from its foundations.

His snoring jolted her out of her reflections. She felt a mournful tranquility that was disturbed by the stinging of the wound in her hymen, which had been ruptured by a dirty fingernail. She placed a pillow over her head to muffle the sound of his snores, and the events that had transpired began passing through her memory. It was as though she'd been hypnotized for months until she found herself at last in the very room where she might have been sleeping with Muntasir rather than Mugahid.

"Does this make any sense?"

Her anger with Muntasir and herself flared in the darkness and the room became redolent with his fragrance, causing his sultry voice to echo in her ear: "How are you, Mubarka?" Her aching womb dilated with desire for the absent one and she fell asleep dreaming of his rib-crushing embrace. Meanwhile, seventy women in al-Ish conceived in honor of the quivering of her breasts in her brassiere as she leapt off the filly's back.

Hafiza knew the limits of her capacity for allurement and Mugahid's capacity to respond. She made no attempt to enter into a competition with the silent enchantress who, with a single look, could ensnare not only men, but women as well. Instead she tried to get closer to Mugahid by talking to him about their children's affairs whenever he passed by to ask after them. She also reminded him of the presence of the hunchbacked Nagiya, who appeared to have no hope of finding a husband, and whose brothers wouldn't think of marrying before she did.

She was emboldened to broach the subject of their daughter, whom he had spent years trying to forget, when she noticed that something about him had changed. She couldn't say what it was exactly, but he'd become less irritable and more able to listen to her. She figured the change was a result of the euphoria he was experiencing on account of the young woman. He was, in fact, distracted after the manner of someone who has discovered life anew. However, it wasn't, as Hafiza supposed, a happy discovery, but a painful one.

Mugahid had always thought sex was something a man did to a woman. After all, by leaving home he had established limits for Hafiza in bed, and it was he who could ignite the gypsy women at the mulid celebrations. But in Mubarka's bed he'd learned how one's manhood could be insulted and rendered of no account.

After the kick she'd delivered on their wedding night, Mubarka stopped preventing him from undressing her. In fact, she would take the initiative to undress herself, and would then lie on her back with her breasts at full mast. He would lie down beside her, his mouth watering. He would massage her body and pinch her nipples, but there was no response of any kind. Even when he slipped his finger into the dryness between her legs, he saw no sign of the alarmed rejection he'd encountered on their wedding night. He couldn't find any way to arouse her desire. Rather, she remained as unmoved as the dead. He would withdraw from contact with her to see if she might approach him. But she didn't. He would come up next to her once more, seeking pleasure in her warmth and waiting for the moment when her body would give some sign of acceptance, which would be his cue to make the next move. But no sign ever came. He began obsessing over ways to take her by force, but thought better of it for fear of causing a scandal. After all, no one knew about their situation yet, with the exception of Aunt Hamida, who slept in the adjoining room.

He knew now what it was like to lie awake at night waiting for a woman's acceptance and approval. He went back to spending his evenings out. However, he would cut them short and come back to the farmhouse, drawn to Mubarka's bed like a moth to a flame. All night long he would listen to her steady breathing, the howling of the dogs, and the meowing of the cats, and every now and then he would raise himself up slightly and look at her eyes to see if she was awake. Then he would collapse in rage over the soundness of her slumber.

Nothing rescued him from this torment but the dawn call to prayer. He would get up and go to the mosque, then return from the prayer seeking refuge in the morning light and the stirrings of Aunt Hamida, who would be busy making his breakfast.

The neighbor lady who'd helped Badr care for Mubarka when she was a little girl, and who used to say that the late Fatima had entrusted Mubarka to her charge before she died, had been asked by Mugahid to stay on in the young bride's service in hopes that she might help to soften her hard head and ease her adjustment to married life. The elderly woman had no objections, and thus became the first live-in maid in a village that had no history of resident domestic servants, including even the household of the Turkish mayor before he fled and left the mansion to be inhabited by ghosts. Aunt Hamida, who had found herself alone after the death of her husband, saw no problem in closing up her house and coming to live in the farmhouse with Mubarka, inspired not by the role of servant, but by the role of mother.

Mugahid was doing everything he could to win Mubarka over. To this end, he lost no time in fulfilling her request to go to Bilbeis, hoping that riding together on the filly would bring them closer. However, she requested a carriage. Hence, al-Ish woke early one morning to the sight of a horse-drawn carriage. When it stopped in front of the farmhouse, it piqued everyone's curiosity, since carriages didn't generally come to al-Ish for anyone but well-to-do individuals who were critically ill. When it did happen, it was usually the person's first and last trip to the doctor, who would invariably declare that they had brought him or her too late, at which point they would take the person out to the shrine of Sidi Sa'dun in hopes that the visit paid to the saint would ease his arduous journey back from Bilbeis. Sometimes the person would die right in front of the saint's tomb, and so be taken away and washed for burial. Then they would pray over him and bring him back to be buried in al-Ish, envied by all for the blessing he had received, and which was certain to ease his passage into eternity.

Curious eyes peered from every door, window, and rooftop as Mugahid emerged with Mubarka and settled next to her inside the carriage. The coachman cracked his whip over his horse, and the carriage began to creak as its wheels furrowed the soil's dewy crust.

The sun had just risen over the silvery dew that garbed the fresh green clover, and they set off down a road flanked by rows of beech oaks which made it into a tunnel of shadow. Mubarka worked to avoid touching the person seated next to her, who attempted to brush up against her with the lurching of the cart. She pondered the surprising antics of delicate sunbeams that stole through the trees like bundles of light and landed in succession on the desolate old horse's back. Meanwhile, a pigeon on the ground cooed, swinging its tail back and forth in front of the horse until, when there was only a step between them, she would fly a few meters away, alighting again in the horse's path.

When the coach arrived at the entrance to the city, Mubarka noticed that she wasn't anticipating Muntasir's appearance the way she had been on the day they'd come to buy her trousseau. She had no idea what might happen if she actually met him. Mugahid got out of the carriage first, and she followed, leaning on the hand he extended toward her. Then she walked behind him, gazing thoughtfully at the street. The aromas of the spices were sufficient to tell her that they were now in the very navel of the city, just steps away from the bazaar whose shops she'd walked among before.

Mugahid didn't feel the trip had done anything to bring her out of her despondency. Nor had it diminished the aloofness with which she treated him. She remained distracted the entire day, her eyes wandering here and there. She expressed no wonder or gratitude in the market, where she bought everything that struck her fancy, or at the tomb of Sidi Sa'dun, at which she cast an indifferent glance amid crowds of weeping visitors who fought and pushed each other aside for a chance to touch the shrine window's iron bars.

Nevertheless, he responded without hesitation whenever she asked to go back to Bilbeis or Zagazig. Every trip made Mubarka all the more distracted and resulted in new eyebrow-raising purchases, such as the water pump that came to occupy the center of the farmhouse yard. The first device for drawing clean water in the entire village, it allowed Aunt Hamida to stop going out to get water from the irrigation canal. It also came to be used by the other village women, who were impressed by the purity of the water that came out of the ground, and that was cool even on the hottest summer days.

Not willing to give anyone the chance to gloat over his misfortune, Mugahid endured the nights in Mubarka's bed like a prisoner who gained his freedom each morning. He became more diligent about caring for his land and started paying more frequent visits to Hafiza, giving himself over to the brotherly-sisterly affinity they'd come to share.

One day Hafiza was engrossed in telling him about the nightmares that had been plaguing her spinster daughter every night when Mugahid said hazily, "All that's left is the Rafah Market."

"Rafah!" she replied, horrified. "Would you sell your daughter, Mugahid?"

Yet, despite the sharpness of her initial response, she began turning the matter over in her mind. After giving it some more thought, she began to feel that it wasn't fair for the girl to have to live and die alone without getting a taste of life or having offspring to keep her company in her old age. Little by little, she resigned herself to the decision. Fortune might grant her daughter some elderly man who still had enough spark left in him to plant the seed of a child inside her.

Hundreds of years earlier, Rafah had been a slave market. After being closed down, the market had continued to be a meeting place for elderly men for whom beauty had lost its importance and who wanted a wife to assuage their loneliness, and for unattractive spinsters whose families would bring them in the hope that they might come to know the warmth of a man. The man concerned might be from Rafah itself, or from Jerusalem, al-Arish, al-Tur, or even from Aqaba or Amman.

Mugahid gave Hafiza two days to get ready for their trip to the matchmaker's market in Rafah. Hafiza gave her daughter a thorough bath and packed her clothes in a satchel together with a number of flat loaves of bread rolled into a bundle, some old cheese, and a bottle of water. Mugahid set off on his filly under the cover of the early morning mist with Nagiya seated behind him, clinging to him with one hand and clutching her bundle of clothes with the other. The only people in the streets of al-Ish at that hour were three men clutching the lead ropes for three buffalo cows who stood waiting impatiently for their turn with the bull. The three cows kept bellowing, spraying urine about in nervous, intermittent bursts. Meanwhile, a fourth cow stood receiving the bull, which was attempting to balance himself on top of her with guidance from his owner and hers. The two men quickly grasped the bull's slender red organ, which was curved like a scythe, and thrust it into the cow's vagina. Missing his mark, the bull would come back down to the ground and reposition himself, then make another leap, pawing the air with its forelegs as the cow, her head to the ground, spread her rump, her vulva pulsating nervously and revealing its moist pink interior.

The scene prompted Nagiya's womb to contract and expand in imitation of the cow's vulva, and her heart opened to the journey ahead. However, she soon recoiled again when she found herself on the outskirts of al-Ish. She cast the village a poignant look that might have been interpreted in any number of ways. It was a look of reproach for the brothers among whom she'd never felt she truly belonged and who were now fast asleep. It was a look of exhilaration at the prospect of deliverance and a dream of the unknown. And it was a look of regret at having to part with her mother who, at the moment of their departure, had flung herself on the ground after letting forth a long cry that startled the pigeons, who had been cooing in joyous courtship on the rooftops of the houses, into sudden flight.

The filly plodded evenly over the soil of the village's main road, urged on by Mugahid's thighs. As they went, he whispered to her continuously—with words of reproach when she stumbled on a brick in the road, or of encouragement when she managed to keep her balance in a patch of mud caused by flooding from the drainage ditch at a low spot on the shore.

"No, sweetheart. That's my girl!" he murmured.

By the time they reached Bilbeis, Nagiya was feeling parched and dizzy from the filly's constant swaying and the heat of the sun. Mugahid dismounted in front of the inn for riding animals and helped her off the horse. He handed the filly's halter to the stable hand with wages for hosting the horse for three days.

"You take good care of her now. When I get back I want to find her in tip-top shape, just the way she is now," Mugahid said, cautioning the stable hand not to neglect her. After going in with him to make sure her stall was clean, he returned to where Nagiya stood, motioning for her to follow. She walked along looking at the streets as though she were in a dream, or in one of the enchanted cities of *The Arabian Nights* described by storytellers during the evening gatherings that accompanied the mulid celebrations. She followed him into the train station and sat down on the platform, looking in the direction the train would be coming from. When she heard the blast of the train whistle, she wasn't the only one who jumped slightly at the iron monster's approach. When the train ground to a halt, she stepped into the car behind her father, satchel in hand, watching the other women so as to do as they did. Mugahid took her by the hand and sat her down next to him on one of the wooden benches.

Hours went by in silence as she watched the trees and telegraph poles running past outside. When she felt herself on the verge of getting nauseous, she would close her eyes until her insides settled. Then she would be prompted by curiosity to look out again, with such excitement that she nearly thought of jumping.

When they reached Rafah, the passengers scattered hurriedly in the direction of the square, which was surrounded by rows of tents whose owners offered their hospitality. Mugahid turned to go into the first tent, at the entrance to which stood an elderly man. The man took a look at the hunchbacked woman, but withdrew his gaze with a disappointment that broke her heart. He began closing the door to his tent as though he wanted to go back on the welcoming gesture he'd extended at first. By this time, however, Mugahid was standing directly in front of him, so he reluctantly invited him in. Following her father hesitantly like a frightened animal, Nagiya looked around at the tent, and was tempted to flee as she timidly fingered its colorful carpets. The elderly man gestured to Mugahid to join the men gathered in a circle around the fire, then stepped forward to show Nagiya the way to the women's tent.

"Boys!" he called, pulling the tent flap aside.

His wife poked her head out of the other tent and invited Nagiya to come in.

By sunrise the tents had ejected guests and hosts alike into the marketplace. The men stood there with their daughters, each of whom had removed some of her clothing in order to reveal what she considered to be her most appealing features. Nagiya let down her long silky hair, which flowed luxuriously from beneath her long, colorful bandana, undulating down her back and camouflaging her hump. The men her father had become acquainted with in Sheikh Mas'ud's tent were the first to walk around her to get a better look. They were followed by others, but one after another they all withdrew.

The day was nearly over. Though they didn't look each other in the eye, she knew the weight of the sorrow her father must be feeling, while he, for his part, knew what pain his daughter must be suffering. Time after time Mugahid had made conversation with the middleman or the escort, turning his back to the elderly matchmaker as he lifted Nagiya's dress with his stick in order to see her rounded thighs, peered into her face in amazement at the frog's mouth he found there, or folded her lower lip down to find teeth implanted in a jaw that had no chin.

When one of the elderly men completed his round of inspection with less displeasure than those who had preceded him, she suspected that she might have found her match. So she in turn began examining him as he set about making her father's acquaintance. Mugahid cheerfully returned his greeting, then waited for the next word. However, the man suddenly reached out and placed his hand under Nagiya's hair. Drawing back in alarm, he said, "May God provide for you, my daughter," and went on his way.

When Hafiza saw her husband on his filly's back with the poor hunchbacked girl seated behind him, clutching her bundle, she was stricken with conflicting emotions. On one hand, she rejoiced at the return of a piece of herself so dear to her that she'd stopped eating out of sorrow over her departure. On the other hand, it grieved her to realize the degree of unsightliness that afflicted the poor girl, who hadn't found even an old man of unknown pedigree who would be willing to have her.

When the two of them were alone, Mugahid told Hafiza briefly about the trip. After that, neither said a word to the other. However, they were both determined to make another trip to Rafah. On that second trip, thanks to a coincidence that played a kindly role as coincidences are sometimes wont to do, an elderly man from Majdal, a village in Palestine, agreed to marry Nagiya.

After a violent sandstorm concealed the train tracks, the train stopped between al-Arish and Rafah, so many of the travelers cut their journeys short. Only a few continued on foot, plodding ahead like a line of captives and struggling to remain upright under the raging wind that was sending the tops of palm trees flying.

Mugahid, who had come out this time determined to return home alone, would plant each foot in front of him like a tent peg for fear of flying away. He grasped his turban with one hand and with the other beat on his gilbab, which would fill with air and billow like a sail, sending him reeling backward. Behind him, the hunchbacked girl quaked, clinging mightily to the satchel on her head, until the two of them reached the desolate marketplace of which nothing remained but palm trunks. Its palm-leaf booths were flying in all directions, leaving a state of chaos reminiscent of a battlefield where the fighting has just come to an end.

The sun, veiled behind the curtains of fine sand, was about to vanish completely. Not long afterward, the sandstorm abated and was followed by a light drizzle, which turned little by little into torrents of water and hail that pelted down on them in the open space alongside the tiny houses and the rows of tents.

Mugahid headed for Sheikh Mas'ud's tent, reassured by the thought of dealing with someone he knew despite the fact that he'd exhibited no enthusiasm as a matchmaker on the previous occasion. The only other people in the tent were an elderly Palestinian man and his jovial son, who joked nonstop. The old man wore a keffiyeh on his head under a camel-hair headband, which he fiddled with from time to time without saying a word. Hardly visible, he only spoke in order to affirm something someone else had said or to answer a question. After the cups of coffee were passed around, the elderly man said that he liked Mugahid, and asked for Nagiya's hand in marriage without having laid eyes on her. The son said she would be the sister to five men, and that they would protect her and take care of her as one of their own so long as she feared God in the service of their father, who was sinking deeper by the day into a slough of loneliness, and who felt himself a burden to his sons' wives.

After they recited the Fatiha, their host drew up the contract and collected his commission. Then they spent the rest of the evening around the fire until every one of them dozed off where he sat, wrapped in his cloak.

The following morning Mugahid bade them farewell and went to the train station, in his pocket a gold pound and a marriage contract bearing the fingerprint of Sheikh Rub'i Abu Sharkh, whose wealth in the form of vineyards and looms was the stuff of legends. In the other direction, two horses set out. One of them carried Sheikh Abu Sharkh, while the other was ridden by his son Ziyad, who held the reins of his father's horse with the bride seated behind him.

A l-Ish was inundated by the flood.

As the waters overran the shores of the irrigation canal, piles of harvested corn floated about and cotton plants were submerged. Alongside dead grasses and dry corn leaves, white tufts of cotton floated like lamps on the frothy, turbid water as it invaded the houses. Ducks and geese swam, while the dead bodies of rabbits and featherless baby birds sank to the bottom. The villagers began evacuating young children and the elderly on the backs of buffalos to Mit Suhayl and al-Balashun. These towns, to the north and south of al-Ish, had suffered less damage. The young men carried sacks of grain and jars of cheese so they would be less of a burden to their hosts in the neighboring villages to which they would be emigrating temporarily. Each family chose its destination in keeping with bonds of kinship and intermarriage.

Mubarka insisted on staying alone in the farmhouse. Mugahid sought out Badr's help in forcing her to leave, but her response was final: "I'm not going anywhere. I'll live or die by myself."

But she didn't die. She placed enough on her bed to keep her alive: bread, water, and a big jar of cheese, then closed up her room to keep the water at bay. However, it began seeping under the door and through its interstices until it was as deep as the water in the courtyard. She had resigned herself to circumstances, not having taken a stance in favor of either life or death. She began amusing herself by watching things bob up and down in the water, delighted by her sense of fearlessness and lack of expectation. She watched the water level rise along the bedposts, waiting to see how far the water would go and whether it would immerse her or not. She waited with a coolness that was devoid of anything but the pleasure of seeing probabilities fulfilled, as though it were an ordinary game of perception that had nothing to do with her own life or death.

The water stopped rising just below the edge of the mattress, and she happily imagined herself floating about on a flying carpet. She would reach out and play in the water until she dozed off. She wasn't afraid of the dark or of being alone in the village, where the only sounds one heard were the croaking of frogs and chirping of crickets. She didn't see any need to leave her bed in order to answer the call of nature, since the outhouse was full. Its tank had overflowed under pressure from the gushing water, its contents mingling with the floodwaters and its stench now noticeable all over the farmhouse. She tried urinating from a standing position the way men do, and laughed when she found that she had wet her bed, which had yet to be reached by the floodwaters.

As the days passed, the water began soaking into the earth, and Mubarka watched the descent of the water level along the copper bedposts. By the seventh day she could see the contours of the ground beneath a hand span of murky water, and she placed breadcrumbs on top of the oven in the farmhouse courtyard to feed the pigeons, which had returned to their nests in the walls and in the open-sided earthenware jars that hung from the ceiling.

For many days thereafter, the pigeons' morning cooing was her happiest diversion, and she wished life could go on this way forever. She listened from her bed to the flirtation of the enamored pairs, anticipating the males' charming pursuit of the females, the brief fluttering of wings, the hopping from place to place, and the increasingly rapid rhythm of the singing before the females yielded beneath the males, who were more beautiful than they.

She watched the dampness recede day after day, and when she heard the sound of someone trying the farmhouse door, she didn't rise from her resting place. Instead, she went on calmly observing the rays of the sun as they slipped in through the window and were refracted toward the ceiling as they collided with the stained-glass figurines that adorned the bed rails at her head. Meanwhile, she could hear the joyous honking of the homeward-bound geese.

She didn't look at Mugahid, and didn't ask about her father. In fact, she noticed that she hadn't thought about him once during the entire week of the flood. She hadn't stopped to wonder whether he'd left the village with the others or stayed home. Aunt Hamida came up to her and looked into her eyes. Tears flowed down her cheeks when she saw how gaunt and lackluster her face had become. Mubarka's lips moved in what appeared to be a smile, and the old woman took her hand and kissed it. Mubarka hurriedly withdrew her hand, gesturing to her in welcome, and sat up straight.

The old woman took her by the hand and they proceeded to clean the farmhouse with Mugahid, though Mubarka didn't exchange a single word with him. They gathered the bloated rabbits in the inner courtyard and shoveled up the piles of feces, dung, and firewood that had been deposited by the floodwaters in the inner rooms. They released the geese and chickens they'd brought back from al-Balashun, the nearby village where they'd gone to stay briefly, and closed the door that separated the inner and outer courtyards. By nightfall they had finished cleaning the front rooms, including Mubarka's bedroom, and had collected everything in a huge pile in front of the farmhouse to be taken to the field as soon as the streets were dry.

Aunt Hamida prepared some asida. It was the first hot meal Mubarka had eaten for two weeks, and she came back to her bed dead tired, not knowing how or when. However, at midnight she awoke to the sound of Aunt Hamida's snores. The old woman had spread a mat for herself not far from the bed.

For fear of making himself a laughingstock, Mugahid had decided to endure Mubarka's treatment of him in silence. Hence, he spoke to no one about the matter, not even her father, whose house he began frequenting in the evenings, and where he would stay late into the night. The two men thus nurtured a friendship that was sustained by a shared sense of guilt, and by solidarity in the face of Mubarka's rejection. They would drink strong tea and take turns puffing on the shisha, breaking the silence occasionally with a memory or terse comment.

Mugahid held out patiently for as long as he could. However, he couldn't avoid the thought that she might interpret his patience as a sign of the weakness of old age. What pained him most of all was the feeling of rejection, and he devised a plan to put an end to the situation. One evening he dismissed Aunt Hamida before sundown and, telling Badr he was feeling tired, didn't come back with him after the final evening prayer as he usually did. For the first time since her wedding night, Mubarka found herself alone with Mugahid, who instructed her to get the stove ready, then sat smoking until midnight.

When he came into her room, he didn't give her a chance. He flung himself on top of her, pinning her arms with his hands as he ripped her underwear with his foot, and pressing with all the strength in his thighs to keep her legs apart. She resisted, but to no avail. Then, suddenly, she went still, like a dead woman with her eyes open. She didn't allow herself even to be pained by the dry thing that had penetrated her. Her stillness and glassy stare provoked him, increasing his agitation, and he discovered in himself a violence he hadn't known before. He wanted either to cause her pain or to see her enjoy herself. However, she showed no sign of life apart from her calm, steady breathing.

The moment she was out from under his weight, she had a bout of vomiting that spattered his face and soaked the bed. He left the room in a fury, and only returned when he was called in by Aunt Hamida, who came the next morning and found Mubarka drenched in sweat, writhing with fever and deliriously repeating Muntasir's name.

At dawn he set out for Zagazig on his filly's back. By noon he had returned, followed by a doctor in a horse-drawn carriage. The doctor examined the patient. He gave instructions for cold compresses to be placed on her head and changed at regular intervals, and prescribed medicines which he asked them to bring as soon as possible. Mugahid took charge of the patient, while her father followed the doctor's carriage. He returned after the final evening prayer with the prescribed remedies, only to find Mubarka in a coma and unable to take the medicine.

Not expecting her to live out the night, Badr bought a burial shroud and issued instructions for a grave to be dug. The two men spent the night smoking beside her bed. From time to time one of them would get up to bring more corncobs to feed the fire or change the water in the shisha, while Aunt Hamida sat next to her on the bed wiping her brow.

Suddenly, Mubarka gasped deeply, and both men leapt to their feet. She gestured with her hand, whereupon Mugahid left the room and rushed back in with a glass of water. Her father helped her sit up while Mugahid brought the cup to her lips. After taking a few sips, she pushed his hand away. He dried her sweat-drenched face and let her rest again. She was like someone who had just returned from a long trek in a desert.

She opened her eyes and ran her hands over the wetness on the bed. Looking at Mugahid before her heavy eyelids shut once again, she saw him as feeble and genial, and his smooth, rectangular head seemed to her as tiny as a newborn's. As she alternated between sleeping and waking, she felt as though she were on a swing: sometimes in the sky, sometimes on the ground. And all the while her mind was occupied with Muntasir, whom she would see approaching in the distance. At times he would wave to her from the top of the minaret, and at other times she would feel his hand on her cheek and hear him saying fondly, "How are you, Mubarka?"

She spent long days between melancholic wakefulness and the stillness of coma before managing at last to stand on her feet again.

Mugahid didn't blame her for her delirium. On the contrary, he appeared content, his spirit light with the relief of having been spared the burden of being responsible for her death, which had come so very near. When she began to lose her pallor and regain her good health, he went back to lying down beside her.

Nevertheless, she didn't surrender. Instead she developed new methods of eluding him. She started to get her period twice a month, and would fast every Monday and Thursday in gratitude to God for her recovery. However, the surest protection came from the Sandman, whom she could summon whenever she hadn't managed to find some other excuse. As for Mugahid, he had no need for all these precautions to realize that he was unwanted.

He went back to Hafiza, leaving the big farmhouse to Mubarka and her servant. With every new sunrise he would emerge bathed and clad in a new change of clothes. Hafiza would leave the bathwater in the tub until midmorning, at which time she would throw it into the street in the presence of the largest possible number of witnesses. Then she would head for the gathering of women seated in the shade behind the wall and chatter about her husband, saying, "Abu Salama ate such-and-such," "Abu Salama said such-and-such," "Abu Salama asked for my advice on what he should plant on the feddan to the south of the farmhouse," or "Abu Salama registered half a feddan in my name in case I might need it someday."

News began traveling from the small house to the farmhouse about the man known as Abu Salama. The fact that he was thus named with reference to his son highlighted the difference between the two wives and served as a reminder that a man's return to his wife and children is inevitable. None of this news succeeded in moving Mubarka, who saw in Mugahid nothing but an old man who smelled like a billy goat. Nor did Aunt Hamida's advice do anything to make Mugahid acceptable to her. Not, that is, until Hafiza came strutting by the farmhouse one day like someone who had delivered the coup de grâce to a mortal foe. When she found herself face to face with Mubarka, who stood inside her half-open door, she crowed, "When a man's got children at home, he's bound to be back even if he's roamed!"

In response, Mubarka opened the door and, standing up to her rival, patted the spot below her abdomen and said, "For your information, he'd give anything to have a taste of this! All I have to do is give him the go-ahead!"

Flustered and taken aback by the normally silent young woman's immodest gesture, defiant look, and unexpected retort, Hafiza quickly withdrew without adding another word. She could see in the lioness's eyes a determination to carry out her threat. However, she wasn't proud of the fact that she was so thin-skinned that she quaked like jelly under the force of the blow.

When Mugahid took Mubarka away from his nephew, Hafiza had looked upon her as a victim, just as she had Muntasir. She'd only begun to feel bitterness and hatred toward her when she found herself and her children despised and relegated to cramped quarters, not knowing what Mubarka might ask for in addition to the farmhouse. After all, the man whose cough at the end of the street had once been sufficient to send all the children scurrying for cover in some dark corner of the big farmhouse was now a mere puppet in the hands of this teenage girl. It was obvious that he'd only come back to Hafiza after being humiliated in the young woman's bed. Hafiza alone knew how frustrated and worthless her husband must have felt when he was on top of the lioness, and she was sure he would go back to her the minute she opened her legs a few inches for him.

The people of al-Ish took pride in their forebears' success in draining the swamp and reclaiming its land, which they had divided among themselves by mutual consent. They also took pride in the fact that they'd been able to establish the renown of their own local saint alongside two other extraordinary men of God. They'd managed to turn the mulid celebration associated with their "silent sheikh" into the third of three mulid celebrations in the region, the other two being that of Sheikh Guda at Minya al-Qamh and Sheikh Sa'dun at Bilbeis. Not once over the course of an entire century had they failed to celebrate the life of the sheikh who had come to al-Ish—they knew neither whence nor how—to summon its people to lend assistance to the Mamluk commander Murad Bey.

During the days of chaos and panic that followed the news that Napoleon Bonaparte's army had taken Alexandria, al-Ish had been visited by a little old man who was so thin he was hardly visible. In the old man's honor, the preacher at the mosque had offered to let him deliver the Friday sermon. The sheikh ascended the pulpit and began his sermon by reminding his listeners that someone who equips another to fight in defense of Islam is entitled to the same reward due someone who goes to battle. He urged the people of al-Ish to volunteer in support of the Mamluk commander who, after losing his battle with the French at Shubra Khit near Damanhur, had rejected Napoleon's ultimatum to surrender and had made up his mind to confront the French in Cairo.

Suddenly, he digressed from the topic of his sermon. His voice took on the sound of thunder and he pointed to the west: "To the west!" he shouted, "To the west, Ibrahim. To the west, O Bey!" Then he fell silent and came down from the pulpit without saying another word. Days went by without his breaking his silence. He made no move to collect the material support he had come for, nor did he seem to have any desire to go elsewhere.

Since he stayed in the mosque night and day, the villagers supplied the sheikh with blankets and began vying for the privilege of bringing him his meals three times a day. They would leave the food beside him, then take it away again without his having eaten more than what would fill a sparrow's craw. He would go on standing, bowing, and prostrating until he was overcome with exhaustion. Then he would curl up and descend into a slumber so peaceful that if you passed him, you could hardly have detected the sound of his feeble breaths.

When news arrived of the terrible defeat the French had inflicted on Murad Bey's army at the foot of the pyramid, the people of al-Ish realized that the sheikh's cry had been an attempt to direct Ibrahim Bey, who was stationed with his troops to the east of the Nile, to join Murad Bey to its west, where the invaders eventually arrived.

They worked together to build him a house, and when it was finished, everyone who'd taken part in the construction gathered to celebrate and to declare the sheikh, whose name none of them remembered, a new resident. Then, as they were all sitting on the roof, it suddenly fell in. But no one was injured. In fact, they remained seated precisely as they had been. Not even the glasses of hibiscus tea in their hands shook. When they'd recovered from their shocked surprise, they cheered, "La ilaha illa Allah—There is no god but God!" and "Allahu akbar!—God is greatest!" They considered the event to be a miracle performed by the sheikh, whom they thenceforth dubbed "the silent one."

The Silent Sheikh then came to live in his new home. The women of the village outdid themselves competing for the chance to clean the house and fetch water for him, and he would bring his clothes to be laundered in their houses. The first cucumbers and tomatoes to be harvested had to go to the Silent Sheikh, and the colostrum produced by every animal that gave birth had to receive his blessing before her young had a taste of it. If anyone, human or beast, became ill, they would bring them to the Silent Sheikh, who would recite verses from the Qur'an over them for healing and protection, and as he performed the recitation with both his eyes and his lips, the patient would be instantly healed. When the Silent Sheikh died, they buried him in the room above which they'd been sitting when its roof fell in. The day of his departure became a mulid celebration. The mulid quickly became famous thanks to the generosity of the people of al-Ish toward the singers, whose food was provided for one night by every household, as well as toward all the other strangers in attendance, including the asaliya vendors, the swing owners who gave the children rides, and even the gypsies, whose mysterious circus was looked upon with some distrust due to the fact that the gypsy girls would strip in front of the young men. You could have sex with them behind a curtain for a piaster and sometimes for free if you caught the girl's fancy. As for the women who practiced divination, made amulets, or cast magic spells to make people love or hate each other, they enjoyed more popularity among the women in al-Ish than they did anywhere else. The villagers had never once missed the mulid celebration for their saint, not even during the days of the plague that had struck some eight years earlier. Despite the decree issued by the authorities forbidding public gatherings, al-Ish received everyone who came to visit the saint's tomb and the mulid celebration went on, albeit with the least fanfare possible.

Despite the destruction wrought by the flood that year, they didn't break with custom. After everyone had returned to the village, they went out looking for elderly folks who had no children and had been forgotten in the panic that attended the flood. They buried what they were able to recover of their corpses, whose guts had burst inside the ruined houses. Then the men began clearing the streets of the corpses of small animals and birds and burying them in the fields. As soon as life had regained its usual rhythm, they sent word to the singers, informing them that the mulid celebration for the Silent Sheikh would be held at its regular time. The singers then spread the news among the vendors and circus performers.

The strangers came at the appointed time. When Hafiza heard the commotion, she ran to the door to watch them as they dragged their chests along, holding the hems of their robes up with their teeth. Delighted, she knew that the ammunition that had fallen into her hands would enable her to decide the battle with Mubarka, who had taken her place in the farmhouse while exiling Hafiza to a tiny, cramped dwelling. She hadn't slept a wink until her man had come back to her. Yet even now that he was back, the young woman went on living comfortably alone in the farmhouse, and he might go back to her at any moment.

She waited until the gypsies had pitched their tents in the village square and their fortunetellers had begun going up and down the streets, baskets on their heads. She waved to a woman who was shouting in a cracked voice, "Whatever you want to know, I'll make it crystal clear!"

Hafiza opened the door for her and pulled her inside, looking this way and that to see if there was anyone out and about despite it being siesta time. Pleased to find no one, she shut the door.

The woman, whose forehead was adorned with a tattoo in the shape of a reclining lion and whose features were concealed by a veil from which round silver bangles hung, realized what Hafiza's complaint must be.

"So you're afraid of a little dove that's distracting your man, and you want to keep him at home," said the gypsy woman. Without uttering a word, Hafiza eyed her fearfully. The woman then began speaking with invisible beings, and before long her voice disappeared beneath a frightening manlike rasp. From deep inside her, the jinni began dictating in terse phrases what Hafiza was to do. The jinni demanded a pair of white roosters devoid of all markings, as well as a keddah of crushed wheat, to be brought by the gypsy woman. He then commanded Hafiza to bring all her gold and an earthenware jar. The woman placed the gold inside the jar and sealed it with mud, all the while reciting words that Hafiza, who stood there in a trance, couldn't understand. Finally, the gypsy instructed her in the jinni's voice to open the jar again after the moon had completed an entire cycle. Then she was to put on the gold and take a bath, and her man would never leave her house again!

The seven days of the mulid celebration came to an end and the strangers went back to where they'd come from. Hafiza began counting the days and watching the moon's progress across the sky, determined to abide strictly by the timetable she'd been given. But when she opened the jar, all she found inside was a handful of potsherds. She closed her heart over her sorrow, not daring to talk about what had happened for fear others would gloat over her misfortune.

She'd lost the gold, and hadn't been able to confine the man!

Mugahid went back to the farmhouse, not because Hafiza's magic had failed, nor because of the success of some counter-magic on Mubarka's part. Rather, he went back in fulfillment of a duty to protect the young woman now that al-Ish had been occupied by squads of dromedary riders who roamed the streets night and day. Armed with riding whips, the tall, lank black men on camelback would flay the back of anyone who dared come out of his house at night, and they had destroyed any sense of privacy inside people's homes. There was no longer a single woman who could remove any of her clothing in her inner courtyard. At any moment she might catch a glimpse of two gleaming rows of teeth that looked as though they were suspended in midair beneath a white turban, since the teeth were all one could see of the black face in the dark.

The dromedary riders had come to al-Ish following the theft of Sultan Hussein Kamel's livestock. It was the largest theft that had ever taken place in the region, and news of it was on everyone's lips. It was being reported that Muntasir was behind it. According to some of the numerous rumors in circulation about where he had gone after leaving al-Ish, Muntasir had taken up residence in Mit Suhayl, where he had married the daughter of Sa'id al-Ghul, his late father's best friend, who had helped Muntasir bring together the surviving members of his father's gang. Of these men, even the toughest had been unable to hold back their tears when Muntasir walked in. When they saw him they felt as though Salama had come back from the dead, and when he'd gotten settled among them and began popping his neck with sudden turns of the head the way his father had been known to do, they recited the Fatiha and swore him their allegiance.

They say the gang became as powerful as it had been before the ill-fated robbery that had scattered its members, driving some of them into hiding for many long years, and putting others behind bars. Salama's death had ignited a fire that only cooled when his son took over the gang leadership and raided the cattle pens of the man the British had installed as Egypt's sultan after deposing his nephew for declaring enmity against them.

The occurrence of the most recent theft had been confirmed. Many of the people living in the region had gotten a taste of the meat, which had been passed around in secret by the butchers. They had sold it for a quarter of its original price, and those who had no money had managed to get some by bartering a keddah of wheat or corn. The gang that had carried out the operation hadn't kept so much as a single calf alive lest it serve as evidence that might lead to its members' arrest. However, the authorities managed to trace the rotten stench back to the skins that had been thrown into drains, and identified a number of villages in Sharqiya, among them al-Ish, as being implicated in the crime. Huge forces swept through the village, combing every inch of it, and imposed a curfew from sundown to sunrise. However, they failed to lay their hands on the perpetrators.

The existence of Muntasir's gang hadn't been confirmed, and Mugahid didn't know whether he ought to be worried about what strangers might to do to Mubarka, or about what might happen to him if his nephew returned. He came back to the farmhouse visibly aged, and made no attempts to crowd out the ghosts that inhabited the bed of the young woman, who'd lived for so long with her mother's spirit that she'd become like the living dead.

He began dividing his time between the field, where he would help his sons, and Hafiza's house, taking care to be back at the farmhouse before dark. He would smoke the shisha alone in the sitting room until it was time for the final evening prayer, then pray and lie down where he was. Mubarka didn't know whether to be happy or sad. She felt protected in her rigid world. At the same time, though, she felt the weight of memories—not only of her short-lived romance, but also of loneliness and silence on long winter nights. And worst of all was the fact that she took seriously Hafiza's threat—a threat she had voiced more than once: "When a man's got children at home, he's bound to be back even if he's roamed!" She felt she was losing a battle without a fight. But in order to win her war with Hafiza, all she needed was a look: an altogether new look, and an overtly lascivious invitation of the sort that Mugahid would never have expected.

He came back from the field one day with a sullen expression on his face. He rushed straight into the storage room, picked up a rope, and rushed out again. Just then he was waylaid by Mubarka, who blocked the farmhouse doorway. She was wearing her black nightgown, which was now loose on her. She had let her hair down behind her back, leaving a lock of it in front to cover her cleavage. She asked him coquettishly if he wanted anything. As she did so, she looked up at him. Then she glanced down toward her bosom as though directing his gaze there, confirming to him that her breasts were still youthful despite her thinness.

The message came through loud and clear. He was able to penetrate the words' delicate outer shell and hear the invitation that he'd waited for for so long and received so unexpectedly. He pushed her nervously aside as though he wanted to avoid a scandal, then rushed out, looking around without giving himself the chance to wonder whether what he'd done was right or not: Should he have shaken off the prudence born of old age, or had he done what he was supposed to do in order to put her in her place as a woman? He didn't know any more. However, he was astounded at the rapidity of his heartbeats and intoxicated by the buoyant movement between his thighs that had been triggered by the wink of an eye heavily and coquettishly outlined in black.

He rejoined his sons, who were in the field reinforcing barriers they had set up to contain the water they had flooded it with. They'd drenched the field using a couple of Archimedean screws that they took turns rotating, and now all that remained was to smooth out the muddy earth before they planted the clover. He threw them the rope they needed to hitch the leveling device to the buffaloes. Then he returned to the woman who lay on the bed in her nightgown with one leg dangling off its edge.

He pushed her gently to the center of the bed, then immediately undressed and kicked his trousers onto the mat at the foot of the bed. With an agility he hadn't imagined he was capable of, he leapt onto the bed and lay down beside her. He reached inside her nightgown, where he found the softness of the freshly plucked spot. She started at his approach, but he quickly passed over her vagina, choosing instead to massage the soft, fleshy mound to the front of it. Then, with all the force of the pleasure that was packed into the expletive, he cried excitedly, "You little bitch!" However, he regretted using the phrase when he noticed how inappropriate it was for his age. He unhurriedly drew the nightgown down to reveal the breasts that had been peeking out of its neck opening. On top of her, he thrust while watching in the wardrobe mirror, and for the first time in his life, he saw his buttocks moving as though they belonged to someone else who was imitating him. In the midst of his feverish agitation he began ranting deliriously about her female organ, referring to it by its most vulgar name. Meanwhile, he looked in the mirror to see if his reflection would repeat his profanities. As for her, she was silent, her eyes closed, trying to avoid the sweaty odor of the aroused man atop her, who cussed and thrust with ever-increasing speed.

Then, suddenly, he went limp and collapsed at her side. She felt stifled, because there was a peak she hadn't reached. She'd experienced it with Muntasir even though he'd never gone into her, since he'd been able to take her by the hand until she rested there. His face hovered sadly before her in a hazy image that then dissipated and left her in a state of disquieting forlornness. It reminded her of the coma she'd gone into when she was ill, and that had brought her to the exhausting edge without delivering her over to death's blessed rest.

Mugahid withdrew from the room without her opening her eyes to see him, and she heard the door close. Then she heard him call Aunt Hamida to spread a mat for him in the cold courtyard. He began recalling what had happened to the sound of the gurgling of the shisha as the water went round and round inside it. Seated in the cloud of smoke, he recalled the erection of her distinctive nipples. Through the curves of Mubarka's firm body now coming back to life, he'd discovered that he had never really known women before. He thought about the fact that Hafiza's body had never been like this. On the contrary, she'd had flaccid breasts and a worn-out body from the time she was a teenager. Casting his sixty years behind him, he noticed as he sat there that his joints weren't aching any more. Little did he know that he would spend the rest of his life hoping for even the most fleeting erection in those same breasts, and that the memory of that night would recede into the past until he came to doubt whether it had ever happened.

As for Mubarka, she reverted to her former indifference toward him, and his sense of chagrin became more overpowering than ever before. The only relief he found was in dreams, where he would recapture the moment of her blissful enjoyment. He would wake up ecstatic, only to fall quickly back into emptiness, yet without ceasing to hope for another moment like it.

B adr died alone in his house during the curfew that had been imposed on al-Ish, and his son-in-law only learned of his death when he failed to show up for prayers in the mosque two days in a row. When he went to check on him, he was met by the odor of the disintegrating corpse.

When Mugahid left Mubarka and went back to his wife and children, Badr had continued visiting his daughter every night after the final evening prayer to make sure she was all right, but he'd received no welcome from her. Instead, she left it to Aunt Hamida to serve him. If he kept calling to her, she would come and sit across from him in silence, and only say as much as was necessary in order to answer his questions. Consequently, he started visiting her less and less frequently until, with the arrival of the squads of dromedary riders, he stopped coming altogether. She no longer knew anything about him until, one day after the noon prayer, Mugahid came and conveyed the news to her in the least cordial way possible.

"Your father's passed away."

She made no reply, and he didn't wait for one. He simply delivered the news, then went back to help get ready to wash and wrap the body and to oversee the burial. She rose unhurriedly and called Aunt Hamida. Then the two of them gathered up the things they would need for the three-day wake, and she headed for her father's house. It was obvious that he'd made all the necessary preparations prior to his death. He had lain down facing the qibla with his arms crossed over his chest, and with the graveclothes that Aunt Hamida had made for Mubarka beside him. After her recovery he had taken them to his house and instructed Aunt Hamida not to let Mubarka know that their preparations for her death had gone this far.

He had removed from the graveclothes the head covering that would have been used for a woman and placed it near where he slept. However, this wasn't the only preparation Badr had made. He'd even paid the undertaker his wages in corn and wheat for washing his corpse, burying him and reading the Qur'an from beginning to end at his grave over a period of forty weeks, with one reading every Thursday.

Mubarka didn't go out behind the men who carried the bier, and she didn't shed a single tear to silence the gossiping of the women who'd come to offer their condolences. Her silence and dispassionate expression prompted them to recall in whispers the story of her wedding day, which she thought had been long forgotten by everyone but her.

Mugahid went to live in his late father-in-law's house in order to be near Mubarka, who began a period of mourning dictated by duty. Since the nightly curfew was still being strictly enforced, she received the women who came to offer their condolences during the day. When the last of the women had left the house, Mubarka would stay with Aunt Hamida while Mugahid sat in the sitting room. As he sat there, he recalled the night when he'd come to ask for her hand on behalf of his nephew only to find that Badr had misunderstood him and thought he was asking to marry her himself. He thought back on how he hadn't corrected Badr by telling him that he had come on his nephew's behalf, not on his own. And over and over he recalled the glimpse he had caught of her as she fled from his path—a glimpse that had robbed him of his senses.

Hafiza attended the wake with a look of exaggerated gloom on her face, trying her best to stave off the worst feeling anyone in al-Ish could possibly be accused of: malicious glee over someone grieving a death.

Mubarka went out to the grave on the first Thursday after her father's death, then came back and began gathering up her things to return to the farmhouse. As she did so, Mugahid told her of his desire for her to stay in her father's house.

"It wouldn't do for us to leave this house to the jinn, especially when the children and their mother are living in a cracker box."

Contrary to his expectations, Mubarka welcomed the suggestion, and for a moment she imagined that staying in the house she'd been raised in would turn her into a little girl again and erase what had happened as though it had never been. Mugahid began moving her trousseau to her father's house while his sons set about moving their things back to the farmhouse, eager to return to their childhood home.

They thus resumed their lives in the house they had left against their will, which made it possible for Salama to become engaged to Tafida al-Fahl, the girl of his choice. He had refrained from asking for her hand officially throughout their stay in the little house, not only because it was so cramped, but also on account of the sense of degradation at being a virtual stranger, living away from the house he'd been born in. Mugahid's wife and children ignored him when he was around as they'd been accustomed to doing for so long, maintaining only the degree of contact necessary to ensure that they were respected among other families.

"It's as if we have to rent him when we need him," Salama remarked to his two brothers when he came back from the bride's house, where he'd struggled to shake off a feeling of phoniness as he introduced his father so that he could speak on his behalf with the father of the bride, Abd al-Ra'uf al-Fahl. Once the engagement had become official, Mugahid was oblivious to the wedding preparations, and he attended the wedding as a stranger as well. Even the service of escorting the bride on the back of his filly—a service he'd often provided to humor strangers—he didn't perform for Salama, who insisted on walking his bride from her home to the farmhouse.

He no longer paid any attention to the brusque treatment he received from his family if he went to the farmhouse or encountered his sons in the field when he came out to get the filly. All that mattered to him any more was Mubarka's approval. Like a gambler who tries to recoup his losses by gambling still more, only to lose all the more, he became less able to part with her with every passing day. When Mubarka began eating burnt mud out of the oven and suffering from bouts of exhaustion and vomiting, Mugahid felt a thrill he had never felt before. He didn't care about fathering any more children. However, he received the signs of her pregnancy with the pride of someone who could now declare to all that he'd taken possession of his young wife. He now had something with which to respond to the looks of malicious glee that he'd seen so clearly in people's eyes, and as Mubarka progressed in her pregnancy, he experienced greater and greater solace. He no longer needed to justify staying at her side, even to himself, on the basis of the danger posed by the squads of dromedary riders. In fact, he didn't even notice when the strangers departed after despairing of laying their hands on Muntasir.

He went back to receiving his old buddies, who always found something to marvel at when they came around. Every time they visited his house they were met by some new curiosity Mubarka had bought in Bilbeis. It was as though they hadn't been living before. It was the first time, for example, that they'd seen ceramic containers that one buys not to use, but simply for decoration. They also became acquainted with drinks other than hibiscus, coffee, and tea: things like cocoa and salep, whose white color and thick consistency amazed them the first time they had it.

"You'll have to take a bath after drinking this stuff!" they quipped, since it looked so much like semen, and they wondered aloud if it would require them to wash off their ritual impurity.

The sitting room in Badr's house was transformed into a gathering place for guests, and it was never empty. Its door remained open to the street to receive friends at any time, even when Mugahid wasn't at home. As for the door that connected the sitting room to the house proper, it remained closed, and would only be opened in Mugahid's presence when someone wanted to ask for a glass of water or a sugar cube. Mubarka received her firstborn into the world against the din of a meeting they had convened to resolve a problem that had been caused by Yusuf Abu Lughud, who for the life of him didn't know how to hold his tongue.

It was a Friday evening, and the men in the sitting room were all talking at once, yet without arriving at a solution to the problem Yusuf had caused during the Friday sermon. The preacher had been talking about the merit that attaches to arriving early for prayer, saying, "Those who come early bring a camel nearer to God, those who arrive after them bring a cow nearer, those who arrive after them bring a ewe, and those who—" when Yusuf looked around him and said, "In that case, I'll just barely manage to come in with the sheep!"

Those who heard him waited until the prayer had finished. Then they asked for an investigative council to be convened, and it was decided that the session would be held that same evening.

Aunt Hamida handed Mugahid the large teapot and pulled the sitting room door tightly shut so that the men wouldn't be able to hear Mubarka, who was struggling with labor pains. Smarting from the gravel that covered the oven on which she lay, she was striving mightily to obey the instructions of the midwife, Aunt Fahima. Suddenly, she let out a long scream, and out slid the newborn, followed by the slimy red placenta, which gushed out over the tiny pebbles.

"This was a victory from God. I'm going to name him Mansur," said a groggy Mubarka as she gazed at the tiny baby. Even though he realized the connection between the proposed name and that of Muntasir, Mugahid offered no objection.

He poured all the passion he felt for Mubarka into Mansur, who was a miniature spitting image of her. Whenever Mugahid left the house he would have him on his shoulders, his tiny legs dangling over his chest and his tender little hands clinging to his head. In the house he would spend his time on all fours, carrying him around the room on his back as the boy, giggling, grabbed hold of the collar of his gilbab and goaded him on with his little legs. As for Mubarka, she would look on in detached silence.

Mugahid continued to wait for a repeat of the moment of approval she had once granted him, and which had caused him to take pride in his masculinity for the first time in his life. Night after long night he would lie beside her, yet not once did she relinquish her deadly calm. The only exception to this was that now she would bring out her breast and give it to Mansur whenever he woke up. Mugahid would go searching with his fingers for her other breast, only to have her wince, then curl up around her baby.

He began asking himself how she could possess such self-mastery. He had to admit, in all honesty, that he wasn't exactly an alluring young man any more. But still, didn't she get the urge now and then? Was she seeing someone? If so, when? After all, he never left her side!

There was no longer any place for him. He was an exile in Mubarka's bed, and had been exiled from the farmhouse where Hafiza and his sons lived. He thought every night he spent in her bed would be his last. He would listen to the dawn call to prayer in the mosque, then leave for prayer. He would follow the imam absentmindedly, with a burning in his belly like the thirst one feels after eating salty old cheese. Prompted by a combination of heartbreak and rage, he would decide to leave the mosque and go back to his house and his wife, trying to imagine how his family might receive him. He was so distracted, he couldn't engage in any sort of dhikr or tasbih, so he just recited the words in a loud voice in an attempt to keep his distractedness at bay. However, when he had finished and began shaking hands with those on either side of him in the sole row of worshippers that had lined up behind the imam, his feet would lead him right back to Mubarka as though he were walking in his sleep. When he arrived he would find her awake, having prepared him a breakfast tray of eggs, ghee, cheese, and warm bread. He thought about the fact that her elegant way of preparing food was one of the reasons he kept coming back to her. As he ate what she placed before him, his eyes would devour her nipples, visible beneath her tunic, and he gazed with longing at the contrast between her erect, firm breasts and her trim, flat stomach. In response, he would extend his stay by her side by yet another day even though he knew in his heart of hearts that he was going downhill and that he had to return to the farmhouse.

"Abandon your home, and your strength will wane."

It was a saying he'd repeated to himself thousands of times like a mantra, and with the passing of the days and nights he'd become so convinced of its truth that it was a belief nothing could shake.

On the day he decided to return home once and for all, the European war broke out. The outcomes of the battles being fought between the British and the Germans in places that no one in al-Ish had ever heard of were reflected in the reactive decrees being issued by the British High Commissioner in Cairo. The decrees would reach the villages in the form of money-raising campaigns that descended upon them like thieves' raids. They began by imposing a charge of one Egyptian pound for every adult male in each family. Another campaign came to collect wheat and corn, taking a kayla for every feddan of land. Then came the raids to round up young men for conscription.

As news of the raids spread through al-Ish, its young men rushed to line up in front of the butcher, Sirhan al-Gazzar, who didn't put his cleaver down until every man in the village of conscription age had rid himself of his right index finger. Whoever was next in line would place his finger on the wooden chopping block, then turn his face away and close his eyes. With a single blow of the cleaver, the finger would go flying through the air until it landed wherever it landed, and the young man would be instructed to immerse the stub in a pot of boiling oil next to the butcher.

The fingers filled a bier over which the men prayed the funeral prayer. Then they were buried in a single grave. However, the loss of index fingers did nothing to stop the authorities from raiding al-Ish, since the Egyptian squad that had been hastily formed to take part in the war wasn't assigned to engage in combat but, rather, to serve the soldiers in the British army and their French and Russian allies in the Sinai and Palestine, as well as in distant places, such as Belgium, that no one had ever heard of before.

Two officers, one British and one Egyptian, came leading a squad of dromedary riders that began to hunt down the young men. Mugahid's son Salama, still in pain from the loss of his finger, fell into the soldiers' hands. They led him away to the assembly center they'd set up in the courtyard in front of the mayoral mansion, where crows could be heard cawing.

Hafiza had been fearful that seventeen-year-old Nagi, who had just barely sprouted whiskers, might also have his index finger cut off, and when it became clear that the campaign would be staying to strip al-Ish of its young men and teenage boys, she pleaded with him to hide in the woodpile on the roof. However, he couldn't remain exposed to sun, cold, and insects. So, thinking that the last place they would look for her son would be the house of her co-wife, Hafiza sent word to Mugahid, suggesting that they hide him there.

Mubarka welcomed the suggestion. In fact, she paid a personal visit to the farmhouse, and Hafiza felt that Mubarka's sympathy was genuine. Hence, she in turn welcomed her, certain now that she'd been right when her intuition told her not to be overly resentful of the young orphan girl.

Under cover of darkness, Mubarka brought Nagi back to her house concealed in a woman's gilbab. Once there, she led him to the dark hay storeroom at the back of the house. She gave him a woolen blanket, which he spread over the hay, and a jug of water, and told him to tap on the door three times whenever he needed anything. Then she shut the door from the outside, camouflaging it with empty baskets and sacks.

Mugahid thus found it necessary to go on living in Mubarka's house, which was no longer Badr's house, nor the house of the young woman who had insulted his masculinity. Rather, it had become his own house, since it was now home to half of his family: little Mansur, who romped and skipped from room to room, and Nagi, who lived hidden in the closed back room.

Time closed chapters that no one had ever imagined could be closed, such as memories of the plague, the cholera epidemic, the destruction wrought by the flood, and even the story of the Turkish family that had lived in al-Ish for nearly a century but whose stay there now seemed, to those who remembered it, like the passing of a cloud. However, the passing of the days hadn't succeeded in erasing the image of a certain medium-sized young man with a moon face and a bull's neck inherited from his father.

Muntasir had remained etched not only in the memories of those who had watched him grow up, but also in the minds of generations who had never seen him. However, those most intent on following his news were the generation that came to be known as "the generation of the seventy": the seventy young men whose mothers had conceived them on the day Mubarka was wed to Muntasir's uncle. The libido that had thrust its seed into their wombs had mingled with their sorrow over the fate of a young man for whom everyone felt a special fondness out of loyalty to his father, thanks to whom al-Ish had been held in awe among the surrounding villages for many long years after his death. The people of al-Ish even went on leaving their farm animals under the mulberry trees on hot summer nights without a single one being stolen.

Unlike everyone else, Mubarka had no need of memory. She could discern his scent in something he'd touched or someone

73

whose hand he'd shaken for as long as seventy days after the event. All she had to do was walk over a patch of wilted crops to know that Muntasir had been at the head of those who had demolished them the night before, and when the stench from the sultan's decaying livestock began to spread, she'd been able to tease from congealed blood and rotting hides the thread of the sweet fragrance she knew so well. Whenever she saw a soldier sneaking a peek at her from the back of his camel, her body would tingle with dread. She imagined that they knew her secret, and that they would force her to divulge information on Muntasir. These fears haunted her even in her sleep. She would dream that they'd grabbed her by the arm and led her away, then forced her to follow the scent until they reached the place where he was. Then she would awaken in a fright. She had no peace of mind until Muntasir was too far away for her to smell him.

Two years after Muntasir's disappearance, al-Ish was visited by an itinerant cloth salesman. When he passed in front of her door, Mubarka instructed Aunt Hamida to bring him into the house. Mubarka served him a dish of cream with two round loaves of toasted bread. After he'd eaten, she brought him a glass of tea and asked, "Do you know Muntasir al-Deeb?"

The salesman didn't recall the name, nor could she describe Muntasir's scent, which she had picked up on the man. In order to help him identify the person she was talking about, she began describing his features and the way he had of popping his neck by twisting it right and left. The man remembered selling him a section of coarse calico a couple of months earlier. He also remembered that he was a foreman who had been on good terms with Hagg Khattab, a contractor who was well known all over Sharqiya for overseeing the dredging and building of irrigation canals.

Some years later, a couple of young men came to collect signatures on a draft document demanding a constitution that had been written by Muhammad Farid. As Mubarka pressed her ink-stained thumb to the edge of the document, she looked intently into the eyes of one of the two men.

Then she asked him straight out, "Is Muntasir al-Deeb all right?"

"Yes," the young man whispered, "and he sends you his greetings." He reached into his pocket and brought out a newspaper clipping that contained a drawing of a group of men in shackles who were all holding hands. It was a picture of the terrorist gang that had cut the railroad track at Abu Hammad. They had overturned and looted a British train that was loaded with arms and headed for the canal region. The names of the accused weren't given, nor did the picture have a caption. However, the features of one of the men were identical to Muntasir's.

The young man identified himself as the lawyer who had defended them in court a week after their arrest. The trial had led to the resignation of the Interior Minister and a change in the court security system. The lawyers had devised a plan for their defense of the accused, while the leaders of the clandestine cell they belonged to had made a plan to smuggle them out of the courtroom.

They marshaled huge numbers of people to pack the courtroom, and in the midst of the excitement and confusion that attended the reading of their verdicts, which were quite severe, fireworks were set off. The soldiers guarding the court were the first to come rushing to see what had happened, and the detainees, finding themselves suddenly free, scattered into the crowd.

This was the first operation Muntasir had carried out in keeping with a clear political stance against the British occupation, whereas stealing livestock and destroying crops had reflected a kind of nostalgia for the path his father had taken and on which he had been raised. His desire to seek vengeance for injustice, if not against his uncle, then against any other tyrant, be he a mayor or a sultan, had found a ready response among his father's friends. Even so, seeing the way security measures were tightening the noose around their necks, they made no objection when he decided to disband the gang. However, Uncle Ruzza, who harbored an unrivaled loyalty to Salama, wasn't willing to leave "Ibn al-Ghali."

"I haven't got anybody I need to worry about in Mit Suhayl," said the man with the stooped back, determined to accompany Muntasir wherever he went. He suggested that Muntasir work with a certain contractor who had been held up by highway robbers near al-Ish some years earlier, and who had sought Salama out for protection. By the time the man reached his own town, Salama had apprehended the thieves, given them a good scolding, and recovered the stolen goods, which he immediately sent back with Ruzza. Together with the goods, he sent an apology that the man had suffered such an attack within the territory of a gang that had established traditions requiring them to protect strangers.

Hagg Khattab remembered Uncle Ruzza with some difficulty, although he hadn't forgotten the incident. After welcoming the two men warmly, he agreed to hire them, albeit unenthusiastically, since he was afraid their presence might cause him problems with the authorities. He recorded them in his books under false names, and by early the next morning, they had joined the workers. Uncle Ruzza would strike the mud with his shovel and empty it into a basket on Muntasir's back. The latter would take it up a rope ladder that hung against the slope of the bridge, then hoist his load onto a mound of mud alongside the waterway. At the end of the day the two men built a hut from reeds and willow trunks in the midst of a number of other huts under a stand of ancient sycamore trees whose branches intertwined in all directions.

With his white turban wrapped around a camel-hair skullcap, Hagg Khattab was like one of the elders of al-Ish. As for his son Abd al-Sattar, who helped him and took his place when he was away, Muntasir had been unsure about him from the beginning. A slender young man the same age as Muntasir or a bit older, Abd al-Sattar made a point of wearing a fez with his gilbab. He'd studied at the Azhar Institute in Zagazig, but found his niche with the laborers, among whom he was a king whose every command was obeyed. On the one hand, he would manage to get alone with the few girls who worked among the men, and who returned to their nearby villages in the evenings, and would flirt with the women who came to visit their husbands. On the other hand, he was constantly carrying a book around as though it were a badge of distinction, although he rarely sat down in the shade to open it.

Muntasir spent more than a year on the world's fringes among Hagg Khattab's workers. After dredging a drainage ditch in one location, they would go somewhere else to dig a canal or build canal locks. The city of Zagazig wasn't far away, but he never went there. From time to time they would be visited by merchants who had loaded their donkeys with jars of whey, bunches of onions and garlic, and baskets of tomatoes. Some of them would bring fabric for robes and tunics, ready-made gilbabs, and vests. He would buy what he needed from them without feeling any inclination to accompany Abd al-Sattar, who'd begun courting his friendship and inviting him along on his trips to Zagazig. He was afraid that if he went with him, he would come back and not find his treasure of sorrows, which he had deposited in his hut on the first day he came to live there. As soon as he settled in, he'd been assailed anew with painful memories of Mubarka. In the mornings he would carry on with his work in silence, hoeing the earth with pent-up hostility or hauling the basket of mud without joining in the workers' mournful singing, since it stirred up his memories. In the evening he would lie down on his straw mattress and close his eyes. She would appear before him with her earthen jar on her head, and he would feel the blood rushing noisily through his heart. He would recall his awkward greeting as though he were getting ready to deliver it with greater aplomb, but it would come out just as shakily as it always had: "How are you, Mubarka?"

Given his dignified silence and the vitality in his plump face, it was obvious that Muntasir was different from the destitute workers around him. Abd al-Sattar had concluded that Muntasir must be an aristocrat by birth with a story to tell, and he wanted to know more about it. Consequently, he exempted him from the work and made him a foreman like himself, who could step in for him when he was away or accompany a group of workers who were moving to another site. After their relationship had grown closer, Abd al-Sattar asked him to travel to Cairo with a group of workers to carry out a contract at the British camp in the Abbasiya desert.

Muntasir couldn't conceal his turmoil. However, he consented to the request that had been made by the foreman, who now treated him as a friend. On the appointed day, he was ready with a new gilbab, two tunics, two vests, and a pair of yellow leather shoes that he'd packed into a satchel. After bidding farewell to Uncle Ruzza, who told him he would be going back to Mit Suhayl to live out his last days, he jumped into one of the three mule-drawn carts, and the caravan set off along the Ismailiya Canal. It traveled the entire day, reaching Abu Za'bal just before sundown. It stopped in front of a waterwheel next to a date palm surrounded by a dense stand of mulberry trees. As the coachmen unhitched and foddered the mules, the workers lit a fire to make tea, which they drank with broken pieces of bread before wrapping themselves in their blankets and going to sleep. At dawn the caravan resumed its journey to Mostorod, and from there to the orchards of al-Matariya.

When the caravan approached al-Qubba Palace, a strange numbness flowed through Muntasir's veins as he peered at the wall before him. He stole a fleeting glance inside the palace's imposing gate, and a walkway and a huge fountain appeared through its wrought-iron interstices. He wondered what the sultan was like. In restless curiosity he aimed his gaze once more toward the gate, but saw no one on the long walkway.

The caravan turned onto al-Gabal Canal Street, and before he had recovered from his astonishment at the sight of al-Qubba Palace, he found himself before another, smaller palace that inspired in him more of a sense of beauty than of awe. He would later learn that it was known as the Za'faran Palace. The caravan turned south in front of this palace and made its way around the hospital, at which point the horizon opened onto the vast desert. The sun had nearly vanished on the other side, still visible in the distance between buildings higher than any Muntasir had ever seen.

The carts came to a halt in front of a large space surrounded by a barbed-wire fence, inside of which were piles of stones for use in construction. Two dark-skinned soldiers with rifles on their shoulders opened a wide wood-and-wire gate. The place was teeming with workers, some of whom were unloading stones and arranging them in neat piles, while others sifted sand. The workers were separated by another wire partition from a number of stone buildings that Muntasir recognized as the Egyptian officers' barracks. Some distance from the barracks stood a set of more luxurious buildings that housed the British commanders.

The new project was an expansion of the army camp that involved adding new stables for the horses, an ammunition depot, and underground trenches, and Hagg Khattab's workers had been assigned to do the digging under Abd al-Sattar's supervision.

It was a coincidence as cruel as it was amazing that Cairo, "the mother of the world," was Muntasir's first encounter with a city!

His camp quarters were a large barrack that resembled a stone stable with a tinplate roof that tirelessly collected the scorching heat of the daytime hours, then exhaled it at night in fiendish gusts to the sound of fifty snoring men, each of whom had placed his things next to his head. Every night he would flee from this misery, feeling his way step by step through the adjacent area of the camp with the excitement of a little boy whose feet are probing the ground for the first time. Every day he would go a few steps farther, in an attempt to return to what he had beheld in such wonderment on the day of his arrival in the city, until at last he found himself among a large number of white palaces and gardens with jasmine and bougainvillea trellises along their walls. He looked in stupefaction at the black, basalt-paved streets like someone who has suddenly discovered an enchanted city straight out of *The Arabian Nights*. He expected at any moment to find a hand reaching out to draw him into one of its palaces, where he would find himself surrounded by perils and delights.

Digging the camp was less exhausting than digging the canal had been, and the whey and dry bread that had been their fare was replaced with stewed broad beans and black lentils with soft bread. In addition, Abd al-Sattar got a bed for Muntasir and brought him to sleep in his room. Consequently, Muntasir's face recovered some of its youthful, healthy glow, while his nightly discoveries made him brighter than before.

One night he came back to the barracks looking jubilant. He described to Abd al-Sattar his discovery of the way to the Za'faran Palace, which they had passed on their way to their new worksite, and the women he'd seen strolling through its garden.

Abd al-Sattar began to laugh mockingly.

"So do you think I'm a liar, Abduh?" Muntasir demanded.

This made Abd al-Sattar laugh all the more. "No," he said. "But look here!"

When Abd al-Sattar accompanied him to al-Gaysh Street, Muntasir knew why his friend had been laughing at his excursion among eastern Abbasiya's orchards and palaces. For the first time he saw the tram as it went down the street between two rows of shops with brightly lit display windows, some of which had raised platforms outside them spread with mats. Abd al-Sattar stopped in front of one of the shops. Then he took Muntasir by the hand and they went inside.

Muntasir had learned to conceal his amazement at things lest he be the butt of Abd al-Sattar's jokes. He entered the place with the excited vigilance of someone crossing a drainage ditch atop a palm trunk or a log wobbling beneath his feet.

Inside, men sat here and there on wooden benches, drinking tea and coffee and smoking shishas. In one corner of the coffee shop sat a band, in front of which writhed a belly dancer who winked at the coffee shop goers.

On their way back, Muntasir felt a swarm of ants roaming wildly through his head. The basalt pavement under his feet had a fragility that reminded him of the feel of the dirt path he'd trodden when he left al-Ish. However, there was hardly any comparison between the fragility born of weakness and fear and the lightness he felt now and that nearly had him floating on air.

"Did you see the dancer, Abduh?" he asked.

"Her name is Tahiya," replied Abd al-Sattar. Muntasir didn't want to ask him how he knew her name.

The following morning as he was watching the workers, he was distracted. He was trying to recall the previous night's events and his return with Abd al-Sattar at midnight so as to determine whether the two of them had really talked about the dancer, or whether he'd been dreaming under the influence of the hashish he'd smoked for the first time.

From that day on, coffee shops were the most wonderful part of Muntasir's new life. He also became acquainted with the bars and brothels on Clot Bey Street when he and Abd al-Sattar began taking the tram to Ataba Square. It was in one of these brothels that he would come to know Samiha, with whom he had his first complete sexual encounter and a rush of pleasure that banished Mubarka's memory far, far away. He would even try to conjure her before going to sleep, but his memory could just barely put together the image of her carrying her earthenware jug. She would come to him only faintly, and without arousing any sense of regret.

On the nights when they decided not to go out, he began borrowing Abd al-Sattar's books. He would sit there trying to spell out the words, and little by little began reading quite adequately. The experience took him back to memories of his boyhood when he used to read *The Arabian Nights* to the men in Guda al-Khayyat's corner store. However, Mugahid, who had forced him to stop attending elementary school, had deprived him of this pleasure as well.

He learned the way to the printing houses and bookstores on al-Sanadiqiya Street, which gave him the opportunity to get to know some students at Azhar and to sit with them in places such as al-Fishawi Coffee Shop on al-Hussein Street, and al-Qazzaz Coffee Shop on al-Muski Street. Their encounters made him feel as though he were back in al-Ish, since most of the coffee shop goers were from the countryside. It was as though he were sitting in Guda's corner store or in front of the mosque, the only differences being that instead of sitting cross-legged on a straw mat as they would have in al-Ish, they were seated on benches, and the fact that there was a waiter nearby to take their orders. However, the most important difference lay in the nature of the discussions, which, instead of revolving around irrigation, the harvest, and the injustices perpetrated by tax collectors, had to do with the relationships between the sultan, the hated British governor, and his Egyptian collaborators; the efforts being made by Muhammad Farid, who had taken over the leadership from Mustafa Kamel in the struggle for independence; news of the European war; and other topics that had become Muntasir's newest source of enjoyment. These things gave him the sense that he was where he belonged, especially now that he could move about on his own rather than being tied to Abd al-Sattar.

Some students took him to the Matatiya Coffee Shop on Ataba Square, where he was dazzled by the experience of sitting with intellectuals and men of letters. His friends pointed out to him an elderly turbaned man surrounded by a circle of rapt listeners, and he could hardly believe that he was sitting in the presence of Sheikh Rashid Rida, who occupied the place once held by his teacher and mentor, Imam Muhammad Abduh.

When he got to know members of the resistance cells, he fled from the army camp and went to be trained in the use of arms and hand grenades. He took part in a number of successful operations, the most dangerous and critical of which was the attack on the Abu Haddad train. The operation that had involved smuggling them out of the courtroom had been another victory that intensified the occupation powers' rage at the Egyptian authorities, whom they deemed not serious about supporting the British in their war effort. In the midst of the hubbub that attended the defendants' liberation, someone slipped an envelope into his hand. It contained three pounds, a recommendation that he flee to Palestine with a brief description of the best ways to get there, and a suggestion that he stay in Nablus. As he sat on the train, Muntasir went over his seven-year journey, in the course of which he had known fear, joy, and a sense of power. He felt no regret now over what Mugahid had done to him, since he would otherwise have lived and died in al-Ish without realizing how vast the world was, or that a person can move from place to place and create his destiny rather than surrender to a life of stagnation, bound by a strand from a spider's web.

One of the two boys was fighting in the war, and the other was hiding from it. Mugahid threw himself into work like someone discovering a new pleasure. Ali, who had learned everything he knew about farming from Muntasir and Salama when he was a little boy, was amazed when he saw how little experience his father had. However, he was pleased with the signs of kindheartedness that he'd begun observing in a man he had once feared more than death.

He remembered how his father had mercilessly left him to work in the field when he was Mansur's age. As for Mansur, Mugahid would have him ride behind him on the filly and, upon their arrival, would seat him at the edge of the waterway. And however engrossed he was in the work, he wouldn't let this prevent him from responding attentively to the inquisitive boy's questions.

On the days when he didn't bring Mansur, Mugahid would drive the filly in front of him along with the livestock instead of pampering her the way he'd done before. And rather than strutting about with Mugahid on her back, she would come back laden with clover like a donkey, something he never would have allowed in the past.

After leaving everything for his son in front of the farmhouse, he would go back to Mubarka's house, happy to see Mansur beginning to recognize his brother. In the beginning it had frightened Mansur to see Nagi rushing ghostlike, with lightning speed, between the hay storeroom and the outhouse, especially given the fact that, since his confinement to his hiding place, Nagi had left childhood entirely behind. His body had filled out, and he was bigger than Muntasir had been when he left al-Ish. His face had rounded out, and his features looked more and more like Muntasir's. However, the fear-filled nights had planted in his eyes the terror of a wounded animal, while the constant inhalation of dust and sleeping in the straw had taken their toll on him.

Every inch of his body was plagued with boils and sores. Mubarka began cleaning them for him and daubing them with honey. Then, when armies of ants made their way into the honey ointment, she replaced the honey with coffee. The authorities continued combing the villages in search of young men to fuel the government's war. The raids would subside when there were signs of peace among the warring parties, and intensify when the battles raged anew.

For long months the only light Nagi saw was the rays that filtered in through a small crack in the ceiling of the dark storeroom, which he would close with some rolled-up rags tied to a long reed. Aunt Hamida would bring him his three meals, as well as a basin and some water for his weekly bath, and when he wanted to relieve himself, he would tap on the door. Before opening the door for him, she would check to make sure the coast was clear. He would sneak hurriedly to the outhouse and back, whereupon the old woman would shut the door behind him from the outside, then pile the hoes, ropes, and baskets in front of it once again.

When the frail old woman went blind and could no longer see her way around, she stopped leaving her room, and Mubarka had to serve Nagi by herself. When she handed him his breakfast or picked up his bathwater, their eyes would meet in a kind of mournful affection. Sometimes she would sit next to him until he'd finished his food, and the two of them would exchange commiserating looks that reflected nothing more than the sense of solidarity that unites fellow victims.

When she reached out to clean a lesion that had developed on his cheek, he showed her a suppurating abscess under one of his nipples. Seated directly across from him, she began digging into the sore. He let forth a moan that sounded like the howl of a wounded dog. He doubled over until his bare chest came in contact with hers and she could feel his breath brushing against her. Her heart was in turmoil as she found herself encountering, once again, the smell of manhood that she'd known in his cousin.

As he moved toward her, the faint rays falling through the tiny opening in the roof illumined his bright face with the yellowish hue of cotton blossoms. A happy tension made its way deep inside her, and she felt as though her spirit had exited her body and was exposed before him. This only heightened her turmoil, since she knew from the look in his pained, imploring eyes that he'd seen what the ball of fire he'd rolled between them had done to her.

"Kiss me," he said, with the cheekiness of Muntasir and the innocence of Mansur. He didn't bat an eye. However, although the pressure from her fingers wasn't painful to him any more, he jumped at her touch. He drew up close until they were touching—on purpose this time—and held his cheek out to her. She leaned toward him and placed her lips on his forehead in delighted surrender. He exposed her breasts, then began alternately scratching them and squeezing them as he sucked her nipples. She lay down and pulled him on top of her. He started to rant deliriously while she remained silent, guiding his hips to show him how fast, and in what direction, to move them. Finally she lost all sense of herself and responded to his cries by etching lines on his back with her fingernails, which added the pain of the wounds to that of the sores.

After straightening her clothes, she sat down across from him again. Then she resumed cleaning his sores and treating them with coffee grounds.

"Was it nice?" he asked with the same cheeky innocence. She made no reply, engrossed in her work. She carried out her task with a gentleness that was felt by his organ, which began responding in jumps until it had hardened completely. He looked at her in such a way as to direct her gaze to the miracle.

Pressing her again, he demanded, "Aren't you happy?"

She fixed her gaze for a few moments on his face, which concealed beneath its innocence the cunning of manhood. She placed her fingers on the erect organ and rubbed it until it wet her hand.

"Let me smell it," he said with joyful curiosity. She gave him a taste of her hand, which was dripping with the liquid, and let forth a laugh that was quickly submerged beneath a wave of pain. It was pain that welled up out of her memory, which hadn't preserved a single laugh from the past. Then her features recovered the bliss of satisfaction and the delight of discovery. It wasn't just a discovery of the secret of masculinity in another man in the family. It was the discovery of laughter. She'd never thought of herself as any more sorrowful than people around her who had the ability to laugh. She'd just lacked the ability to laugh herself.

Her hands moved, kneading his chest from under his armpits to the depression between the mounds on either side. Once in the center, she knit her fingers together, then moved them apart again. When she saw his organ stirring again, she pinched his nipples and, picking up the handleless basket with the plate and the jar of coffee on top of it, left without looking behind her.

All she felt was the happy turmoil she'd known with Muntasir. She was filled with energy now. However, she started dropping things again, and smiled to herself as she remembered the way her father had once wondered aloud if she'd grabbed a cat's tail.

With the readiness of a hungry animal waiting for prey to fall into its clutches, Nagi spent his days with his ears pricked for the sound of the slightest movement. Whenever the house was quiet, he would knock on the door and Mubarka would drop whatever she was doing and run to him. She would forget what she was cooking on the stove or the bread in the oven, drop the water pail at the door to the room where thirsty birds waited, or leave clothes in the washbasin. As one encounter followed another, she began using her knack for making her voice sound manly and gruff. Her stifled moans mingled with his howls, which would get louder and louder until she fell silent and clapped her hand over his mouth as a reminder of the presence of the blind woman nearby.

As the dromedary riders' siege wore on, Hafiza began venturing out to see her son. Salama's absence had revived the anguish she felt over Nagiya, of whom she'd received no news since the day of her departure. All she had left of her children were Nagi and Ali, whom she would send out on a reconnaissance mission before wrapping herself in her black shroud and scurrying over to Mubarka's house.

She would knock on the door and Mubarka would come out. They would first look around to make sure no one was watching, and then come in and stand behind the door until they were sure it was safe to proceed. Then Mubarka would go back to the hay store-room, open the door for Nagi, and return with him. She would sit down, doing her best not to look in his direction lest his animal eyes rob her of her composure in front of his mother, and she made a point of not commenting on anything he said. When Mugahid came back to the house to find Nagi playing with his brother while the two co-wives sat exchanging whispers, he felt as though a new world was coming into being without him, and he would withdraw to the sitting room to smoke his shisha and wait for one of his friends to come spend the evening with him.

When Mubarka began showing signs of a new pregnancy, Muga-hid felt unsettled as he went back over his servile attempts to get a response from her. He noticed that she'd become less hostile of late, while he for his part had become less eager and determined. Had he gone into her one night when he was half-asleep and didn't remember it? Was she really a consort of the jinn after all? He thought a thousand times of confronting her with his suspicions, but didn't have the strength. Nor did he dare risk besmirching his dignity by confiding in anyone else about it. So he buried his pain deep in his heart. Meanwhile, Hafiza had begun bringing food she had prepared from the farmhouse. She would even come help Mubarka with her chores, and when she saw how touched Mubarka was by the gesture, she put her arms around her and patted her on her back.

"You're like my long-lost daughter," she said, sobbing with anguish and fear for the daughter she'd lost touch with in a distant town whose name she couldn't even pronounce right, and for the absent son now fighting in a war that had nothing to do with them. There was no evidence of his existence apart from a tattered post-card that she kept in the pocket of her gilbab with a picture of a spacious square on the front and a few words written on the back. After several months en route it had reached al-Ish one morning with a postman from Bilbeis. Hafiza had sent him back to the city laden with ducks, rice, and broad beans so that he wouldn't be lax about delivering any future letters. But he'd never been back.

The war not only stripped the villages of their young men; it also milked them dry by imposing taxes and the payment of protection money. Whenever the government was about to go bankrupt, it would overtax the people. Not content to collect what the authorities demanded, the tax collectors took protection money for themselves until hunger was rampant and the farmers grew increasingly rebellious. Meanwhile, the villagers began taking interest in the news of the nationalist movement, and loyalties were divided between Muhammad Farid, Mustafa Kamel's successor, and Saad Zaghlul, the justice minister who'd resigned his post in order to be on the side of the people rather than that of the imperialists.

Thefts became commonplace once again. Now, however, there were no codes of honor associated with them as there had been in the past. No longer did the thieves target only the cattle pens of mayors and members of the ruling family; they targeted everyone without distinction. Hafiza, fearful of being in the huge farmhouse by herself, began closing the door to her room and barricading it with a wooden ladder to fortify it against any attempt to open it by force. Then she would hold Ali in her arms. When she woke to the sound of the filly beating her head against the door to her room, she looked out through the peephole onto the street, where she saw the livestock in the hands of masked men on the run. She screamed in terror. Then she heard the thieves running away, leaving the livestock scattered here and there in the street. Mugahid approached in a crowd of people who'd been wakened by her scream. After seeing light coming through the large hole the thieves had made with crowbars in the cattle pen wall, they rounded up the animals that had been left in the street and examined the filly, whose belly had been pierced by a pack needle and was dripping with blood.

It was obvious that the thieves had been goading her to get her to move. However, she had insisted on disobeying them despite the pricks that were doing such damage to her body. She began butting against the walls of the room, whinnying fretfully and stamping her hooves on the ground against the thieves' angry snarls.

The filly survived only three more days. Finding her dead from her suppurating wounds, they dragged her away with ropes and left her to be ravished by dogs at the edge of the drainage ditch far from the village. Hafiza wept over her despite the fact that she had once hated her, considering her to be one of Mugahid's most disastrous caprices. She had shared the crops with the family while Mugahid frittered away his dignity by riding her as she danced at weddings and mulid celebrations. For as long as he lived, Mugahid remembered her with an ache that he hadn't known she would leave in his heart. Until his dying day he told his children and grandchildren who had never seen her about how skilled he and she had been, and what a harmonious team they'd made. And he would conclude his narrative with her final act of heroism, which could bring tears to the eyes of an entire generation that had never seen her.

When the occupation authority's raids on al-Ish came to an end, Nagi emerged from his hideout. When Mubarka brought him the washbasin and a cooking pot filled with hot water so that he could bathe in an ordinary room, he began looking at his body in the light and getting reacquainted with it. Wet from his final bath in Mubarka's house, he bundled up the clothes she'd gathered for him, bade farewell to the shadowy paradise, and headed back to the farmhouse.

"We've gotten used to having you around, Nagi," said Mubarka, unable to conceal the shudder that came rushing from deep inside her and caused her voice to fade out in the middle of his name. She felt exposed in front of Mugahid, who sat puffing noisily on his shisha only a few steps away. Nagi made no reply, pretending to be preoccupied with Mansur, who had grabbed the tail of his gilbab to prevent him from leaving. Turning, Nagi lifted him with one arm, and with the other picked up the bundle of clothes and prepared to be on his way. Mansur, who wanted his brother without having to part with his mother, flung himself toward Mubarka, who found herself drawn into contact with Nagi as she took the little boy from his arms. Nagi left without looking behind him, running his hand over the spot on his chest that had received a touch in which she'd condensed all her longing.

Hafiza continued visiting Mubarka and spending her evenings with her, whereas Mugahid would go to sleep right after the final evening prayer. She spoke to her the way a mother speaks to her own daughter, relating to the young woman memories of things she had never witnessed. Mubarka would ask her about things happening in the present in an attempt to get her to talk about Nagi, who had gone back to working in the fields with Mugahid and Ali. Hafiza would go on talking until she got so tired that she would lie down in front of her. But even then she didn't stop talking, and would often fall asleep with the words still in her mouth. Mubarka would position her head more comfortably and leave her where she was until she wakened, astonished, to the dawn call to prayer.

"Why don't you let me relieve you of making the men's lunch once or twice a week?" Mubarka suggested after Hafiza mentioned her need for rest. "At least when they're working on my land." It was more of an entreaty than a suggestion, and Hafiza agreed to it without questioning it even to herself. After all, she thought, it might be motivated by the pregnant girl's weariness of staying in the house.

Nagi was delighted at the news, and began looking forward to the days when Mubarka would bring them their lunch. Anticipating her arrival, he would think up excuses for leaving the field ahead of the others so that he could be alone with her for a few moments before Mugahid and Ali came out from among the cornstalks. She would remove the cover from a large copper tray to reveal one of the rich, elegantly prepared dishes that made all three men look forward to the days she cooked. As Nagi ate in silence, furtive glances would pass between them like sparks of electricity. Pregnancy had made her fuller and more beautiful, while sunburn and fresh air had made him more manly, and fatigue had graced his body with a seductive languor. They pursued each other voraciously with their eyes, while at the same time doing their best to avoid the spark that was ignited if they happened to meet until, flustered, she picked up the leftover food and left without his recalling a thing he'd just eaten.

Hafiza suggested to Mubarka that she come live with them at the farmhouse so that, together with Salama's wife Tafida, she could take better care of her after her delivery. Mubarka's heart fluttered at the suggestion, since once again she would find herself living under the same roof with Nagi rather than having to steal glances, fleeting touches, and a few riotous moments alone together on rare occasions. At the same time, she trembled in fear at the thought of living next to him in the crowded, noisy farmhouse. She began imagining herself making wild love to him in her bed only to find someone standing over them. The head that popped in the door would change depending on the scenarios conjured by her apprehensions, and her heart raced as she imagined each person's reaction.

Her inner turmoil reached its climax when she remembered Tafida, the woman she disliked more than anyone she'd ever known. The two of them would see each other while delivering wedding dinners, waiting in line at the steam mill, or filling their water jugs at the canal. She'd been a mean girl with a broad, manlike, straight-up-and-down body and a harsh face with a large mouth, huge lips, a big sharp nose, and wide, insolent eyes. She never blinked when she was speaking or listening, and would peer down from above as though she were undressing the person in front of her.

Mubarka remained silent for some time before replying to Hafiza's suggestion, and the colors of her face changed several times before she said at last, like someone in a hypnotic trance, "All right. That would be better."

Mugahid, who knew his cousin Hafiza well, didn't rule out the possibility that her invitation had been motivated by the desire to save money, particularly in view of the fact that their financial situation had deteriorated to the point that they'd had to pay the previous year's taxes by selling the two women's jewelry. He was distressed at the suggestion. However, he saw no need to squelch the good will that had developed between the two wives.

The bed and the dresser were taken apart, while the stored grains, legumes, and ghee were moved to the farmhouse along with the rabbits and birds — including the pigeons, whose feathers were trimmed to keep them from flying off and, in this way, help them adjust more quickly to their new quarters.

Hafiza let Mubarka decide which room she would put her bed in. She chose an isolated room, not the one she'd occupied when she'd lived alone in the farmhouse. It was a spacious room located next to a smaller one that she reserved for Aunt Hamida so that she could take care of her. This decision was prompted by the pangs of conscience she'd suffered for having forgotten about Aunt Hamida for so long. In fact, she'd only noticed her again as she began preparing for the move to the farmhouse. She was aware of how thoroughly Nagi had turned her upside-down: so thoroughly that she'd lost touch with the woman who for so long had assuaged her loneliness in her mother's absence, and in Mugahid's presence.

When her mother died, Mubarka had had a vague notion of what death meant, but she hadn't realized that those who go there never come back again. She'd watched the bier as it left the house, and she remembered knowing that her mother was inside it. But she hadn't cried. And when the neighbor women vied for the opportunity to send food to their home during the days of mourning, she'd eaten voraciously, possessed by a curiosity to try out each woman's culinary skills. Whenever she saw Mubarka's mindless elation, Aunt Hamida would take her into her arms and weep, and never once did she go to sleep for the night without first checking to make sure she was all right.

On religious holidays and in the evening mulid celebrations, Aunt Hamida would take Mubarka to her own house with her new clothes, give her a bath, and style her hair. She would instruct the other children to take Mubarka with them on their morning holiday outings, while she herself would take her out in the evenings during the mulid celebrations. She and Mubarka would sit with the women on a housetop overlooking the courtyard where the dhikr was taking place so that they could watch and listen to the singing.

Mubarka had once overheard someone talking to her father about the possibility of marrying Hamida, since she'd been so attentive to his daughter, but at the time she hadn't understood her father's reply.

He'd said, "Once you've had a gazelle, you're not going to want a she-goat."

It was only many years later, after she had grown up, that she understood the meaning behind his words. And when she did, she herself proposed that he marry Hamida, who had seen her through childhood with a mother's tender affection. But in reply he'd said things that it had taken her several more years to comprehend: "Ah! Shall I marry her and tell her, 'Cover me up and wail over me'?"

Though she hadn't understood it at the time, her father was referring to the fact that he'd lost his ability to be intimate with a woman. She remembered how distressed he'd been at Hamida's attentiveness and concern and how, in spite of this, he'd honored her wish to take care of his little girl. He began accepting her gifts of cooked dishes and hot loaves of bread, and would return the favor by giving her grain in the wheat and corn seasons. Little by little, Hamida began cooking, cleaning, and doing whatever else was needed at their house, such as taking home clothes that needed washing, mending, or buttons sewn on. She didn't need anybody to tell her what to do, since she knew everything about her neighbor's household. She would wait for Badr to leave in the morning, and when she heard the loud expectoration that marked his departure or arrival, she would peek out her door to make sure he was gone, then visit the neighbor who was dearer to her than a sister. The two of them would talk nonstop as Hamida helped Mubarka with her chores or as they ate together, and she wouldn't leave her until she heard the expectoration that signaled his evening return.

For many years Aunt Hamida never felt weary or resentful of serving, even though, when Mubarka become a young woman and the mistress of her father's household, she stepped back somewhat. Yet even then, she continued her relationship with her, just as she had with her mother. Mubarka was no different from Fatima. She even resembled her in her tendency to be quiet, a trait that was to Hamida's liking since she enjoyed taking a double share of the conversation. Mubarka didn't know whether the intensification of her interest in Aunt Hamida was simply a way of assuaging her conscience, burdened as it was by the guilt she felt over forgetting her for a period of time, or whether the feeling of fullness that came with pregnancy had made her more complete. She no longer felt the blazing fire that had once swept through her whenever she looked into Nagi's eyes. However, she knew her endurance wasn't without its limits, and that she was still too weak to resist his fervor and the male bravado that could paralyze her the way a cat paralyzes a mouse until it abandons any attempt to flee. She began avoiding opportunities to be alone with him, and was careful not to look at him when he had just finished taking a bath and had nothing on but an undershirt that displayed his bronzed body, his bulging forearms, and his black, half-kinky hair as it spread out in wild disarray like the branches of an acacia tree with their needle-like thorns.

She not only distanced herself from Nagi, but became less involved with the rest of the family as well. Even her little boy Mansur, who now spent part of his time at school and the rest of the time in the field with his father and his two brothers, had become more independent of her, and no longer insisted on staying at her side.

When she entered her ninth month, she did nothing but prepare for childbirth. She went looking for pieces of old fabric to use as diapers for the newborn, and for scraps of new fabric that she used to sew clothes the size of a person's palm, most of them tiny, doll-sized dresses. Aunt Hamida had once placed her hand on Mubarka's belly and discovered that it was larger than it had been during her previous pregnancy. She passed her hand over her face, then let it slide down over her breasts.

"Have you gotten prettier during this pregnancy?" she asked.

"Well, yes, if I do say so myself!" Mubarka replied with a giggle.

"Hasn't the man told you so?" she asked coyly.

Mubarka winced, and made no reply. Then, peering at her out of her dimmed eyes as though she could see her, Aunt Hamida declared, "You're carrying a girl!"

Mubarka was overjoyed, since she longed for a daughter who could be her confidante, and who was sure to take better care of her in her old age than ten men could ever have done. Seeing Aunt Hamida draw up to her with her wizened face, Mubarka decided to prevent her from going on with her questions by taking matters into her own hands.

"Tell me honestly: Why didn't you marry my father?" she asked.

The woman stepped back with a smile on her face. "If I'd married him, wouldn't people have said that I'd sent two men to their graves?"

"No! Tell me, really!"

"I could never have filled Fatima's shoes, and your father could never have filled Ibrahim's."

They fell silent for a few moments. Looking up at a ceiling she couldn't see, Aunt Hamida said dreamily, "When a woman's known a tiger, she could never be satisfied with a pussycat."

Everyone took Aunt Hamida's prediction concerning the pregnancy as gospel truth, while the countless dresses that Mubarka had made served to cement it in people's minds. Consequently, it had become a foregone conclusion. When Mubarka gave birth, the midwife removed the placenta and tied the umbilical cord, leaving it to Hafiza to dry the infant and wash off the blood that clung to her. As she was busy performing these tasks, her hand stumbled upon a sleeping noodle between the baby's thighs. With the embarrassment of a woman who has just seen a man step naked out of the irrigation canal, she cried with visible disappointment, "It's a boy!" It was then that she realized that the secret behind her happiness over Mubarka's pregnancy and her thrill over the prediction that she would give birth to a girl had been her hope that, through this baby girl, she would be able to recover humpbacked Nagiya's childhood—a childhood she'd let go to waste because of her grief over the poor creature's unsightliness. The midwife, Fahima, who'd gone outside to smoke the shisha with Mugahid, came back into the room at the sound of Hafiza's cry to make certain of what she had seen, and asked that her wages be doubled.

Mugahid, who'd felt neither ecstatic over Mubarka's pregnancy nor worried about her delivery this time around, came in response to the women's raucous excitement, and stopped in the doorway. Contemplating the scene with his arms outstretched and his hands resting on either side of the doorframe, the word slipped out of his mouth: "Salem."

He uttered the baby's name in the form of an irrevocable command, pleased that he'd beaten others to the punch. Then he withdrew without so much as asking about the mother's health, and with the serenity of someone pronouncing his final will and testament before closing his eyes and breathing his last. Nevertheless, the two women didn't surrender or easily relinquish their hope for a girl. So they went on calling Salem "Salema," supported in their rebellion by the girlish baby clothes the boy wore until he had sense enough to be embarrassed by them.

Salama al-Deeb returned from the war after four years that had left nothing but a faint trace of his old features. If it hadn't been for the thick eyebrows and black eyes that marked him as a member of the Deeb family, Hafiza wouldn't have known that the scrawny, middle-aged-looking man she saw before her was her son, who had been as huge as a bull when he left.

The celebrations that were held in honor of his return went on for seven days, during which time they slaughtered everything that moved on the farm with the exception of two milk cows. Not once did the fires go out for those seven days, since Hafiza had made a vow at the Silent Sheikh's shrine to feed all of al-Ish if her son came back to her safe and sound.

The women repainted the farmhouse's inner rooms with silt and ashes, while house painters and artists from Bilbeis took care of its façade and front rooms. They painted the walls with white lime and decorated them with drawings of ships. The painters joined the evening gatherings where Salama related his memories of the war, which helped them to draw the cannons and the soldiers on the ships in such a way that one could distinguish between them and the pictures they drew on the houses of people who had returned from the pilgrimage to Mecca.

Tables were spread for the entire seven days from noon until after the final evening prayer, and the evening gatherings would go on past midnight. With the exception of a quick question or a request for clarification on the part of one of the listeners, the only person who spoke at the gatherings was Salama. Once a question had been asked, an inquisitive silence would reign in anticipation of the answer. Salama, who had returned from the war a nervous man with a smoking habit, felt at ease among them during their evenings together. He would speak slowly and deliberately, and they listened with such rapt attention that you could have heard a pin drop.

He learned how to divide up his story in such a way that he could create the needed suspense. He would sigh during the moments of silence or squeeze his head to get himself to remember something. He would begin his story with short statements interspersed with long silences, and when their eyes began to glisten with curiosity, he would take out his can of tobacco, open it, remove a thin paper from a small package, and spread it out on the lid of the tobacco can. Then he would take a bit of tobacco between his fingers and place it on top of the paper, pick it up with both hands, and begin calmly rolling it with everyone's eyes on him. Lastly, he would wet the edge of the paper with his tongue so that the roll would hold together. When their curiosity had reached its peak and they looked as though they were about to pull the words off his tongue, he would light the cigarette, take a drag, and ask, "Where were we?"

"Natwarab," somebody said.

"Antwerp," Salama corrected him with a smile. "That's the name of the Belgian port on the North Sea. It's way, way north, near the end of the world."

Everyone would be very quiet so that they could catch everything he said, since his voice would rise and fall like the waves of a calm sea. He talked about the port city where the French destroyer had dropped anchor and in whose streets he'd been able to breathe fresh air for the first time in three years, during which time they'd learned the names of the ports without even seeing them. The city's cloudy weather differed little from the darkness of the galley, where he'd been confined with his shipmates in the gloomy hull.

Hardly had they finished preparing breakfast before they had to begin making lunch. In Antwerp, at least, he'd been able to breathe fresh air. He described the city's fair-skinned, slender women. He had found them unattractive, not because of their pale skin, but because of the short, tight dresses they wore, since they left nothing special in reserve for their husbands.

The small, neutral country of Belgium wasn't the only source of Salama's stories. He also told them about Khalifa, his shipmate from the southern city of Akhmim, which specialized in silk weaving, and about the foreigners who babbled away in strange languages.

Every night he would take them to a different country that was under British occupation or in alliance with the British. He'd seen numerous countries through the eyes of his buddies from other British colonies who, like him, had been recruited into the service teams. He would talk about their customs and the strange foods he'd learned to make, and how they used to prepare them for themselves after they'd finished feeding the French officers and soldiers on deck.

His eyes would well up with tears when he talked about his best friend, a fair-skinned Romanian youth with reddish hair and blue eyes by the name of Don Francisco. Don Francisco hailed from a little village, located at the far end of the Danube Delta on the Black Sea, that still enjoyed the same spirit of equality that al-Ish had known in its early days. The people of his village would go out by boat to their fields, which were on an island across from the village. They would take their livestock over to the island in early spring. Leaving them there to graze freely, they would go to milk them every day, and wouldn't bring them back to their pens in the village until autumn, since no living creature could bear the cold of winter when the island was covered with snow.

"Fish is cheaper than plain bread there," he said, probing their eyes for looks of amazement. He went on to explain how they could gather up huge numbers of fish from the river bogs or from the sea, whereas importing flour from distant locations cost them huge sums. Don Francisco had taught him a hundred different ways to prepare fish, whereas the people of al-Ish had never known what to do with it but fry it. His Romanian friend, who in the beginning had thought the Muslim way of praying strange, had come to love it, and would look on inquiringly as Salama bowed and prostrated.

Salama would talk and talk, then fall into a wordless trance, no longer aware of the people around him. Other times he would suddenly start to tremble and look down at the floor. When he sensed their unspoken bewilderment, he would gradually, cautiously lift his head again and look probingly in all directions before going back to his story.

Their amazement at the changes he'd undergone was matched only by his amazement at the changes he'd found upon his return—changes he never would have thought possible. He was surprised not only by Mubarka's presence at the farmhouse, but by the state of harmony among the three women that was roiled by nothing but minor disagreements. As for the state of conflict in which he'd left his mother and his wife, it had subsided to a significant degree. Hafiza had become a beloved mother-in-law to the two young women, like an empress who's established her authority on a foundation of justice. The two young women shared in the household chores while Hafiza held Salem in her lap, until he wriggled out of her grasp and went crawling away to put everything he came across in his mouth.

They would arrange everything together: what they would cook, which days each of them would take lunch to the men, what tasks each of them would be responsible for on laundry and baking days, how to arrange the men's things, and what rank each of them would occupy in the household. Salama was surprised to see Nagi's progress toward becoming an authority figure in the household, and shocked to see his father's torpid state and increasingly unkempt appearance, whether due to indifference on his part, or negligence on the part of his two wives. Even his food wasn't distinctive the way it had been in the past. He was now just about the least important person in the household—the very least important being the blind woman who, like the mice, slept all day and began stirring in the evenings out of embarrassment over her tendency to trip and stumble when she moved about.

It was a new thing for Salama to see the elderly man take part in the field work. He contemplated his gnarled fingers with their bulging joints, which had turned blue from the effort that was so new to them. After all, he hadn't exerted such effort when they were children who needed care, but had instead let their tender bones wither under the weight of the heavy hoes.

After a few days of rest and recuperation, Salama ceased to be a guest and joined the other men. However, he found that he no longer had his old stamina for farm work. After his first day out in the field, his palms and fingers were covered with blisters. He no longer worked as a supervisor on the French destroyer, but he was certain now that farmers were no better off than slaves, since their work is the harshest and the least remunerative of all the jobs a person might do. He started thinking of getting a number of looms and setting up a weaving enterprise in Mubarka's house, which now stood abandoned.

Mubarka welcomed the suggestion, which promised to bring her deeper into the heart of family life. It was as if she sought refuge in this acceptance from the burden of her secret with Nagi. Salama left for five days, and came back with Khalifa Abd al-Al, the young man from Upper Egypt whom they'd met previously in his stories. After inspecting Mubarka's house, Khalifa indicated the necessary modifications and expansions, showing them which windows would need to be closed and which ones would need to be opened in the various rooms in order to maintain the proper humidity for the spun cotton and the cloth that was to be produced. Soon thereafter a cart arrived, laden with smooth beechwood rods of varying lengths and thicknesses like the ones used to roof special parts of people's homes. Khalifa began putting the rods together to build a series of looms, which looked like small but imposing mazes that he alone knew how to navigate. Then came the spun thread.

Their first experiments were disappointing: meter after meter of cloth filled with irregularities and poorly executed roses and stripes. He used them to make pillowcases, comforters, and underwear for the men of the family. The work improved little by little until, by the time Khalifa left al-Ish, the factory's output was in demand all over Sharqiya, and people were even ordering in advance.

Salama began devoting all his time to the factory, and before long he'd managed to break even and even achieve a surplus. Before the first year was out they'd bought an additional feddan, and Salama had begun coming back from his trips with perfumed soap, sweets, fruits, and bottles of fruit-drink concentrate. Influenced by his association with foreigners during his military service and with city folks from the time when he established the factory, Salama did away with the family's old ways of doing things, and everyone began sitting together at two large, low, round tables and eating the same food.

With some difficulty, Salama persuaded his father to stop working in the field now that he was more than seventy years old. Ali came to work at the factory, and Nagi took over sole responsibility for the field work. He would work the land himself and hire as many laborers as he needed to work alongside him. Meanwhile, Salama began talking to him about the need to get married.

It had been a natural thing to avoid bringing up the subject of Nagi's marrying as long as Salama was gone. However, it had been more than a year now since Salama's return, and the young man still expressed no interest in marriage. Tafida, who had noticed the furtive glances he and Mubarka were exchanging, had wanted to let Salama know what was happening. However, fearful that he might react sharply, she held her tongue. Meanwhile, Salama began pressuring his brother to choose a girl whose family they could approach on his behalf.

Tafida wanted to establish certain boundaries before Nagi married so as to reserve the profits from the factory for her own children. As far as she was concerned, it was thanks to her husband's efforts that the family was enjoying its new prosperity, so she began pampering herself: sleeping till mid-morning while Hafiza and Mubarka were finishing the household chores, and acting irresponsibly and arrogantly. If a bar of soap slipped out of her hand into the trough under the water pump, she wouldn't reach in to get it. Then Hafiza would find its mushy, slimy remains when she came to clean out the trough and empty its contents into the street.

Hafiza, who had begun making efforts to win her daughter-in-law's approval, no longer punished her, scolded her, or complained about her. Not content even with this, however, the shameless young woman began thinking about the communal profits being used to buy land for the entire family in Mugahid's name, and goaded her husband to move out of the farmhouse and establish a life apart from the rest of the family.

"You work like a maniac for the whole family while your own kids go on being treated just like everybody else," she told him. As she spoke, she reached over to where Salama lay beside her, took his hand, and passed it over her distended belly.

"Don't forget that the factory is in Mubarka's house," said Salama.

Pressing his hand to a spot below her belly, she moaned with pleasure, then replied in a broken voice, "So would it really cost that much to rent a house in al-Ish?"

"Everybody does whatever God's given him the ability to do," he said, and withdrew his hand. However, convinced that her husband was a cut above his brothers, the woman would stop at nothing to get him to keep his profits for himself, and was determined to settle the matter before they married Nagi off so that Salama wouldn't have to bear the expenses. When she failed to get the response she was after, she left the farmhouse in a huff, saying she wouldn't come back until she knew she was going to have a house of her own.

Salama let her have the baby in her father's house, and only went to get her after her family sent word that they wanted a reconciliation, asking him to take her back and promising to abide by his wishes.

So Tafida lost the round, and her husband didn't separate from the family. He did, however, make arrangements with two poor women to come work at the farmhouse in order to relieve himself of the disputes among the women over how to divide up the work. By continuing to divide a single income between himself and his brothers, he unwittingly set off a baby-making competition between the two young women. Having two live-in maids made it easier for them to carry on with their race, and every year a new baby was welcomed into the farmhouse. It wasn't long before Ali had married as well, and his wife joined the race, which meant more than one newborn every year.

As Mugahid and Salama were making arrangements for Nagi's engagement to Zakiya al-Gahsh, Nagi had been stealing into Mubarka's room, and was now immersed with her in another world.

She hadn't needed the ravenous looks of collusion over dinner. Rather, she had already been prepared for the stealthy visit he paid her after the two other men had left the house, Hafiza and Tafida had gone to bed, and Ali had lost his mind in Mas'ada's arms the way he did every night.

"It's all right. It's something that's got to be done, you know," she whispered to him as he squeezed her so tightly that it hurt.

They'd begun pressing Nagi even more insistently to choose a bride since Ali's "shotgun wedding," which had resulted in his marrying before his older brother contrary to the dictates of custom. Nagi had expected people to forget about him in the wake of the stories about Ali and the tall, svelte bride with fire between her legs. Instead, however, they began pressuring him all the more, arguing down every excuse he offered until it became impossible for him to go on refusing.

"Whatever you say," he replied halfheartedly as they sat together at the dinner table. He stole a glance at Mubarka, who trembled as her eyes met Tafida's. As they sat around the brazier that held the large teapot, they went over the names of eligible girls until at last, with the frustrated resignation of someone choosing the least onerous of a number of punishments, he agreed on Zakiya.

Tafida enthusiastically volunteered to check out the situation with the girl's mother in preparation for the men's visit to ask for her hand. At the time set by Mahmoud al-Gahsh, Mugahid and Salama paid the family the first visit and recited the Fatiha with them. Meanwhile, Mubarka was wiping away two rivulets of tears that had flowed down Nagi's cheeks as he lay beside her. She brought his fingers under her loose-fitting gilbab, beneath which she had nothing on. He pulled it up beyond her navel and lay down on top of her in a state of turmoil. Moving his gilbab out of the way the best she could, she began licking him, and dug her fingernails into his back to reinforce his convulsive thrusting until the two of them went limp and he lay back down beside her.

"Don't you dare leave me," she said. A cough coming from Aunt Hamida's room gave him no chance to reply. He jumped to the floor and left on tiptoe, not for fear of the blind woman, but for fear that her cough might wake his mother or Tafida. When he found himself far enough away from Mubarka's room, he resumed a normal gait and proceeded brashly to the sitting room to wait for the other two men, who returned in good time.

"Congratulations," said Salama. He shook his brother's hand and began telling him about the warm reception Mahmoud al-Gahsh had given them. When he noticed his lack of enthusiasm, he said jokingly, "Don't worry. Your dad didn't ask to marry her himself!"

Infuriated by the joke, Mugahid left the two of them without saying a word. He withdrew to Mubarka's room, where she was pretending to be asleep. He deliberately made a commotion and she turned over in bed. When he lay down beside her, she rested her arm on him in what seemed to be a spontaneous gesture. He sensed a warmth that he hoped was intentional when she said to him lightheartedly, "Congratulations, Abu Salama!"

"Thank you," he replied, suddenly happy and relaxed. When she turned her back to him, he reached out to hold her. He caressed the roundness of her still-firm buttocks, and felt her easing toward him until she filled the hollow between his thighs. He gave himself over to a warmth he'd been waiting for for years, pained by the fact that he hadn't found it in Hafiza's bed. Though he was finding it in Mubarka's bed, he knew it was nothing but the warmth of her soft, youthful body, which took no real notice of his presence.

He began trying his hand again at the silent game of advance and retreat that had exhausted him over so many years. He felt a kind of mournful jubilation when he pressed up against her and found that she didn't withdraw or wince. He tried moving away slightly so that he no longer felt the warmth of her body, although he could tell that her gilbab was still in contact with his and, to his surprise, he found her drawing close to him again in a way that appeared to be intentional. The message coming from the body that he had waited for in torment for so long came through loud and clear, and he was sure she would let him enter her. Maintaining contact with her, he turned over and began rubbing his buttocks gently against her back while reaching down to fondle his organ as though he wanted to reach an agreement with it before turning around again. However, it remained limp. He began rubbing himself vigorously, like someone trying to revive a person from a coma. Before long the vigorousness of his rubbing had given way to an ill-tempered relentlessness, and his battered glans looked like a date that had been tied to his body with a flimsy cord. He found it strange that his buttocks could derive such ecstasy from being in contact with Mubarka while the lifeless object in his hand felt nothing at all. As she turned around to hold him, he withdrew his hand from between his thighs and went to sleep, giving himself over to the warmth of her breasts on his back.

Had his spark gone out? Or was it just that his body had waited for her so long that it had finally developed a mind of its own, and was exacting revenge for the long nights of unrequited longing? Maybe it was both. Whatever the case, the sympathy that had warmed him on that night began to recur, and his body came to anticipate that gracious gift in spite of itself. Mubarka no longer concerned herself over what he might know about her relationship with Nagi. However, she feared Tafida, and was paralyzed by those stinging glances of hers that said something halfway but never said the rest. And now there would be a confrontation with a new party: a woman who belonged to Nagi and who, by virtue of her sense of ownership over her man, would be able to pick up the scent of any other woman.

She decided to do everything she could to appear natural as the fiancée entered the scene. Not only did she become more gentle and solicitous toward Mugahid; she also began talking about wedding preparations with an enthusiasm sufficiently restrained that it wouldn't give her away. She asked when the marriage contract would be finalized and when the wedding celebration would be, and made suggestions to Hafiza regarding the wedding cake and the other things to be baked for the occasion. She also made a point of enumerating the virtues of the al-Gahsh family and the new bride, describing Zakiya as an "Arabian filly." And Zakiya merited the compliment. The girl that Nagi had agreed to marry, however unenthusiastically, would have given any man reason to feel jealous: she had a rosy complexion, a charming gap between her two front teeth, and narrow eyes that concealed an indolent sensuality. She was tall and willowy, with a tiny waist and plump buttocks that even her loose-fitting gilbab couldn't hide. Her only shortcoming was her small breasts, which made up for their smallness by the sweet, graceful way they bounced as she walked. Nevertheless, Nagi wasn't prepared to appreciate these delights.

When he visited her for the first time with his mother, he didn't look at her once. It was obvious that what kept him from looking at her wasn't the bashfulness a suitor feels on his first visit under the watchful eyes of others, since he had no difficulty engaging in conversation with her father and mother.

After that his visits were few and far between, and when they did occur, it was only in response to pressure from Salama, who'd begun to marvel at his brother's indifference toward the girl. He never once tried to be alone with her or to touch her the way young men do during a courtship. He didn't spruce himself up for the visit or bring even the simplest gift with him the way grooms-to-be normally do when they come to see their prospective wives.

As for the girl, she responded to his disregard for her with proud disdain. She stopped sitting with him, and in her father's absence would leave him with her mother, with whom he'd established a relationship of profound mutual understanding. The woman wasn't young enough to arouse her daughter's jealousy, nor the jealousy of the father, who would come back to find the two of them engrossed in a whispered exchange.

And things went on this way. He began making more and more frequent evening visits, but when he came, he would start a tête-à-tête with the mother and talk nonstop.

Mahmoud al-Gahsh, who had to sit in silence until midnight while a young man reveled in talking to his wife, became convinced that Nagi wouldn't make a good husband for his daughter. He waited month after month, not knowing what he should say whenever Mugahid broached the subject of formalizing the marriage contract. What reason could he give for his refusal? Should he say, "He never looks into my daughter's face"? Or, "He's constantly whispering to my wife"? He kept putting things off with flimsy excuses. He waited and waited, but nothing changed. On visit after visit, Mahmoud and his daughter would sit there like a couple of silent guards as Nagi and his future mother-in-law engrossed themselves in whispered conversations of which they could make out nothing but a word here and there.

A whole week would go by without his feeling any need to visit his bride, and every time he did visit her, he would come home with the certainty that he could never desire any woman but Mubarka. Longing for even a look from her, he would make a racket when he came back to the farmhouse in hopes that it would give her an excuse to come out of her room so he could see her. But she paid no attention to his silly pranks, and he would go to his room and fall asleep frustrated.

Mahmoud al-Gahsh began waiting for some coincidence that would give him an excuse to break things off. But that coincidence never came, and at last he found himself obliged to put an end to the situation.

"It isn't going to work out." He settled the matter with Salama one day after the midafternoon prayer without offering any explanation for calling off the engagement. Zakiya told her mother afterward that when they'd shaken hands the first time he set foot in their house, she'd known from the feel of his hand on hers that she would never be his wife.

Zakiya was married to the first new suitor who approached her, and the pressures on Nagi started up again. Hafiza, who wanted to hold his son or daughter in her arms before she died, began praying and hanging on to the window at the Silent Sheikh's tumbledown shrine, vowing to have the shrine renovated if her son finally had the sense to get married. And whenever the two of them were alone together, Salama would rake him over the coals, saying, "You don't hear the things we hear!"

"I'm just not interested in women. What of it?" Nagi would reply with stubborn impudence. Time after time, however, he found himself faced with the prospect of marriage to a girl Hafiza and Mubarka had picked out, and in the end he had no choice but to follow through with it. It was a short engagement, in the course of which Salama busily engaged himself in preparing for the wedding the way a father would for his eldest son. He took care of buying everything: the gold, the copperware, the bed, the bride's hope chest, and her wardrobe. He also gave instructions for two rolls of fabric to be woven with special one-off designs for Nagi's mattresses and blankets. As fate would have it, however, the bride only slept on them for a month before asking for a divorce. And since no secrets ever remained secrets in al-Ish, word got around that he'd never once had an erection with her, and that the only part of him that had gone inside her was the finger he'd used to deflower her on their wedding night. As the rumors multiplied, people heaped more and more blame on the bride's family for having inflicted this experiment on their daughter when they knew he wasn't a real man. When the prattle began reaching the ears of those concerned, a pall of sadness descended over the farmhouse and, with it, a sense of strain.

"Why did you go through with it if you didn't want her?" demanded Salama of his brother, who made no reply. Just at that moment, a frightening sound burst forth from the small forgotten room, and they found Aunt Hamida standing there and leaning against her door.

"That's enough arguing!" she cried. "The boy's been consorting with the jinn, Salama!" She fell silent for a few moments before swearing to the truth of what she'd seen but had told no one about. She told them that when Nagi had been hiding in the dark in Mubarka's house, she would take him his food, then close the door to the hay storeroom from the outside. One time she removed the baskets, hoes, and ropes that she'd piled up in front of the door and opened the latch, but didn't find Nagi inside even though she'd bolted the door herself. She put down the meal she'd brought and locked the storeroom again without saying anything. When she came back several hours later, she found him in the locked storeroom, still wet from a bath, and sound asleep on the thigh of a girl more beautiful than any she'd seen in her life. Nor had she ever smelled a perfume sweeter than what she smelled at that moment.

"You saw her?" asked a terrified Tafida.

"And I never saw her again," Aunt Hamida replied.

Filling in the blanks in her story, they gathered that the jinn had found their way to him in the darkness and married him to one of their daughters. Consequently, his unseen consort would never allow him to find happiness with a human wife. However, their curiosity couldn't budge her another inch.

"What more do you want to happen to me? I'm already blind!" Her angry question struck fear in their hearts, so they didn't dare press her. Seven days later, Aunt Hamida died without having uttered another word. However, what she'd related that night made its way outside the farmhouse, and it was sufficient to change Nagi's image from that of a man afflicted with impotence to a man possessed by jinn: phobic, pitiful, and stricken with the evil eye.

A fter the hasty departure of Ismet, al-Ish's third Turkish mayor, the authorities showed no interest in appointing a new one, and the village enjoyed a return to being unknown and forgotten the way it had been for the first three centuries of its existence. However, the authorities continued to pay the salaries of a generation of sentries, each of whom hid his weapon in a safe place in case he might need it. They went back to taking care of their farms, happy to have the additional income, and one of them would go pick up the salaries in Bilbeis on everyone's behalf. When death took them all, one by one, al-Ish's last ties to the authorities came to an end. However, whenever the state went bankrupt it would go looking again at its rosters and maps, then send out its assessors to collect new taxes, which kept increasing to the point where no one could pay them any more. Gold merchants began making the rounds of the villages, where they would swindle the peasants out of the value of the gold they bought from them. Consequently, the authorities decided to accept in-kind taxes in the form of jewelry.

The money changers raised eyebrows in al-Ish when they began bringing a gold scale with them on their visits. At first the villagers couldn't believe it. However, they knew that what they were seeing was real when the employees began examining and weighing the items being presented to them, estimating their value, deducting their taxes from the price of the items, and returning the difference to them in cash with a receipt.

As the years went by, the scales ceased to be of any use, since people didn't have anything left to sell. Yet the taxes went on rising. Some people began emigrating, leaving behind the few carats they owned, or looking for someone who would buy them for any price just to get the tax collectors and the exploitative cotton merchants off their backs. Some started refusing to pay, either with tears and complaints of poverty, or with assaults on the tax collectors. Not long after this a couple of soldiers came to summon Salama to the office of Sharqiya's chief of police.

From the day he received the summons, Salama didn't sleep a wink, and at the time appointed, he was standing outside the chief of police's office. A soldier opened the door for him and left him standing before the officer, who was engrossed in his paperwork. Salama froze in place, not knowing how to act, until the chief of police looked up and gestured for him to have a seat.

"Do you know what's been happening to the tax collectors in al-Ish?" he asked.

"I've heard about it, sir."

"So what should be done?"

"Whatever you think is best, sir."

The chief of police opened an envelope that lay in front of him and took out a decree appointing Salama as mayor. He showed Salama the decree and asked him to choose seven sentries along with a village elder to maintain security.

He chose the regular sentries and the elder from among the conscripts who had been discharged from military service, and when they'd gone to the governorate to sign their appointments and be trained in the used of shotguns, he began renovating the neglected arms depot. Within two weeks they all knew their responsibilities, and the arms depot came to serve as the new mayor's administrative office. When the tax collectors arrived in the village they would first come to see Salama, and from his office they would send for whichever of the villagers they wished to see.

Salama didn't dispense with the services of the special sentries whose help he'd been obliged to seek out when security deteriorated. However, he exempted them from having to keep a night watch in front of the factory, contenting himself with securing the road against the highway robbers, who would come out of the cornfields and attack the carriages that brought spun cotton to al-Ish and transported finished cloth elsewhere.

As the factory began making progress, Salama bought land with whatever he'd been able to save up. He would register half of the land for the entire family in Mugahid's name, and the other half in his own name. He began doing this after Tafida convinced him that he was the source of the family's wealth, and that it wasn't right for Mubarka's or Mas'ada's children to be treated the same as her children, especially now that Nagi and Ali no longer did physical labor. It was Salama himself who had asked his two brothers to content themselves with overseeing the hired workers—Ali at the factory and Nagi in the field—and neither brother objected to the new division. The only problem that remained, then, was how to protect what the family had achieved.

After things settled down Salama felt relieved, since he now had time for some thought and reflection. In the late afternoons he would sit on the stone bench along the front wall of the farmhouse to get away from the racket made by the looms and the singing of the workers, who would jump on top of the looms and turn their wheels like monkeys in a tree. He would make his own coffee on the alcohol burner, pour it into the cup, and inhale its fragrance with the first sip. However, his first sip was often his last, since he would open his ledger and lose himself in his calculations.

Household provisions began coming regularly from Bilbeis on a cart filled with rounds of cheese, sesame halawa, cone-shaped packages of sugar, and sacks of black-eyed peas and kidney beans. The mothers in the household had no work to do but oversee the hired bakers and cooks, milk the animals, and make cheese.

Salama had asked them to take charge of the milk and cheese production since he didn't trust strangers to ensure the cleanliness of the milk, which he liked to drink raw and still warm from the cow. The baby-making contest at the farmhouse had produced eleven children in eight years. After giving birth to Mansur and Salem, Mubarka had Mustafa, Mahmoud, Yusuf, and Zaynab; Tafida had Ahmad, Abd al-Maqsud, Deeb, and Umm Ali; and Mas'ada had Samiha, Kamel, and Sanad.

"In a few years we'll be able to form an army and declare independence!" Salama chuckled, pleased with the steady succession of births. He was also pleased to see the factory's work steadily expanding. Things were going so well, in fact, that there wasn't enough room in the factory for the surplus spun cotton and fabric, so some of the women crowded their families by winding spools of spun cotton and storing them in the spare rooms of their houses or in the empty corners of rooms that were in use. Merchants would come from other villages and cities in Sharqiya, and some of them would stay in al-Ish for several days waiting for their orders to be completed during the wedding and holiday seasons when consumption was particularly high.

"My God!" he said in amazement, looking at the abandoned mayoral mansion as though seeing it for the first time. His coffee cup halted in mid-air before the fragrance reached his nostrils, his mind wandering over to the dry fronds that dangled from the towering royal palms. As he thought back on the childhood fear that had centered around the mansion, he realized how far away his childhood was now and how old he had grown.

It wasn't only the children who avoided the mansion. Everyone went out of his way to keep from having to pass it in the dark, and many a story had been told about the drumming and pipe-playing that went on all night there, and about the beautiful fair-skinned girl who would stand in the window wearing nothing but a bride's veil to lure young men. They used to say she was a demonic apparition of Nadiya, the daughter of Matin Agha, al-Ish's first mayor, who'd been buried alive by her brother Hikmet in the mansion's garden because her husband had sent her home on their wedding night after discovering she wasn't a virgin.

"Demonic apparition my foot! There's no such thing!" mused Salama with a smile as he took his first sip of coffee. He knew now what he had to do. He disappeared for a couple of days, and returned with two strangers. He walked through the gate of the dilapidated mansion with the two men, who removed a bunch of keys from a small chest they were carrying and opened the mansion door. Then the car that had brought them took them back to wherever they'd come from. It was rumored that Salama had gone to Cairo to look for Ismet Oghlo's sons and that he'd bought the mansion from them. No one challenged him or asked to see the deed to an abandoned building haunted by evil spirits. So he set about doing the needed renovations.

He couldn't find a soul in all of al-Ish who dared cross the threshold of the mansion gate, so he had no choice but to bring workers from Bilbeis to restore the mansion to life. When the boys in the village passed the workers they would run as fast as they could, imagining that the demons whose voices they heard in the evenings had begun coming out during the day, while the adults cast anxious glances through the gate. Never before had they known what lay beyond it, with the exception of the palms and a few other trees that they used to see from the top of the wall in the mornings. However, they'd always avoided looking at them in the dark, since it was during the nighttime hours that the demons liked to play in the branches and jump from one tree to another.

The work dragged on for weeks. There was nothing in the garden around the mansion but four royal palms with small green wisps and dry branches that hadn't been trimmed for years, and several generations of lemon trees that had reproduced from the seeds of fallen fruit to form a huge dense forest. Alongside the trees, tufts of withered grass were interspersed among mounds of salty soil that bore the tracks of black ant caravans.

The building proper, now marred nearly beyond recognition, was in no better shape than the garden. Its walls had been eaten away by moisture, the beds with their dusty mattresses were falling apart, and what remained of the windowsills had been scorched by the sun. Every corner of the ceiling was now home to sparrows' and pigeons' nests, while the surface of the soil that had piled up at the base of the walls glistened with the shed skins of lizards and snakes together with broken pieces of the stained-glass windows, which had been a source of wonder and awe when the mansion was first constructed.

Every day, from early morning till sundown, the workers were busy removing the effects of neglect both inside and outside the mansion. Then they would leave to go to their barracks, have their suppers, and fall quickly into a mindless slumber. People coming home from the final evening prayer would hear the communal snoring of the fifteen workers who were being housed in a small abandoned cottage that Salama had rented and whose floor he'd spread with a mat for them.

When the mansion renovations had been finished off with a fresh coat of paint, a cart arrived laden with carpets, beds, and chairs to replace the Turks' worm-eaten blankets and cushions and the bed frames the workers had used for firewood when they wanted to make tea in the garden. Salama decided to host a house-blessing celebration before moving into the mansion. After slaughtering two calves in the garden, he sent the raw meat from one of them around to people's houses, and kept the meat from the other for his immediate family, his other relatives, and the workers. He requested the attendance of two Qur'an reciters, who agreed reluctantly to sit on the veranda.

The two blind men began their recitation after the midafternoon prayer, bobbing their heads up and down as they chanted with quavering voices and looking about with their dimmed eyes as though they expected to encounter some danger they couldn't see. By the time the sun went down, kerosene lanterns had been lit and hung from the trunks of the royal palms. However, they soon started going out so quickly that the person lighting them couldn't keep up with them. Fear spread through the place, tying the tongues of the people who, during the daytime hours, had been talkative and full of merriment as the animals were being slaughtered and skinned. Salama couldn't convince anyone that it was the wind, and not evil spirits, that had put out the lanterns and burned up their wicks.

One by one the guests began withdrawing. Then the mass flight began. Even the workers who'd spent long days laboring in the mansion and whom Salama had kept on to attend the celebration; even the family members and the women who had served the food with knees knocking, fled back to the farmhouse. Meanwhile, the Qur'an reciters began stammering and making mistakes. Then they hurriedly rose to their feet and withdrew, groping for the exit with their white canes.

Salama found himself alone among the tables piled with left-over food as smoke rose from beneath the kettles on the stoves as though the garden were a war camp that had just been overrun. Dragging his feet, he departed with the others, leaving the fire to burn itself out.

Those who had received raw meat in their homes swore that it had jumped around in the cooking pots, screaming and sending the lids flying against the ceiling. Some of them said that after the meat had been boiling for several hours they'd had to carry it outside, still uncooked, and throw it to the dogs, which sniffed it uncertainly, then ran away. The two blind Qur'an reciters swore that they'd run their hands over the meat that Salama had placed before them, and that, within moments, the loaves of bread in front of them had turned dry as though no broth had ever touched them.

Salama didn't want to force the family to move, realizing how awkward it was to talk about evil spirits on account of Nagi's situation. He'd hoped the people would forget the story of the housewarming celebration as time went by. However, the mansion, which had been there for decades and had been neglected so thoroughly that it was hardly visible any more, was no longer invisible now that it had been renovated. On the contrary, it was the center of attention, and the stained glass that sparkled once again in its windows compounded its mysteriousness even during the day.

Mugahid, whose old age had turned him into a little boy again, was the most fearful of all. He was no longer open to any sort of discussion, and would dismiss Salama with a wave of the hand whenever he approached him about moving to the mansion. As for Tafida, she would resort to banter whenever he tried to persuade her.

"All right, then, let Nagi go! Isn't he the one who consorts with the jinn?"

If he rebuked her with an angry look, she would try to fix what she'd said before.

"Well, so what if I fall in love with a goblin or a jinni?"

"All the better for me!" he would retort crossly, ignoring the joke. He couldn't help but obsess over all he'd spent on the renovations, and during his late-afternoon sessions in front of the farmhouse with his coffee and his ledger, he went on thinking glumly about the mansion. Then a certain defiance sprouted in his head, and he decided he would move there alone.

He made sure the factory was closed up tightly, the way he usually did at the end of the day, and went back to the farmhouse. After having dinner with the family, he took the keys to the mansion, got a lantern, and headed out, leaving the family still seated around the table. Tafida tried to talk him out of his decision, but he pulled the hem of his gilbab out of her hand and left.

Lantern in hand, he made his way through the tunnel of darkness in the large parlor to the room he had decided would be his when he distributed the mattresses and blankets among the various rooms in the mansion. He set the lantern on the floor so that it would light up both the room and part of the corridor. It was as though he were creating a wall of light that would protect him from the demons whose existence he had insisted on denying whenever arguments heated up over the mansion. He lay down on the bed, his ears pricked for the sound of any movement, but all he heard was the rustling of the palm branches, which was amplified by the silence of the night and the howling of dogs in the distance. He had one nightmare after another as he alternated between sleep and wakefulness. No sooner would a wave of slumber carry him away than he would find himself being chased by monsters. He couldn't move his legs, which were as heavy as bags of salt. A scream would jolt him awake, but he found no trace of monsters among the undulations of shadow and tremulous light.

By sunrise he was back in the farmhouse. Hafiza, who'd been sitting near the door, sprang to her feet with an agility that was out of keeping with her age. It was easy to see that she hadn't slept a wink all night, in terror of the adventure from which she hadn't been able to dissuade him. She ran her hands over her son's face, his red eyes betraying an exhaustion that, however visible it was in his features, couldn't conceal the pride and satisfaction of a hero who had returned to lead his people into a liberated land.

He went into his room, where he found Tafida sound asleep. He slipped into bed beside her, and before long his snores could be heard, his features etched with triumphant euphoria.

When Ali saw the place that had been suggested to him as his bedroom in the mansion, he refused to move, preferring his room on the farmhouse roof over this prison with its stingily meted-out spaces. The worst thing about the mansion was that, being built from stone, it had an echo that made sounds much louder than they would be otherwise.

"This is a personal matter, Mr. Mayor. I mean, can you imagine Mas'ada's snore being four times louder than it is now?" He said it with a touch of ironic humor lest Salama be angry over his refusal to move to the mansion. As a matter of fact, Salama had no objections to their sleeping in the farmhouse provided that Mas'ada was willing to come to the mansion in the mornings to look after her children and help with the chores. He also wanted them to eat with the family at the mansion, fearing that if they cooked at the farmhouse, which was being turned into a warehouse, they might start a fire that would consume the spun cotton and stored fabric.

"Your scandals set enough fires as it is!" Salama whispered jovially to his brother. His tone betrayed a hint of admiration for Ali's nocturnal escapades with his wife, whose voice could be heard by people coming home from the final evening prayer and going to the dawn prayer, and whose screams were accompanied by the barks, howls, and meows of the dogs and cats in the streets and on the rooftops.

The newlyweds' bed didn't hold out for more than a week before its joints started creaking, and not long afterward it collapsed under them, so they started sleeping on top of the oven in the farthest room in the farmhouse. Mas'ada, who by this time wasn't a guest any more, dispensed with the pillow she'd held between her teeth during her first month of marriage and allowed herself to scream however she liked, since it was the only way she could reach orgasm. So Salama decided to build them a room on top of the roof in hopes that her voice would be dissipated into the open air. However, although it couldn't be heard with the same intensity by the farmhouse residents, it now carried all over the village.

"At the very least, try to keep it down during the call to prayer," Salama told his brother. "It drowns out Sheikh Hasanayn. He's an elderly man, and his voice has gotten weak." He uttered the words with a mixture of admiration and exasperation, since the problem might hurt Mas'ada's reputation, making it harder for her to live down her past and be accepted as one of the women of the family.

Mas'ada Ta'lab was the first and last girl ever to work at the factory. She considered factory work preferable to getting sunburned and scratched up picking cotton or wading through mud to plant rice. Her mute widowed mother saw no reason to prevent her, since she would be mixing with men wherever she worked. Besides, she'd never attracted anyone's attention, either because of her poverty, or because her femininity was disguised beneath a boyish figure that wouldn't have tempted a soul. She was too tall, and up till the age of fourteen she went around with a runny nose. Nothing had sprouted on her chest but a couple of little bulges the size of cotton bolls, and her behind was as flat as a board. There was nothing interesting about her apart from an enigmatic beauty in an elongated, nondescript face, a chin adorned with a deep dimple, and eyes that made up for their smallness with their green hue and that glistened with the indolence of a contented cat.

After she started working in the factory among young men who stripped down to the bare minimum and who sang and told off-color jokes, nature began endowing her with additions of flesh that were deftly aimed at her breasts and hips. So, while Salama kept an eye on the growth in production, traveling to Cairo to take in the latest designs in high-class fabric shops, Ali, who was in charge of workflow at the factory, was keeping an eye on Mas'ada's curves. The two little bulges he had rubbed for the first time with just three fingers had turned into a couple of tomatoes that filled his palms, and the flat backside was being endowed with a roundness that increased from one day to the next.

The One who shapes all things had given her a girlish figure at last, then left her at the mercy of Ali, who, trying to ignore the bewildering inscrutability in her face and her now-flawless physique, began deliberately subjecting her to harsh treatment in front of the other workers. He would scrutinize the movement of her hands with a doggedness that bordered on harassment as she removed the yarn from the spool, then rolled it into a skein between her fist and her elbow. He would assign her to more than one task at a time, and when she got flustered, would call her names and smack her bottom with whatever he could get his hands on.

When they heard her screaming one day in one of the store-rooms, they figured the huge cylinders of spun yarn had fallen on her, and those who had glimpsed Ali sneaking in behind her thought he was giving her a brutal beating. They gathered outside the door, which was locked from the inside. They rammed it with their shoulders and half the workers broke through, spilling in a heap onto the floor of the room, while the others froze where they stood at the door. They saw the two of them naked on a bed of spools of spun thread which, set in motion by the force of their embarrassment, flung its load of flesh gone berserk onto the stunned workers.

"The wedding will be in a week," said Salama to the men who came to ask him what he intended to do to provide for the orphan girl. He could have spurned her as the sole girl who worked in the factory and prevented his brother from marrying her, in which case she would have lived the life of an outcast with no one who cared enough either to defend her or to kill her. Nor would anyone have agreed to marry her. However, Salama settled matters and, by honoring the girl, made her part of a family that enjoyed such respect that others had no choice but to forget, or at least pretend to forget.

No one at the farmhouse objected openly to the marriage, with the exception of Hafiza. She wasn't concerned about the girl's poverty or her family's size or social standing. What worried her was not knowing who else the girl might have dallied with before snaring her son.

"Why should he take a girl who's done a number on him?" she asked, trying to recruit support from Mugahid. However, he just waved his hand dismissively, exempting himself from having to comment on a marriage that would reinforce the image Salama was establishing for them as a family of gallantry and integrity. As far as Ali was concerned, gallantry had nothing to do with what bound him to Mas'ada. She would be his woman even if she were a highway robber's daughter, and nobody was going to keep him from marrying her just because she'd given herself to him before he'd made things official.

She stopped working, and by the end of the week everything was ready just as Salama had said it would be: a hundred grams of gold, a hundred kilos of copper, a bed and a fancy wardrobe, mattresses, blankets, comforters, sheets, nightgowns, colorful gallabiyas, a silk wedding dress, and a black bridal veil—in short, all the things that made no difference to a bride who dreamed of nothing but a safe and socially acceptable state of undress in Ali's arms.

A wedding celebration fit for the family was hosted: Animals were slaughtered, singers came, and shots were fired into the air. All the fanfare proper to a joyous celebration was in evidence, though it seemed more like a funeral. The bride came out of her ramshackle house and Ali lifted her onto the back of a horse, the sight of which caused Hafiza to relive the sorrow she'd felt on the night when Mubarka was wed to Mugahid. As for Mugahid, his eyes welled up with tears as he thought back on his filly and relived memories from his youth.

Mas'ada paid no attention to the cool, almost hostile reception she was given by her mother-in-law. Nor did she worry about the looks of disdain or mockery she detected in the women's eyes when her mother would visit her with a boiled egg and toast and insist that she eat them in front of her. She would laugh at Mansur as he stood behind the mute woman, mimicking the hand gestures she used to complete the gusts of air that came out of her throat in her attempts to say something.

Mubarka was the only one who'd been openly delighted over Ali's marriage and the circumstances that had led up to it, since they drew people's attention away from her and Nagi. Things had cooled off between them by this time and their trysts had become fewer and farther between. Even so, Tafida seemed to be alert to the slightest gesture or look that passed between them.

After Mas'ada's arrival, Tafida ignored Mubarka and began focusing all her curiosity on the new bride. From the day of Mas'ada's morning-after bridal party, she scrutinized her belly, searching for signs of an unborn child that might have begun forming before the wedding.

None of this meant a thing to Mas'ada. All that mattered to her was to see the day end at dinner with the family, then withdraw lickety-split to start her nightly love battle with Ali. As the days passed, the farmhouse residents lost their bet that things would settle down eventually. In fact, the flames of desire kept growing night after night. And once her screaming had ceased to be a secret, the two of them were freed from the need for restraint. Consequently, the bedroom was no longer their only battleground, nor were the nights their only meeting times. The minute they found themselves alone in the farmhouse courtyard, on the roof, or in a hayloft, storeroom, or cattle pen, he would lift her gilbab and enter her whenever circumstances permitted.

More than a year after they were married, Mubarka and Tafida left Mas'ada with the task of milking a refractory buffalo cow that would only give milk when a trough filled with clover or fodder was close at hand. A man would sit on the edge of the trough holding a huge stick to threaten her while a woman milked her.

"Mas'ada could squeeze milk from a stone! You'll see!" said Tafida playfully. However, she won only half the challenge. After managing to get the cow's udders to fill with milk and her teats to go erect, Mas'ada brought her milk gushing down into the pail. However, she didn't get out of the place with a single drop. The two women went in at the sound of her screaming, and came back out trying to suppress giggles. The story didn't remain a secret, since Tafida told it to Salama, and Mubarka told it to Nagi.

Ali was aroused by the sight of Mas'ada's hands going up and down, up and down on the cow's swelling, hardening teats. So, rather than staying put on the edge of the trough, he got up and came over to where she sat with the milk pail between her thighs. Grasping her under her arms, he pulled her upright, sending the pail tumbling to the ground. Then he lifted her hands onto the cow's back, pressed into her from behind, and silently sank his teeth into her neck, like a donkey mounting his mate while she did the braying for him.

Unmarried Nagi, who was hiding out in the obscurity of his clandestine love affair, wasn't at liberty to go into the story. However, Salama managed to circulate it at the dinner table in an attempt to bring his father out of the isolation into which he'd been sinking.

"A little river of that cow's milk came out of the cattle pen with your son's cream on top, Abu Salama!"

They all burst out laughing, while Mubarka, red in the face, shot Nagi a glance that Tafida picked up in a flash. Ali's romantic escapades with Mas'ada were no longer known only to the family. The stories had begun spreading among the young men of the village, who, in keeping with traditional protocol, related events without mentioning the girl's name. Despite the fact that the voice they heard at night was hers and not his, they would joke with him about it as though he'd been doing it all by himself. They jokingly attributed to Sheikh Hasanayn a complaint that he couldn't compete with Ali's shouts, so attendance at the dawn prayer had dropped off to the point where he was praying in the mosque all alone, and the only reason he was regular about his own prayers was that he didn't have anybody beside him to mount!

The children's shouting and rowdy games didn't give the evil spirits a chance to appear anywhere in the mansion, which had expanded thanks to rooms that had been added in the backyard and on the roof. Nor did Salama get a chance any more to close his eyes after lunch and take a break from the tiring tasks of managing the family business and fulfilling his mayoral responsibilities, which had increased after the provincial government installed telephone lines. They had placed one of the remarkable gadgets in the guardhouse, which was now dubbed "the telephone." The new marvel might ring at any hour of the day or night, and he would find himself confronted with someone on the other end giving him orders to take this or that measure, or reprimanding him for being lenient with farmers who'd been late in paying their taxes whereas the other mayors were extracting the state's dues with riding whips.

Salama wasn't prepared to use this sort of violence against neighbors and relatives from whom it still felt strange to hear the word "mayor" when they addressed him by this title. His awareness of the farmers' circumstances and the pressures to which he was subjected by his superiors in the city set up a painful conflict in his heart from which he would try to escape for a while by sleeping. However, there wasn't a moment when the children weren't shouting and moving around. Tense, he would scold them and chase them away, then not be able to get back to sleep. So he set up a room for himself in "the telephone" where he started to go for his naptime, but the children's voices reached him even there, chasing away the slumber that was being guarded by a sentinel at his door. During the family times after dinner, he would turn the anger he felt during his interrupted naptimes into laughter. He told his brothers, for example, that he hadn't wanted to inform them of what he'd seen a week after the family moved into the mansion: "With my own eyes I saw the goblins throwing themselves off the roof!"

However, the din produced by the children's playing, running, and arguing, which had succeeded in driving the evil spirits to suicide, hadn't succeeded in driving the shadow of grief from the mansion. A deadness had stolen into the chambers that lined the narrow corridor, and the noise coming from the children's rooms had become the only sign of life in the old building. The regnant state of indifference had enveloped Tafida, who abandoned even her unseemly prying. She no longer showed any interest in either Mubarka or Nagi, who for their part no longer had anything between them that was worth hiding.

The only person who escaped the deadly ennui was Mas'ada, who hadn't moved out of the farmhouse. She went on spreading her legs for Ali and screaming every night, and spreading her legs and screaming for the midwife every nine months. Every newborn would banish his older sibling to the mansion, where the other women would take care of him on behalf of Mas'ada, who was constantly busy with an infant.

Hafiza secluded herself in her little room next to the door of the mansion, where dreams had begun assailing her again. She was beleaguered by the dead, most of whom were women she had hated. The one who paid her the most frequent visits was her mother-in-law Alhaz, who was always rushing about and screaming at the dog-sized cats that were running after her and tearing at her legs and buttocks. She would see the gypsy woman who had swindled her out of her gold jewelry carrying red-hot shards of pottery in the hem of her gilbab, which would then catch on fire.

Her most painful dreams were the ones in which she saw Nagiya. She would come to her with a beautiful face, in her eyes the same look of sorrowful reproach she'd cast her the last time she saw her. But the dream she had most often took the form of a woman with her legs spread, and a fire that emerged from between her thighs and seared her abdomen. The face of the woman, who was in a reclining position, wouldn't appear, but somehow Hafiza knew in the dream that she was Nagiya.

She would wake up early as if to flee from her nightmares, then go out to the garden, where she would sit in the sun during the winter, and in the shade during the summer. If, out of politeness, one of her daughters-in-law tried to ask for her advice about cooking or baking arrangements, she would dismiss her with a wave of the hand. When the children crowded around her, she would bring pieces of candy out of her pocket. Knowing that she would ask them their names, each of the boys would introduce himself the minute he shook her hand. Not content to hear the name, she would ask, for example, "Are you Mubarka's son?" "No, grandma," would come the reply, "I'm Mas'ada's son." Then she would place a piece of mint candy or Turkish delight in his hand. Not satisfied with these formalities when it came to the girls, she would take each one in her lap and search her hair for lice, and if she found any, the girl's mother would be in for a tongue-lashing.

Mugahid's powers were failing, and he could no longer tell the difference between sleeping with Hafiza and sleeping with Mubarka, whom he would brush up against with a behind so wizened that he couldn't feel a thing. Nor did it matter to him whether the reason for this was old age, or the fact that her body also had begun going downhill. He couldn't even remember why he'd felt so let down when she used to ignore his advances.

He tried to be regular about praying the noon and midafternoon prayers in the mosque, where he would prop himself up on Salem. He said that out of everybody in the new "litter"—the term he used to refer to the little children who now filled the mansion—Salem

133

was the only one whose name he could remember. Salem was also the only one who called Mugahid "Daddy." Mustafa, Mahmoud, Yusuf, and Zaynab all called him "Grandpa" the way his actual grandchildren did. By this time, however, he no longer paid any attention to what they called him and, like Hafiza, had started asking them the names of their mothers, not their fathers.

Forgetting the children's names wasn't the only thing Mugahid and Hafiza now had in common. A brotherly-sisterly affection had developed between them, and he had moved permanently to her room. The two of them would wake up before everyone else. She would go to the kitchen and make him a glass of tea that he would drink in their room, and after sunrise they would come out to the garden, where they would sit for long hours on the ground among the well-tended shrubs. They would move with the shade until Mugahid got sleepy. Then she would take him by the hand and lead him back to bed, where he would sleep for a while before waking up for the noon prayer.

In his old age Mugahid began eating more voraciously than he had as a young man. He would also eat so nervously and rapidly that his remaining teeth couldn't chew what he was shoveling into his mouth. Unable to control himself, he would eat until he began vomiting, and sometimes he would go to sleep so sated that he was on the verge of death. Afterward he would stop eating for days, but once he recovered, he would resume his gluttonous ways all over again.

Hafiza became protective of his appearance, and would try to conceal from the younger women anything that might shame or humiliate him. She asked Salama to put a lock on the pantry door and attached the key to a string that she tied to her braid so she could keep him from devouring sweets, which he did with a voracity that brought amused looks from the women and provoked laughter among the children. She would look this way and that before wiping cake crumbs from the corners of his mouth and brushing them off his gilbab, or when she wiped off the mucus that dripped from his nose onto his upper lip. After discovering that he'd lost control of his bowels, she began hiding his underwear so that she could wash it herself out of other people's sight.

From time to time she would think back on how he'd left her for Mubarka and inflicted all manner of suffering on her and her children, before they grew up and he began to respect and fear them. Meanwhile, her treatment of him had changed. Sometimes she would scold him, but he would accept her reprimand meekly. She contemplated the huge difference between the little boy who now bowed to her will and the monster who had once left her and gone out to spend the evenings with his friends after setting her body on fire with a bamboo stick, and this thought would calm her down again despite the anger she might be feeling. Even so, she would help him get dressed with muffled resentment. After all, they were the same age and, as far as she could tell, the only reason for the infirmity that had afflicted him was the way he had so shamelessly spilled his seed on Mubarka's thighs.

"If only you'd shown yourself some compassion!" she would say to him irritably when the spasms in his arm wore her out as she was dressing or undressing him. However, his resigned silence would restore her spirit of tolerance.

A moment later he would break the stern silence, saying, "Let's recite the Fatiha for your daddy."

No sooner had they finished a mumbled recitation than he would repeat the request all over again, until she was so frazzled that she had no choice but to get away from him on the pretext that she was worried about a child stuck in a tree, or that she smelled something burning and was afraid one of the other women had forgotten something on the stove. He wouldn't tell her why he'd mentioned her father rather than his own father or mother. However, she knew this was his way of expressing his gratitude to his uncle, who hadn't given in to his wife's insistence that they divorce Hafiza from Mugahid after he took Mubarka as his second wife. As the mistress of the household, Hafiza's mother had seen nothing wrong with Mugahid's beating Hafiza, or being the selfish individual his mother had raised him to be, when her daughter was his only wife. However, she didn't say a word to him from the time he married Mubarka. After the children were grown, they would joke with their grandmother about how Mugahid's marriage to Mubarka had given their mother more freedom in her house than she'd ever had when he was around. When they made fun of the elderly grandmother's grief over a man who was no use to anyone, she would fire back without hesitation, "That's just the point! If only he'd been of some use!"

Caring for Mugahid and keeping an eye on him all day weren't the only cause for Hafiza's weariness, since his failing memory coincided with a fondness for hiding things. He would hide something, then forget where he had put it. She would go in circles looking for a plate he'd eaten from or a glass he'd drunk tea from just moments earlier, only to find piles of dishes with rotting leftovers on them under the bed or in the closet nestled among the clothes. In addition, he'd become more and more reckless in his confrontations with the children. Unable to leave them alone, he would turn to see if any of the other adults was looking before he pinched or hit a little child to keep him from playing. Consequently, she had to watch him every minute lest he hurt someone and get a scolding from Salama. If that happened, he would burst into tears like a little boy. His words coming out tremulously between sobs, he would say, "Yes, sir. Yes, sir. I'm wrong!"

"You bet you are!" Salama would retort. Then he would feel guilty for having gotten so irritated to his face. As for Mugahid, not an hour would go by before he'd forgotten the confrontation and hurt another child.

Salama wasn't the only person who was pained by his father's hostile behavior, which was excusable now given his senility, whereas there had been nothing to excuse his cruelty toward him and his brothers when they were young boys. Nagi and Ali were no less bitter toward this man for whom none of them felt the least affection. However, whereas Salama's responsibilities to the factory and his mayoral post, and Ali's responsibility for keeping Mas'ada happy in bed, had restricted their thinking about the children to the matter of how to protect them from their father's hostile antics, Nagi's intense isolation led him to think about things more distant, about providing them with a level of education that went beyond what he and his brothers had received in primary school and that would befit the family's new station in life. He discussed the idea with Salama who, quick to respond, decided to send the school-age boys to Zagazig.

He rented an apartment and furnished it with beds, tables, notebooks, pencils, and kitchen utensils. Before school started, he was seated next to a taxi driver taking Mubarka and a load of kids between the ages of six and eight to the city. There were seven boys: Mubarka's sons Salem, Mahmoud and Yusuf, Tafida's sons Ahmad and Abd al-Maqsud, and Mas'ada's sons Kamel and Sanad. The trunk and the rack on the car's roof were weighed down with their clothes and food: a jar of old cheese, bundles of dried mulukhiya and okra, rice, vermicelli, a huge amount of onions, garlic, jerked meat immersed in congealed fat, and dry bread.

Within two days Mubarka had everything in place, and the apartment looked as though it had been her home since time immemorial. She felt as though she'd been liberated from the heavy atmosphere that had nearly suffocated her in the mansion in spite of the fact that she'd had to leave Mansur, who had learned to weave and gone to work in the factory, and her daughter Zaynab. As time went on she would have painful recollections of the way Zaynab had gone running after the car until it disappeared into the distance, and how she'd cried for days, not only over having to separate from her mother, but over her desire for an education. It was a wish her brothers had denied her, since in those days no one even considered the possibility of teaching a girl anything but how to bake, milk cows, and do housework.

Mubarka began getting acquainted with the other women in the building, some of whom had come from outlying villages to educate their sons as she had, and some of whom were city dwellers to begin with and married to men employed in the city. After the boys had gone to school the women would have tea together, then head for the market to buy the things they needed in order to have lunch ready when the boys got home in the afternoon.

Mubarka knew what time they would be home by the size of the patch of sunlight on the living-room floor. She would set the food before them, after which it was time for a communal nap that enveloped the apartment in silence. After they woke up, the boys would do the day's homework as she sat among them learning letters and numbers, then words and how to spell them. Once she'd seen the shape of a letter or number, she wouldn't forget it or need to ask about it ever again. Hence, within a few months she was able to move ahead of them in their schoolbooks and help them do their lessons. However, her greatest pleasure was bath day.

When the boys got home from school on Thursday afternoons she would be ready with a tin pail of water boiling on the burner in the bathroom. She would toss a piece of mastic and a few bay leaves into the water, and their aroma would waft upward with the steam. After neatly laying out clean underwear beside the washbasin, she would have them get undressed in turn. She'd dip boiling water out of the pail with a long-necked pitcher and mix it with the cold water in front of her. After dousing the boy with the water, she would begin lathering his head and scrubbing him down with a loofah. As she worked, her breasts bobbing up and down, a numbness would spread through her body from the aromatic steam and the feel of the boy, who would rest his hands on her head with his eyes closed to keep from getting soap in them. She would see his scrotum wiggle and shrink until it was nothing but a tiny firm tip. At the same time, his little birdie would move and stiffen with innocent pleasure as he stood facing her. With happy hands she would turn him around and scrub his back before pouring water over his head, wrapping him in a towel, and dressing him in clean clothes so that he could come out and give someone else a turn. When she'd finished, she would come and relax with them, not as a nanny or a babysitter, but as a queen among her subjects.

The only times she felt her throne shaken were when Salama came to visit for a few hours every two weeks on baking day. He would bring them fresh bread, jerked meat, duck, and slaughtered geese with their livers, which the boys loved. During the hours he spent with them, she would feel as though she'd been banished from her realm for the sake of a man who was issuing commands to her children, and that she had to wait on him hand and foot. However, this discomfort on her part did nothing to improve her position with her sister-in-law, who was jealous of Salama's visits to her husband's stepmother. Tafida, who, whenever she had a chance to be alone with Mubarka, hinted that she was aware of her relationship with Nagi, thought it unlikely that Salama would be attracted to her. At the same time, she wasn't comfortable with the idea of her husband being alone with a woman whose magical charms seemed to numb men, making them obedient to her and as tame as orphaned children. Her magic had even made her own boys the calmest and most obedient children in the family.

"I'm coming with you!" Tafida said one day with an insistence that left Salama no chance to think. Thereafter she accompanied him on two visits that were a source of such distress to Mubarka that she asked him not to trouble himself any more, and to send the money and provisions she needed with any emissary he could find. She felt good about this solution, which had been brought about by a woman who had no appreciation for the pleasure of a life lived without men in a paradise inhabited by little boys, and which Mubarka only left against her will during the summer vacations, which they spent in al-Ish.

In this paradise of hers, Mubarka learned how to love herself. After the boys left for school she would take off all her clothes and contemplate her nakedness unhurriedly in the mirror. She would examine her thighs in search of the puckers and varicose veins that other women her age tended to complain of, but which she

139

found no sign of on her still-youthful legs. With her fingers pressed together in the shape of a bird's beak she would roam with her hands over her thighs and pinch the area below her abdomen. Then she would bring them up to her breasts, which were still full and firm, and pinch the nipples, which glowed with a coppery redness, examining their cracked appearance and the orifice in the center of each one and imagining them to be the heads of sleeping twins. Then she would put on a calico dress that rested voluptuously on her bosom to begin her lazy morning routine with the neighborhood ladies.

Salama served as mayor of al-Ish for ten years, during which time he tasted the bitterness of power more than its sweetness. Nevertheless, he came to understand the responsibility that went with his stature.

He wouldn't have minded if al-Ish had gone without a mayor forever. However, if there was going to be a mayor, it would have been unthinkable for the position to go to anyone but him. Then the unthinkable happened when the government changed hands in Cairo and the new leaders chose their interior minister, Abd al-Raziq Asfur, as al-Ish's new mayor. Like Salama, Asfur was in his mid-forties, but with his shortish stature and a potbelly that protruded visibly from under his woolen gilbab, he looked at least ten years older. He'd been a conscript during the same time period as Salama, but hadn't come back to al-Ish after his discharge. After working in the vegetable market in Rod al-Farag, he'd started trading in scrap metal that he bought from British military camps. He'd amassed a huge fortune and taken an interest in politics, moving back and forth among political parties the differences between which were lost on him.

After long years away from home, he remembered al-Ish and began coming for visits. He rebuilt the family homestead that had been abandoned years earlier and suggested to Salama that they build a primary school for the children of the village. Salama welcomed the suggestion and donated half a feddan for the project, while Asfur offered to cover the building expenses. He had six classrooms built on one half of the land, and on the other, a small house to serve as quarters for the teachers who would come from the cities. When the construction had been completed, a sign was hung on the building that read "Al-Ish Primary School." The village was visited by a delegation of senior officials that included the governor, the chief of police, and the deputy minister of information. These men officially opened the school, and it began receiving students.

All Salama could see in the new mayor was an emigrant who felt nostalgic for his home town but who would never be able to give up his life in Cairo. Yet, in spite of everything he'd accomplished in the capital, Abd al-Raziq saw himself as a stranger there. Consequently, he planned to come back to al-Ish so that those who had known him as a child and as a young man could see him again and appreciate what he'd achieved during his years away. He paid regular visits to al-Ish at the beginning of Ramadan and on the two major Muslim holidays, Eid al-Fitr and Eid al-Adha, with his wife and two young boys, who always wore European suits, fezzes, and neckties.

In the beginning there was no sign of the worst thing Asfur had brought back: the memory of a feud that went back years—no one knew how many. It had happened so long ago that no one in either the Asfur family or the Deeb family made more than vague mention of it any more, since nobody knew what had caused it or which side had initiated the hostilities. What they did know, however, was that the resulting hatred had consumed the lives of an entire generation of both families, who took turns cutting down each other's crops before they were ready for harvest and poisoning each other's livestock. The notables of the region had eventually managed to draw up a settlement that was respected by both sides, but they'd never rid themselves of the hatred that continued to run in their veins from one generation to the next.

Abd al-Raziq gathered his relatives around him and, by handing out gifts and hosting banquets, managed to reunite a family that had been torn asunder by disagreements over things such as paltry inheritances or marriages that had ended in divorce. When the decree appointing him mayor of al-Ish was issued, a force from the central police came to carry out the transfer of power and, for the first time, Salama felt defeated. He felt insulted by the removal of the telephone, and in order to keep the place open, he replaced the government sentinels with sentinels of his own, though they concealed their unlicensed shotguns. The fire over which they'd been accustomed to making tea in front of the abandoned "telephone" continued aflame with the teapot on top of it, but Mayor Asfur wasn't pleased to see the regular sentinels taking breaks from their nightly rounds to have tea with the cloth-factory guards. Consequently, he demanded that the old "telephone" be turned over to him as government property. He had its door bricked over and sealed with mud, and required his sentinels to stay in the new "telephone" that he'd built on a lot he had purchased opposite his residence.

For the first time in his life Salama found himself obliged to defend his status, and to preserve the outward signs of his family's superiority. He bought a car more beautiful than Abd al-Raziq's and learned to drive it himself. He repainted the mansion and began moving about with a group of his workers. And for the first time he hosted a huge banquet for the singers who performed at the annual mulid celebration held in honor of the Silent Sheikh, whereas in the past he'd simply paid them their wages while letting other families take turns feeding them.

However, events intervened to prevent the conflict from escalating. The Nile ended seven years of parsimony with a fury that could be clearly seen in the torrent of foamy, churning water that came rushing out with its red silt, and that continued to rise steadily higher. Everyone worked together to pile debris on the low spots of the bank, but this did nothing to halt the water's impetuous advance.

They removed as many spools of thread and rolls of fabric as they could from the factory and hoisted them with ropes onto the roof of the mansion before the water began raiding the streets and making its way inside the houses. Nagi moved the family's livestock, along with displaced persons and their livestock, to al-Balashun. Salama drove his parents and those of Ali's children who were too young to walk to Zagazig, driving at a snail's pace so that the hordes of family members rushing along behind the car could keep up. Once they were out of danger, he rented a horse-drawn carriage to take them the rest of the way. After giving directions to the carriage driver, he took off in his car at a normal speed.

Mubarka was smitten with conflicting emotions when, after hearing a commotion on the stairs and opening the door in response to urgent knocks, she found the entire family on her doorstep only one week after the summer vacation had ended and she had brought the family's schoolchildren in her charge back to Zagazig. She was delighted to see Mansur and Zaynab. At the same time, she was faced with her elderly co-wife; her decrepit husband whose delirious ravings she'd been only too happy to leave behind; her sister-in-law Tafida, who was worse than any co-wife; and her other sister-in-law Mas'ada, who was sure to disturb her peace and quiet in the coming days.

She discovered that the passage of time hadn't done anything to calm Mas'ada down, nor did the crowded apartment deter her from her nocturnal noise-making. After lying down next to her husband in the living room, which was wall-to-wall bodies, she would give him her lower half under the cover while giving her breast to her baby. If she sensed that someone was listening to her moans of pleasure, she would spank the baby and snatch her breast out of his mouth, cursing him for being so mean and threatening not to nurse him any more if he didn't stop biting her with his razor-sharp little teeth. It was a transparent message to whoever had been listening to her, not to the infant whose crying had blended with the sound of her moans, and without any cessation of her insatiable, pendulum-like movement around the pivot of a not-really-sleeping Ali.

In total contrast to Mas'ada's diligent attempts at concealment, Tafida began resorting to unaccustomed and exaggerated displays, either out of envy for Mas'ada, or as a way of showing off in front of Mubarka. Despite the exceptional circumstances, she didn't leave Salama in peace for a single night, even when he came back exhausted from his trips to Cairo, Bilbeis, and Minya al-Qamh, where he would go to request extensions from the spun-cotton merchants who were demanding money he owed them, or to plead with the cloth merchants to repay debts they saw no reason to repay until they'd received new cloth.

Mubarka tried to convince herself that the worst part of this invasion was the loss of her morning routine. She never saw her neighbors any more except on the stairs or in the market, and her movements were restricted by Tafida and Mas'ada, who went stumbling about in their countrified gilbabs. She was also faced with the responsibility of feeding the crowd that had descended upon her, and of taking some of its members out into the street during the day to ease the crowding in the apartment. But at night, when she heard the two women's hissing, her ears would be filled with the delirious ravings of Muntasir and Nagi, who had fused into a single man who lay on top of her in a haystack, tickling her in a way that was as delicious as it was painful.

"Pack everything up," Salama told them. "We're all going back."

He'd gone out early that morning as he had every other day for six weeks, but on this particular day he'd come back dejected and covered with mud. Mubarka didn't understand why she should have to bring the boys in her charge back to al-Ish when the school year had hardly begun. Salama didn't say anything; nor did anyone ask him anything, piqued though they were by his gloomy silence. As for the boys, they were saddened to be leaving the city. Even so, the silent caravan set out for al-Ish: a heap of humanity and bundles of clothing atop a horse-drawn carriage preceded by Salama's automobile with its mud-caked tires and fenders.

The carriage arrived late, surrounded by a cloud of mosquitoes that were withdrawing with the last rays of the sun from the still-muddy streets. Wisps of smoke wafted from a few houses, and the mansion gate stood open. Even so, the old, depressing silence still hovered about it. As they began getting out of the carriage, they found Salama sitting wordlessly with his mother and father. The three of them looked at the queue with bowed heads.

"Nagi." The whispering of the name did nothing to dissipate the baffling silence. No one added the phrase "may God give you strength" after the name, the way people always did when speaking to those who'd been closest to the deceased. Nor did they add "may you have a long life," as was customary when informing more distant parties of a person's passing. All they did was utter the name, so no one was entitled to consider him dead.

Nagi had disappeared. He'd left his livestock in his neighbors' care among the huts where the displaced villagers had been staying in al-Balashun, saying that he was going to al-Ish to check out the possibility of returning. The entire day had gone by, and he hadn't returned either that night or the night after. So they'd come looking for Salama and informed him of the disappearance.

There was no sign of a corpse in the farmhouse, the mansion, or in any of the canals or drainage ditches. The jinni must have overpowered him in the dark, ruined village. She must have taken him down into the depths of the earth, and he might spend the rest of his life there. He might be able to escape from her at any moment by some sleight of hand or he might remain her captive until she was finished with him and spat him out, sending him back to the surface of the earth as an old man with fading eyesight and replacing him with some other human being—with some young man who could keep her satisfied. This, at any rate, was the readiest explanation for the puzzling absence. In such circumstances it wasn't possible to hold a wake. Nevertheless, the family received visitors, who would sit in silence without trying to think up new words of condolence to fit a situation they'd never been faced with before.

Mubarka didn't let anyone see her tears over the absent one. But when she was alone in her room at night, she would let them roll hot down her cheeks. After a week of gloomy silence that no one dared refer to as mourning, Salama asked her to take the boys back to their schools. Once she was back in Zagazig, she had time to acquaint herself with her tears in the light.

Mugahid, who was busy running after little children, forgot all about it, and went back to asking Hafiza to recite the Fatiha over her deceased father. If he pressed her she would remind him that she was in no position to be thinking about people who were dead and gone when she was so worried about her lost son. When he asked her who she was talking about, she shook her fist at him, saying, "I'd like to know why Death is taking such a long time to come get *you!*"

Yet she herself would exhaust Salama, Ali, and Mansur with her constant harping. "Your brother's been gone a long time, boys," she would say. In the beginning they would answer her. But as time went by they started looking away without saying anything. She went on keeping servings of meat for him until they either went bad or someone found them and ate them. She would go on investigating until she found out who had eaten his brother's share of the food, and once she found out, she would wage war on the offender, and wouldn't speak to him again until she saw another sumptuous meal from which she could keep something back for Nagi. Only this time she would do her best to hide it. She would hide it so well, in fact, that she herself couldn't find it again, and the rotten odor would lead them to it in some out-of-the-way window or under her mattress.

Hafiza took to lighting a lantern every night at the Silent Sheikh's tomb, where she would beseech him to intercede for her son and ask the jinni to leave him alone. When she received no response, she concluded that the sheikh must be angry because they'd forgotten him, neglecting both him and his run-down shrine. So she made Salama rebuild the shrine. He paid the building expenses in spite of the family's financial situation, which had deteriorated due to the fact that the cotton crop found no buyers any more, and when they planted grain, they didn't even break even. As for the factory, it wasn't doing as well as before because, although spun-cotton prices were low, nobody could afford to buy new cloth.

When the Silent Sheikh proved unable to bring Nagi back, she began asking Salama to take her with him to visit saints' tombs in nearby cities. This was followed by visits to the shrines of Hussein and Our Lady Zaynab in Cairo. She refused to give up hope. Eventually, however, she became too weak to leave the mansion, having shrunk to the size of a little girl. Holding on to things for support, she would steal onto the mansion's rooftop at night. Sometimes Salama would hear her and follow her up the stairs. When he did, he would find her with her hair uncovered and her hands raised to heaven. Then he would carry her back down the stairs, kicking and flailing her arms.

"Let me go! He might have mercy on me!"

After having been the one to take care of Mugahid, Hafiza herself had now become a burden like him, and Tafida would complain to her husband about both of them. Mubarka was living comfortably in the city, and Mas'ada didn't arrive to help her until late in the morning, by which time the senile man and woman had worn Tafida out with their demands and their bickering, either with each other or with her. Salama didn't get angry with his wife for her complaints, since he himself could hardly tolerate them any more.

"If we could only find his body!" he would think. He was grieved over his brother and understood what his mother was going through. Yet it wasn't long before he forgot about all this in the face of the threat that now loomed against the reputation and position he had achieved by the sweat of his brow.

The crisis was growing steadily worse. The price collapse had not only hit his factory, but also threatened the giant Tal'at Harb companies. Meanwhile, more and more taxes had to be paid to the state. But what worried Salama most was the impudence being displayed by Asfur, who'd begun threatening members of his family who'd been tardy in paying their taxes. Thus far Salama had managed to avoid a confrontation. In order to do so, however, he'd had to redeem land belonging to some relatives and lend money to others lest they have to sell their livestock for a pittance. As far as he was concerned, any financial loss was better than waiting until Asfur summoned one of his relatives for a stern reprimand—since, once that happened, he wouldn't be able to keep quiet any longer.

He asked Ali to move to the mansion so that they and their wives could help each other take care of their parents and children. However, Hafiza, who no longer slept for even an hour of the night, would move around outside the bedrooms. When she heard Mas'ada's moans, she would bang on the door with both hands and shout, "That'll be enough from you, girl. Shame on you!"

Everything would get quiet for a little while. Then the screaming would start all over again, and she would go away muttering to herself, "One's been kidnapped, and the other one—well, this floozy's going to be the death of him!"

She'd become ghostly thin. Even so, when everything was quiet, she would still creep up to the roof and start in on the nightly entreaties that she brought directly to God, veiled by neither roof nor head covering. She would join her prayer for Nagi's return with a prayer for the lascivious woman's death. Then one morning, they woke to find her draped over the branches of a lemon tree. When Mas'ada saw her, she thought it strange that Tafida would hang a dress on a tree from whose thorny branches she wouldn't be able to disentangle it once it had dried. Little did she know that her mother-in-law lay dead inside the dress, crowned with the fragrance of lemon blossoms and without a drop of blood even on her unprotected face, whose leathery skin the thorns had been unable to pierce. A huge funeral was held for her, while the two daughters-in-law laughed at their husbands' grief over a woman that the angel of death had only been able to ensnare by pushing her off a rooftop.

Before the second European war had decided the fate of any of the warring parties, it destroyed Mubarka's queenly realm. The Egyptian government was in alliance with Britain by virtue of a binding agreement, while the Egyptians themselves were cheering for the Germans. "Go, Rommel!" they cried in celebration of the German commander who had crossed the desert with his soldiers from Libya's Burqa province to al-Alamein. Salama had begun thinking that the boys would have to come back from Zagazig for fear of bombing, invasion, and bullying by British soldiers in the city streets, whereas the villages remained immune to such dangers.

When Mubarka came back, the number of her charges had increased by two. Along with those who'd gone to Zagazig, the caravan included a fair-skinned teenage girl whose face still looked like that of a child, in her arms a baby girl who cried nonstop and who bore more of a resemblance to Yusuf than she did to her alleged mother.

"A marriage, and children too, and I'm the last to know?" asked Salama unhappily.

"Later, Mr. Mayor," replied Mubarka tersely.

She was determined to postpone the discussion in order to protect the young girl. She seemed terrified by the huge number of people living in the mansion, who had begun inspecting her in bewildered surprise. Mubarka had coached her fake daughter-in-law not to speak with anyone and to leave it to her—Mubarka—to answer any questions.

"The boy went too far with my neighbor's daughter."

Mubarka offered no more than this terse, unconvincing clarification when others noticed the untouched look of the pink, firm breast Duha brought out to nurse her baby girl. The girl would become agitated with pain as the baby suckled without getting a single drop of milk, and before long she would spit out the nipple and cry. Then Mubarka would take her and feed her from a bottle filled with goat's milk.

"It's her first baby, poor thing," Mubarka said in response to the inquisitive looks. But it wasn't only the absence of milk that aroused people's suspicions. The absence of any mutual interest between the two teenagers was also peculiar. It had nothing to do with bashfulness, or the boredom that couples experience from time to time. Rather, it was obvious that there was no attachment of any sort between them. Of this Tafida was certain.

"There's no trace of his smell on her," she declared confidently to Mas'ada, who felt sympathetic toward the girl and had no inclination to interfere in her affairs or press her to talk about things she didn't wish to discuss.

During Duha's two weeks at the mansion, she exchanged nothing with its other residents but silent nods of greeting, as though she were mute. At the end of the two weeks Mubarka dictated to her son the words he would need to take an oath of divorce. He repeated the words after her three times in the presence of the young girl, who gathered up the few things she'd brought with her and went back to Zagazig, leaving the infant in the grandmother's care.

Tafida's curiosity about the teenage girl who had left didn't last, and before long she'd forgotten all about her and begun focusing her attention on how to relate to Mubarka herself, who in her absence had turned the clock back twelve years. Youthful and delicate again, she'd taken to wearing dresses instead of gilbabs the way city women did. She would put the radio, which she'd saved up for out of the boys' spending money, in the mansion entranceway and, a cup of tea in hand, listen to songs with the volume turned up. She talked about her routines, her likes, and her dislikes the way men do. She gave Tafida haughty looks in spite of the fact that her long stay in the city had yielded nothing but a single graduation from primary school that had enabled Salem to go on to military school in Cairo, whereas none of the other young men had even made it into middle school, and had come back to al-Ish to be farmed out to work in the factory and the fields.

Tafida began accusing Mubarka of ruining the boys. They'd come back brutes, she said, just the way they'd been when they left, since she'd blunted their intelligence by feeding them so much flat bread drenched in ghee and duck and goose fat. All they'd learned was bad manners. And on top of that, one of them had come back mixed up in a dubious marriage, and God knows what might come to light next!

Tafida couldn't help wanting to protect her husband from Mubarka, even when she could smell Nagi in her clothes. Yet she'd never been able to reveal her suspicions to anyone. Now, however, relying for support on her sons as they grew up around her, she could voice her worries with greater clarity. She also started behaving as she pleased: she would smoke the shisha, cough, and spit on the ground as though she were getting revenge for her long years of walking on eggshells and working like mad to make sure Salama didn't leave her. As she looked anew at him and at herself, she was sure that marriage to a handsome man was an ordeal no woman in her right mind would ever subject herself to.

"Why don't you sleep in Baba Mugahid's room? He's your husband, isn't he?" Tafida asked, wanting to inflict pain on the woman whose eyes, now more than ever, emitted the sort of gleam that could rob even the most otherworldly man of his senses.

Mubarka knew there wasn't a creature on earth who could force her to do anything she didn't want to. But it made her feel sad to be reminded of Mugahid, who only left his room when someone carried him out to the garden to get some sun, and who, even then, would keep moaning until they took him back to bed. It surprised her to find that she no longer carried any memory of him, as if he hadn't been anything. There wasn't a trace, not even the tiniest pinprick's worth, of pain left from the injustice he'd done her, nor any regret for the way she had tormented him. The only thing that hurt was that he was still around. His constant coughing and spitting was the worst possible insult to her hygienic sensibilities, which weren't something she'd acquired only from her stay in the city. But the worst thing of all was the fact that his driveling senility might infect her spirit as well, and she wasn't prepared to go to pot yet. She'd come back to Mansur and Zaynab, and wanted to ensure their well-being by arranging suitable marriages for them. She was still attached to the boys she'd taken care of in Zagazig, as were they to her. In fact, they related to each other as though they were a family within a family, calling her "Mama Mubarka," whereas they called Tafida and Mas'ada by their names. And now she had an infant, Atiya, the baby sired by her baby Yusuf, who had been specially chosen by her neighbor from among his brothers.

Latifa, the wife of a noncommissioned officer who was away in Sudan, had come to see Mubarka one morning after the boys left for school. They made a sticky paste out of lemon, sugar, and water, closed the windows and locked the door from the inside, then took off all their clothes and began taking turns pulling their body hair out by the roots. Suddenly, they heard a tired-sounding knock on the door. They covered themselves up quickly, and Mubarka went to open the door.

It was Yusuf, dragging his books behind him, his face flushed with fever. Mubarka rushed to wet a towel and place it on his head, while Latifa took him into her arms and stretched him out on the couch, placing his head on her thigh. He was a towering fourteen-year-old, but still went to school in shorts that revealed thighs as tender as those of a little boy.

Mubarka handed the towel to Latifa and went to make him a glass of lemonade. When she got back, Latifa had unbuttoned his shirt and was massaging his head, neck, and chest. Mubarka had him sit up, and he gulped down the drink as though he were in a hurry to see the treatment take effect. Then Mubarka had him rest on her thigh as Latifa sat on the floor while continuing to massage the boy. As she did so, she looked surreptitiously at the swelling inside his shorts. The boy noticed it, and drew his thighs together and up to his chest. Then, seeing that this position didn't conceal the bulge, he turned over on his stomach. The tickling sensation produced by her massaging brought him to orgasm, and as the shudders of pleasure mingled with the shudders from the fever, his shivering and shaking terrified Mubarka.

"Don't worry. He'll be better soon," said Latifa. She got up and went to another room, fetched a blanket, and spread it over him. Then she sat back down on the floor, checking his fever with her hand and patting Mubarka reassuringly on the shoulder.

Latifa would visit Mubarka in the mornings and stay until she saw the boys when they came home. Sometimes she would go out and stand on the stairs when she heard them clattering up the steps. Over time, Mubarka began to worry that her neighbor's attention to the boys concealed a kind of destructive envy. When she noticed that her neighbor, who was around thirty years old and who only saw her husband once a year, took such pleasure in teasing them and engaging them in horseplay, she imagined she must be trying to keep her desires at bay through her contact with the boys. It had never occurred to her that Latifa had her eye on any particular boy, least of all Yusuf, whom Latifa knew to be still wetting the bed.

This problem had made him the most bashful and introverted of the boys. He'd begun forcing himself to wake up at night at three-hour intervals. He would stick to this exhausting regimen for two or three nights on the pretext that he needed to study. On the fourth night, he would be so overcome with drowsiness that he would go on sleeping, only to be wakened by the wet spot under him in the early morning. He would change his clothes, wash them, and start drying them over the fire before anyone saw him. Hoping to make him feel better, his mother had told him that this happened to other people too. She even told him her own secret: that she'd gone on wetting the bed until she was a bride. She'd had the good fortune of being an only child, though, and her father had known nothing about her early mornings. At the time she hadn't been able to seek out anyone's advice. However, she had tried to find a way to treat her son. She'd asked the neighbor ladies, including Latifa, if there were any remedies for this type of problem. One day Latifa asked Mubarka to send Yusuf to her apartment to help her write a letter to her husband.

"And why Yusuf in particular?" Mubarka wanted to know.

"His brothers say he has pretty handwriting," she replied without hesitation.

Mubarka considered this better than her asking Salem to come. Sardonically, she thought that her neighbor needed a boy to pee on her, but quickly dismissed the thought and asked her, "Doesn't Duha know how to write?"

"Yes, but Abduh can't make out a word she writes."

All the absent husband ever received were two letters penned in Yusuf's ornate script, since his wife decided that satisfying her longings with the teenager was preferable to dictating them to him.

"Let's write the letter in here, away from the living room and the racket on the stairs," Latifa said the first time she led Yusuf to her bedroom. The boy looked around and saw nothing but the bed with its lace mosquito net. He shot her a questioning glance.

"Don't you know how to write on a bed?" she asked him coquettishly, and took him by the hand. Pen in hand, Yusuf lay down on his stomach waiting for Latifa, who sat next to him, to begin dictating.

"Write, 'We miss you like crazy, Abu Duha!'" she dictated dreamily as she rested her hand on the boy's back. She began stroking him and massaging his shoulders. Then, grasping him by the back of the neck, she turned his head and brought him up against her pulsating bosom. Yusuf smiled craftily and buried his face in the depression between her breasts as she pressed him closer. She lifted his mouth to hers and kissed him, then began licking his face. She stripped him, then stripped herself and lay down on top of him. Within moments the boy had finished. She began kissing his upper thigh, which became wet with tears in which the boy could discern a mixture of turmoil, joy, anxiety, and fear. She dried her tears and gathered up his clothes for him, then began helping him put them on. She nudged him gently out of the bedroom and followed him across the living room. After looking around to see where her daughter was, she drew him toward her, kissed him, and pushed him away again.

"You won't tell your mother, will you?" she asked before opening the door. He promised not to say anything. And before he could ask her whether she would call for him again, she shooed him out of the apartment and shut the door.

Sometimes she would tell Mubarka she needed Yusuf. Other times she would snatch him from in front of her apartment before or after school, and sometimes he would sneak out to be with her while the others were taking their afternoon naps. She would close the door to Duha's room or send her out to buy something on the street, then drag him to her room. Once there, she would unzip his shorts and slide them down around his ankles, where they rested like shackles. Then she would take off her blouse and sit on the floor, his hardened organ level with her head. She would make circles around it with her tongue and slide her lips up and down over it, swallowing it in successive gulps. Then she would shove her captive onto the bed, where he would lie prostrate with his legs dangling off the edge. As she flung herself on top of him, his shackled feet would knock against the floor with the awkwardness of a horse being urged into the water by a ruthless rider.

"My period's late," she said distraughtly one day after Mubarka asked her why she was so distracted.

"Why? Did you get pregnant from reading Abd al-Samad's letters?"

"No, from writing."

Mubarka got Latifa's drift. She didn't blame her neighbor. However, with astonishment written all over her face, she asked, "What are we going to do?"

Latifa told her she was tired of carrying mattresses up to the roof, jumping off the bed, and drinking bitter, stinky castor oil. So Mubarka tried jumping up and down on her stomach. She made a mixture of herbs that the herbalist had prescribed and had Latifa drink it on an empty stomach after letting it steep all night. The woman nearly died from all the things she put herself through, but nothing succeeded in budging the unborn child, who was determined to stay in her womb. As she lay sprawled out half-dead in her apartment one day, Mubarka took her hand and said, "This is the way God wants it to be. Finish out your pregnancy, and we'll say the baby belongs to Duha."

The worn-out woman's jaw dropped. How did Mubarka expect her to lay the blame for her mistake on her young daughter?

"If your daughter had married as soon as she was old enough, she would have had two children a long time ago. So we can marry her to Yusuf."

After arranging to have a justice of the peace come with two witnesses, they finalized the marriage contract in the absence of Yusuf's brothers. When they came home, Mubarka served the boys lunch and informed them of Yusuf's marriage to Duha in as few words as possible, and without offering any explanation.

Yusuf was now expected to give his brothers and cousins the impression that he was Duha's husband. Consequently, he began frequenting the neighbors' apartment openly and staying close to the neighboring girl, who spent all her time sewing dolls and stuffing them with scraps of old clothes as he looked on indifferently. She began sewing him horses and camels and, joining in the game, he began stuffing the play animals with her and making saddles for them.

Mubarka didn't ask Latifa and Yusuf to stay away from each other, since the panic brought on by her pregnancy caused them to avoid each other of their own accord. Thinking back on the moment when his mother's friend whinnied like a mare, the boy would close his eyes and recall the whiteness of her body, which was what had amazed him most when she undressed in front of him for the first time. He would picture the border that divided her suntanned face, neck, and upper chest from the rest of her body, recalling the place where the whiteness began like a sudden brilliance, and his body would tingle with desire. When he imagined himself in her arms, his joints would tremble as though she were going to get pregnant all over again. As for Latifa, whose sole preoccupation now was how to hide her swelling tummy, she hardly noticed the teenager's existence, and wondered how she could have lost her head over him.

She no longer left her apartment, and wouldn't let Duha leave either. Mubarka bought them everything they needed, and prepared herself by getting a clean razor and disinfectant so that she could deliver the baby without anyone knowing.

When Latifa's labor began, Mubarka sat at her head so that she could hold her hand every time there was a contraction. At the same time she would reach down to check on the baby's position. A few hours later her fingers could feel some wet fuzz. She asked Duha to heat some water and began pulling gently on the head until the newborn popped out. She took the baby in her arms, cleaned off the goo between its legs, and cried, "A she-lion like you!"

Latifa, who had dozed off, didn't hear her. After removing the afterbirth and tying the umbilical cord, she gave the baby girl a bath and wrapped her in a piece of clean cloth in the presence of a stunned Duha, who was expected to act as though this were her own daughter.

Mugahid lived ninety years, and died on the day the mayorship was restored to his son. His funeral procession was headed by the district commissioner and his four officers, and condolences were received by thirty-nine sons and grandsons. Salama had been sitting on the bench by the mango tree next to the mansion door drinking his late-afternoon coffee when the British forced the king once again to summon the majority leader, Nahhas Pasha, and assign him the task of forming a new ministry. The British High Commissioner was angered over the minority parties' inability to keep Egyptian hostility toward his government in check.

As soon as he received the royal assignment, Nahhas Pasha summoned his ministers who, like him, had been removed from their posts just a few months earlier, and assigned them their responsibilities. The next day, the minister of the interior summoned his officers and restored them to their positions, and on the morning of the third day, the district commissioners summoned their mayors and restored them to their posts.

Salama brought the decree back to al-Ish and got busy with arrangements for reestablishing himself as mayor. He ordered the reopening of the bricked-over "telephone" and oversaw the reconnection of the telephone line. That done, he reinstalled the telephone, which had been brought back from Asfur's house with a fanfare fit for a wedding procession. Meanwhile, the women bustled about, overseeing the cooking being done for the officers who would be coming the following day to congratulate Salama and confirm him in his post.

When he came in after midnight to go to bed, he remembered his father. He went into his room and found him lying on his back with his legs drawn up to his chest. At first he thought he was asleep. However, the light filtering into the room from the lanterns that were still lit in the garden showed his eyes to be open. Salama greeted him, but there was no reply. He shook him by the knees, and his stiff legs collapsed without falling completely onto the bed. Turning him over, he found no sign of life. He closed his eyes and wiped around his mouth. He expended a huge effort in an attempt to straighten his body so that the undertaker wouldn't see him in this position, since it revealed that he had died alone and neglected. His father's bones cracked beneath his hands, but he finally succeeded in making him lie straight.

He informed no one—neither the young men spending their night hours in the garden, nor the three women who were busy slaughtering pigeons and sifting flour to make pastries for the lunch that would be served the next day to the district commissioner and his escorts.

After reassuring himself that the deceased looked neat and tidy, he closed the door and went to his room after a long, enervating day. He was amazed at his detachment. He felt nothing but a slight pang from memories of childhood, when Mugahid had been like a monster that forbade them to move or speak, and when they could only breathe freely when he had left the farmhouse.

Salama threw off his gilbab and collapsed onto the bed. His cheek sank into the soft pillow, which took him back to the rocking of the waves during his days on the French destroyer and carried him swiftly to the land of Nod.

The following morning they washed the body of the deceased. In order to keep the odor from spreading until he was taken for burial after the noon prayer, they drenched the body in so much musk that the graveclothes were wet. Although the officers' visit had been scheduled beforehand, their presence lent the funeral a festive air. The district commissioner, who headed the procession on horse-back, was trailed by four horses bearing the officers. The officers were surrounded by the soldiers and al-Ish's sentinels, who marched briskly along on either side. Then came the pallbearers, followed by Salama, who walked ahead of his brothers, sons, and nephews.

The only expression on the faces of those receiving condolences was one of pride—pride in a man who had lived until his presence was no longer felt. Among his family members were those who had harbored bad memories of him that time had helped them to forget, others who had watched him grow old with a sense of pity, and others who had no memories of him and no feelings toward him of any kind.

Thinking back later on events, Salama said the only reason he'd grieved over his father was that as long as his father was alive, he didn't notice that he'd entered his sixth decade, but that once his father was gone, he'd suddenly felt like both an orphan and an old man.

"You're young as long as your father's alive." That was how he summed up the situation. For many long years thereafter it was Mugahid's death, not his life, that gave others cause to remember him, because he was the last person to die when death was still comprehensible and meaningful.

A year after Mugahid's death, cases of diarrhea and vomiting began hitting al-Ish. Those who took the sick to Minya al-Qamh and Bilbeis came back without them, and in a state of terror. The factory halted production in order to prevent mixing, the mansion's windows were shut, and they began carrying out the instructions that were being broadcast continuously over the radio along with reports of the spread of the cholera epidemic.

No one asked about the war's outcome. No one waited any more for the German advance, but rather for the retreat of the epidemic, which had stolen into the country on a train with the luggage of the soldiers coming up from Sudan, then spread from the army camps to Egypt's cities and villages. After the death toll in al-Ish began to rise, Salama sent an SOS to the district commissioner. Then he took up residence beside the telephone, waiting for a response. However, the echo of the cry that had been carried over the wires wasn't heard until two days later: "A truck will come every day. You'll be required to report any known cases so that they can be taken to the quarantine the government has set up in the courtyard outside Bilbeis's cotton gin."

The radio continued broadcasting instructions on how to keep the disease from spreading, the most important of which was to give up sentimental habits that could prove deadly, since covering up for a loved one who was ill would kill another loved one who hadn't contracted the disease yet. At the same time, there was a growing terror of the neglect associated with the isolation wards, dubbed "the stink holes," where diseased individuals would simply be abandoned to await their deaths. Sometimes they would be taken alive to an open grave, where their moans could be heard within the piles of live lime being heaped on top of them.

The rumbling of the huge truck had become as dreadful to people as the sound of enemy war machines, and the sight of nurses with medical masks on their faces stopping with a stretcher in front of someone's house was enough to give even a healthy person the runs. The cholera epidemic hadn't created the kind of solidarity and shared sympathy that al-Ish had known during the flood and the fires on the threshing floors, since there was nothing the able-bodied could do for the sick. Instead, fear and rage would drive neighbors to report a diseased person hiding in the house next door. For the first time Salama felt the distance that separated him from the residents of al-Ish and the hatred that accompanies authority. Based on a decree an orderly had brought, and which he signed to show he'd received it, Salama was expected to keep order and to enable the medical teams to carry out their responsibilities safely. However, people now viewed removing a diseased person from his family as tantamount to carrying out a death sentence.

The mansion didn't hold out long in the face of the epidemic, despite the strict hygienic precautions Mubarka had been enforcing based on the instructions being broadcast over the radio. Tafida began vomiting after sundown one day, and when one of the sentinels whispered to Salama that his wife had contracted the disease, he left the "telephone" and went back to the mansion. He gestured to her to go to her room to get away from the others, and didn't go near her. It was clear from the expression on his face that, at that moment, she was nothing to him but a source of danger. She left, in her eyes a look filled with all the sorrow and reproach of a life spent feeling that her presence meant nothing to her man. She knew that the only reason he hadn't taken another wife was that he'd simply been too busy, and that she had only remained in his household thanks to his stubbornness and the pride of success, which he hadn't wanted to tarnish with a failed marriage.

"Fine, then. God's corrected your mistake now," she said bitterly as she struggled to suppress a new wave of nausea. So now he could marry someone else without it being considered a failure that would count against him.

She shuffled to her room. She didn't see him as he rested his brother Ali's head in his lap and began catching his vomit in his hands while Mubarka stood beside him holding a pail and drying his hands and the patient's mouth with a towel. In less than an hour, Ali had died in his brother's arms and his daughter Samiha had fallen ill, followed by Mansur and Yusuf. As the night wore on, one person after another succumbed to the disease, and God only knew who would be next. In the morning the truck backed up to the mansion, and didn't move until the truck bed was filled with a pile of human flesh, feces, and vomit. It wasn't known exactly how many family members had died until after the epidemic was over and the young men, who had fled to the fields and lived for weeks on greens for fear of the ongoing infections in the closed atmosphere of the village, came back.

Neither Salama nor Mas'ada had the strength to stand up to bid farewell to those departing. As for Mubarka, she stood there with expressionless eyes as though she were watching some neighbors move the furniture out of their old house. When two nurses with medical masks on their faces closed up the back of the military vehicle and jumped in beside the masked driver, a tear fell, and she waved to a pair of eyes that gleamed from the top of the pile. She glimpsed the pleading look of her son Mustafa as the vehicle rolled away, and before long the mournful look had disappeared behind a cloud of dust mixed with the soot spewing out of the beat-up engine.

She closed the mansion gate, and on her way back inside she came across Yusuf's daughter Atiya under an orange tree, covered with feces and an army of ants.

After making certain that the epidemic had passed, the military school opened its doors again and gave its students a week's vacation to check on their families. Salem came back as brown and parched as a sunbaked herring, dressed in a khaki uniform with gold braids on his shoulders. He found no one in the mansion but his mother; his two surviving siblings, Mahmoud and Zaynab; little Atiya; his uncle Ali's wife Mas'ada; and her son Kamel. As for Salama, who was now the mayor of a village that had lost half its population, his only surviving offspring was Abd al-Maqsud.

The mansion seemed empty now that it was no longer buzzing all day long with noisy, rambunctious children. Those who remained lived with a wordless sorrow and pent-up rage, against whom they didn't know. Afflicted now with a debilitating absentmindedness, Salama never went anywhere without a little notebook and an ink pen in his hand so that he could write down anything he felt necessary. When someone reminded him of a promise he had made or a job he was supposed to have done, he would open his notebook and shout angrily, "So, is it written here? Is it? You show it to me!" The issue wasn't whether the question was important or urgent. Rather, it was a matter of acquitting himself and his notebook of the charge of having forgotten. Mubarka and Mas'ada intensified their silence, focusing their efforts on caring for the remaining children and a man who belonged to neither of them.

One evening, after a year of mourning, Mubarka was rolling out the dinner table. "We've had enough sadness, brother," she said to Salama, and asked him to agree to set a date for Zaynab to be engaged to Wafiq, Abd al-Raziq Asfur's eldest son. Wafiq had been hovering on horseback around the mansion gate one day when he saw Mubarka combing thirteen-year-old Zaynab's hair. She'd sat her on a high stool in the garden to keep her hair off the ground. He stopped to watch them, and when they noticed him, he prodded his horse and rode away. However, he kept circling the mansion every day, pursing Zaynab with his looks from atop his horse. At first Zaynab would run inside whenever she saw him. But once she'd taken a liking to him, she began hesitating before moving out of sight. When he sent his mother to find out what the girl and her mother thought about the possibility of their marrying, he received a tentative yes, with a promise to broach the subject with her half-brother the mayor, and inform him of his reply.

"You must have loved her father a lot!" replied Salama, indicating that Wafiq resembled the young Mugahid in his fondness for strutting about on a horse and sporting clean, stylish clothes, and the fact that he had no work. The request flustered and surprised him, and he wondered whether joining their families in marriage would bring an end to the struggle between him and his rival, or whether the competition between them would just make his sister's life miserable.

Mubarka kept after him about the proposal until he agreed to it without having found an answer to his question. Later, she would think back regretfully on her insistence, the reason for which she couldn't put her finger on. Had she been thinking of her mother's maxim that "a handsome man is like a pendant around a girl's neck"? Or had she chosen him because of the mutual admiration that had grown up between her and his mother Sakina, the city girl who'd been so delighted to make Mubarka's acquaintance, and who treated her as though she was some sort of rare find?

The suitor was duly welcomed and the wedding preparations got underway. Mubarka let Mas'ada see to the practical matters of choosing the furniture and the fabric for the clothes, and preparing the ghee and dried legumes that the bride would take with her to her new home. Meanwhile, she devoted herself to instructing her daughter in the essentials of married life. Seeing that she was still a child who had no idea what lay ahead, Mubarka explained to her whatever she could: how to act after her hymen had been ruptured, what to do in bed, how to hide her menstrual flow from her husband, and how to determine which days she was most likely to get pregnant.

"When I get pregnant, should I stay away from him until I have the baby?" Zaynab asked innocently. Mubarka looked at Mas'ada and burst out laughing over her daughter's naïveté, saying, "Poor you, Wafiq! You're going to be in agony for nine months!"

After the bride's departure, the mansion seemed gloomier than ever, so Salama began urging Abd al-Maqsud, Mahmoud, and Kamel to get married. At first he tried to help them choose, but after a while he stopped, because he would suggest a girl to one of them and the young man would agree, only to discover to his surprise that Salama had suggested the same girl to one of the other two. After that he began leaving the choice up to them. He devoted a separate page in his notebook to each of them. After recording the name of the girl the young man had chosen, he would make an appointment with the girl's family and write down the appointment on the same page.

Salama would bring all three young men with him regardless of which house they were going to, since it was the custom of most families to bring along the largest possible number of men when making such visits. On the day one of them was to be engaged, Salama would insist that the groom-to-be wear a white gilbab to distinguish him from the others. This way he could ask for the girl's hand on the young man's behalf without having to refer to his notebook. This practice had been rendered a necessity by Salama's failing memory. But because no one outside the mansion knew the secret behind it, it turned into a tradition in al-Ish. In fact, it came to be considered bad luck for a young man to ask for a girl's hand wearing anything but white!

Now that two males in the family were living under other women's care, Mubarka and Mas'ada had nothing to do but compete in taking care of Salama and his son Abd al-Maqsud. They referred to Salama by his agnomen, which included the name of his firstborn who'd died in the cholera epidemic. "Eat, Abu Ahmad," one of them would say. Or one of the women might ask the other, "Have you washed Abu Ahmad's coffeepot and cup?" If one beat the other to serving him a meal, the one who'd missed the chance to feed him would run to wash his clothes. She might even ask him to take a bath so that he could give her his dirty clothes to wash even though he'd only been wearing them since that morning, saying, "The weather's so hot, you must have gotten them all sweaty by now, brother!"

When they washed his gilbab, they would hang it on the clothesline suspended between two trees in the mansion garden. Then they would stand or sit nearby until it dried to make sure it wasn't soiled by a sparrow passing overhead or a fly with dirty legs.

Mubarka remembered how jealous Tafida had been of her, though she'd never known whether Tafida was just being protective of Salama, or whether she envied her beauty, which had sometimes led Salama to make comparisons between them, and she thought back on Tafida's hurtful words and looks. But things were different with Mas'ada. She wasn't competing with Mas'ada for Salama's affection. Instead, she cooperated with her, helping her the way a mother would help her daughter take care of her man. When she calculated Mas'ada's age, she knew why she'd taken to her from the day she came into the family. She was sure Mas'ada must belong to the "generation of seventy" that she felt she herself had somehow conceived, because her wedding-day charm had driven the women of the village into their husbands' arms. But this wasn't the only reason she'd never thought of Mas'ada as her rival. The man who as of yet belonged to neither of them would be allowed by Islamic law to marry Mas'ada, but not his father's widow.

At the same time, her unspoken passion for masculinity added something else to her concern for Salama. It was also what made her invulnerable to women's advances, however loudly her body cried out to her. Ahlam and Nargas, her neighbors in Zagazig, had pleaded with her on occasion, and she'd turned them down. However, she hadn't done so in anger or condemnation.

"I don't feel like it," she would say calmly, as though she were turning down some food or drink she wasn't accustomed to. She also maintained her relationship with them, and didn't stop stripping in front of them and accepting their help in removing the hair from places on her body that her hands couldn't reach. The same thing had happened with Abd al-Raziq Asfur's wife Sakina, whom she'd met at a wake and who, when she came to visit her the next day at the mansion, kissed her on the corner of her mouth as she shook her hand. When the two women were alone, Sakina cried and pleaded and nearly kissed her feet. But Mubarka didn't give in to her pleadings; nor did she express any sort of disapproval. The youthful Sakina, whose charm was evident in her sleepy white flesh, continued to visit Mubarka at the mansion from time to time. She would sit with her for hours, telling her about everything in her life. If she was having aches and pains, she would ask Mubarka to check her temperature. Mubarka would do as she requested and reassure her, saying, "There's no fever." But she would utter the words without emotion, pretending not to notice the limpness in the body of this woman who had succeeded in hitching her son to Zaynab as a way of getting closer to Mubarka, yet without succeeding in winning her over.

"If there weren't a man on the face of the earth, I'd fast till God made one," she muttered to herself. Her clear conviction in such matters hadn't been grasped by the women who'd attempted to seduce her. However, men perceived it without the slightest difficulty: through her looks; through the softness of her voice when she uttered the few words she had to say; through the attentive, listening ear that was so soothing, making them feel as though she was drinking them in; through her cleanliness; and through the cooking that could bring whoever ate it to a state of bliss that bordered on orgasm. All these things had drawn Salama inexorably to her company even when his father was alive, and if he'd had any say in the matter, he

168

would have chosen the woman who was two years his senior, not Mas'ada, who was fifteen years his junior. However, Mubarka didn't give this situation a chance to continue. After setting his food before him, she sat down next to him and took the bull by the horns.

"Why don't you marry Mas'ada, Abu Ahmad?" she asked.

Salama feigned surprise at her suggestion. However, it was obvious that he'd already given the matter some thought, and that Mas'ada was waiting for him to ask her.

When Salama and Mas'ada married, Mubarka became a confidante to both. Mas'ada would chatter away to her about her intimate secrets and make comparisons between the two brothers. Thinking back on Ali's delirious ranting in contrast to the staid performance of Salama, who behaved in bed with the same economy and prudence that he exhibited in the factory, she complained, "He's so serious! He treats it like some sort of business deal where he's afraid he's going to be taken in!"

However, she would add that she too had gotten older, and wasn't the same as she had been. Contenting himself with a statement that he could make in all seriousness to Mubarka when the two of them were alone without feeling guilty, or in affectionate jest in Mas'ada's presence, Salama said, "It's as if I'd never known what marriage was till now."

Mubarka listened to him with interest, whether he was speaking seriously or in jest.

"I know," she replied, adding that she'd always wondered how a man could live with a woman whose breath alone—not to mention the smell of her downstairs—would be enough to send him running in the other direction!

Nine months later Mas'ada gave birth to Adel. Mubarka volunteered to take care of him, and started showing him off to the young men who had married before Salama but whose wives' tummies still showed no effects of their nightly free-for-alls. She also started having to keep her eye on Atiya, who considered the newborn her doll, lest she unwittingly do him harm.

When she caught sight of al-Ish, hunchbacked Nagiya felt a trepidation she hadn't felt years earlier when her father left her with two strange men. She began thinking about what a shock it would be to meet people again. Who had left? Who had stayed? Would she be remembered by the people who'd worked so hard to forget she existed when she'd lived among them? She skipped in front of her daughter along the village's now-paved main road. It was still flanked on either side by the same old beech oaks, which had withered and aged to the point where all that remained of some of them were short, worm-eaten trunks. She noticed that the trees no longer blocked the sun, which had begun sinking behind the golden wheat fields in the distance.

She thought about the fact that she too had changed. She'd gotten old. However, she'd come back with her daughter. They were exhausted, but that didn't conceal the beauty of the thin, forty-year-old woman, who carried a small satchel like the one her mother had held to her bosom when she left al-Ish.

Al-Ish seemed twice the size it had been when Nagiya had left it, and she found her way to the farmhouse with difficulty. The village, which had been circular, had become elongated and snakelike because of the new houses that lined the main road.

When they stopped in front of the farmhouse, the factory workers fell silent, their eyes fixed on the two women, one of whom was the picture of life, the other the picture of death. They found it difficult to understand the women's Palestinian accent, but one of them went out and pointed to the mansion where the family lived.

"So are they living with the jinn?" Nagiya wondered aloud. She drew her daughter, who was clutching her satchel anxiously, along with her. When they were gone, the laborer just stood there, dazzled by the younger woman's beauty.

Nagiya stood outside the mansion gate thinking back on the day of her arrival in Majdal. After dismounting from the horse with help from Ziyad, she'd stood there staring, flabbergasted, at the house she'd seen so many times in her dreams. Sheikh Abu Sharkh took her by the hand encouragingly, but her discomfiture wasn't on account of homesickness, as he imagined it to be. Rather, it was on account of the terror that had stricken her when she saw how precise her dreams had been: the sprawling two-story house, the grass and the delicate moss that grew between the stones in the walls, and even the sparrows' nest from which pieces of straw hung down over the old gate's crossbeam—she had seen it all before in dreams.

Mas'ada had been sitting alone on the bench in the garden when she saw the two women standing at the gate. Thinking them beggars, she went inside momentarily, came back out, and offered them a loaf of bread. As she did so, she scrutinized the young woman, since never in her life had she seen such a beautiful beggar. Ignoring the bread in Mas'ada's outstretched hand, Nagiya pushed her gently aside and went in. Mubarka, who was standing on the veranda at the door of the mansion, saw her.

"Nagiya!" she cried with the astonishment of someone who's just seen a dead person walking. The sight of the hunchbacked woman standing at the gate caused her to see her entire life in a single moment, and her heart began pounding wildly. There hadn't been anything between the two women that would have given her reason either to fear her, or to be happy or sad about her return. However, seeing her right in front of her so unexpectedly made her heart ache over Salem, who had left immediately after graduation

171

with the Egyptian army that was going to fight in Palestine. At the same instant she thought of Muntasir. She knew that Palestine was a country. It wasn't the size of Egypt, of course, but it was still a country. The hunchbacked woman wouldn't necessarily know anything about either Muntasir or Salem. Even so, seeing her brought them both to mind. What might be happening to Salem there? And what if the person returning just then had been Muntasir rather than his hunchbacked paternal cousin? After years of agonizing waiting—a wait whose fires she had quenched with the scent of another male in the family, who had soon left her and disappeared—she wondered whether Nagiya might have come bearing news that would rob her of her peace.

Nagiya stopped in her tracks. Meanwhile, Mubarka regained her composure and rushed up to hug her. Taking her by the hand, Mubarka led Nagiya up the five steps from the garden to the veranda, and the young woman followed.

"This is my little girl Zayna," said Nagiya.

Hearing this, Mubarka gave the beautiful young woman an even warmer hug than she'd given Nagiya. She called Mas'ada, who was still standing at the gate with the bread in her hand, and introduced her to the guest who had left al-Ish as a bride whose time had passed, when Mas'ada was nothing but a bulge in her mother's tummy.

In spite of the warm welcome she and her daughter had received from the family, it had never occurred to Nagiya that she might have come to stay. She preferred to share a single room with Zayna, as though they were guests who would be going back as soon as Palestine was liberated. She also kept her Palestinian accent, which she exaggerated more than Zayna did, and made it known after every meal that the kinds of food being served upset her stomach now that she was used to cooking with olive oil.

She remained suspended in her past, and since no one in al-Ish knew anything about it, she could concoct whatever events struck her fancy. After shaving twenty years off the actual age of Zayna's father when they were married, she filled her days with exciting events and her nights with passionate advances in places with names Egyptians had never heard of: under the old olive tree, on the hill, and in rooms with names like ulliya and barraniya.

"Oh, it was so horrible!" She paused, her mind wandering into the distance as though she were remembering actual events. Then she resumed her sad account of the four births that had resulted from those passionate advances. Of these Zayna was the sole survivor, though her brothers had been even more beautiful than she was. Seeing the curiosity in Mubarka's eyes as she waited for her to talk about the males, her words came out spiced with a pinch of sorrow over the three angels who had emerged from her womb smiling with an effusion of light, only to expire a few hours later.

The tales were so masterfully woven that she almost believed them herself, in raptures over a virility her elderly husband hadn't possessed. On the one occasion when he'd gone into her, she'd felt the saltiness of his semen as it leaked out of a trembling, flaccid weapon that had produced no effect but the sting she felt as his seed slipped into her womb. He'd never done it again, and he passed away when Zayna was two years old. She didn't even remember him, and called her brother Ziyad "Daddy" the way his own children did.

Nagiya burst into sobs and wiped away a tear that had rolled down her cheek. She'd become a stranger all over again. She thought back on the way the women of the Abu Sharkh household had fallen all over themselves for a chance to see their father's bride. As soon as they caught a glimpse of her diminutive, deformed body inside a black gilbab with a piece of black muslin wrapped around her head, they exchanged looks of despairing approval and came up to Nagiya one after another to shake her hand sympathetically and introduce themselves. Then they led her upstairs to the room she would share with her man. Decked out in their jewelry and their gold-brocaded gilbabs, the women went up ahead of her with the frustration of an army called out to fight an imaginary enemy. However, she learned as time went on how to command the respect of her daughters-in-law and wipe off their faces the looks of sympathy bordering on disdain, even if they didn't call her "Aunt" as tradition dictated. She didn't herd sheep in Majdal as she'd imagined she would as she was crossing the desert along the seacoast from Rafah, and although her house in Majdal was different from the one in al-Ish, she did basically the same chores—milking, separating the cream from the milk, and cheese-making—and instead of the buffaloes they'd had in al-Ish, they had cows.

She would stay with her daughters-in-law from morning to evening, and after supper would withdraw to her room with her man, who was happy to have a wife of his own. Unlike his sons or their wives, who were embarrassed for him to call on them when he felt thirsty or hungry, he could undress at his leisure in front of his wife.

"Imagine! A man can fart in front of his wife, but not in front of his son, even though he's his own flesh and blood!" Abu Sharkh said with a laugh as he got ready to let another one out. Nagiya responded with a fleeting smile and handed him a clean nightshirt. Then she lay down in his arms, anesthetized by his breath, which was tinged with the fragrance of tobacco and the anise seed that flavors arak.

He took pleasure in the questions she asked about things she hadn't known in al-Ish and gave lengthy explanations. On the nights when he drank too much, his face would take on a reddish glow. When he lay down next to her, he would press up against her, reach for her breasts, and run his hands over her erect nipples, which were no different from any other nipples that had clung to their days of youth. He would bring his rough hands down below to her abdomen and feel to see whether she was wet. As he did so, what was between his thighs would stir with a warmth that nevertheless wasn't sufficient to make him forget her hump and her wrinkled face. So he would withdraw his hand, wrap his arms around her, and fall asleep. She in turn would doze off in his arms without either of them feeling the least regret. All either of them wanted from the other was a sense of intimacy and security, and a warmth that didn't come from heavy woolen blankets.

Long months later he came home from a wedding party near dawn, and Nagiya was waiting for him as usual. She took his abaya and laid him down. In the light of the lamp that hung on the wall, his shiny, wrinkle-free face looked as though it was going to explode, his capillaries visibly engorged beneath the skin. Suspecting that he might be having a heart attack, or what common folks called a "blood rush," she started massaging his chest and abdomen, and took off his outer layer of clothing. Then, in what she hoped would be an effective way of alleviating his obvious palpitations, she wet an old rag and began wiping his face. Just then she noticed a pulsation inside his trousers that piqued her curiosity, and before long her curiosity had turned into an irresistible urge.

She removed his trousers and began fondling him. The sleeping organ started to raise its head, and finally hardened in her hand. She sat on top of him and felt a salty drop go into her womb, and before long he'd petered out. She lay motionless beside him, enjoying the sensation of the drop that stung her with the sweetness of a honey whose bees had fed on lemon blossoms.

"May God keep you," she said gratefully, running her hands over his face as he broke into a loud snore. She never had the experience again. However, she would never forget it, thanks to Zayna, who came to her as the best possible compensation for her unsightly appearance.

Noticing how distracted the two guests were, Mas'ada began pressing them to talk about the circumstances that had brought them to al-Ish. Zayna told them how they'd gotten news of the massacre at Deir Yassin, and how the Jews had stormed the village and begun targeting pregnant women.

"They would make a bet over whether a woman was pregnant with a boy or a girl. Then they'd split her open." Zayna spoke evenly, as though she'd lived her entire life in the midst of war, her features etched with a faint trace of revulsion more than anything else. She would fall silent for a while as though she were trying to recall events she'd forgotten.

"They were trying to scare us. They wanted us to run away," said Nagiya in an attempt to give Zayna a chance to remember what she wanted to say. But Zayna would lose herself in the silence, squinting as though she wanted to see the world of the unseen. She'd still been in mourning for her husband, who had died in the battles against the Jewish gangs, when the villagers began leaving. Her half-brother had pulled up in front of her house in a truck loaded with his household furniture and with his family sitting on top, and invited her to come with them. But she'd refused to leave her house. So he took her little boy and hoisted him onto the truck along with the rest of his family.

"All right, then, Zayna. Riyad is with us. Meet up with us in Syria."

Ziyad got in beside the driver and the truck took off. However, Zayna didn't meet up with them. Nor did she have any choice about where she would go for refuge. Two weeks later the Egyptian forces entered Majdal and began expelling the people of the village so that they wouldn't be a burden to the fighters. A whole queue of trucks arrived. As soon as one of them had filled up, it would leave and another would do the same. She found herself with her mother in a vehicle heading for Rafah, but rather than staying in the makeshift camp there, Nagiya took her back to al-Ish.

"We'll go see your uncles, and come back after they've driven the Jews out," she said. Like all those being displaced, she had no doubt that she would be coming back in a week at the most. Some people took their house key with them, and others left it in whichever place their family was accustomed to leaving it: under the doorstep, in a crack in the wall, or at the base of an olive tree or grapevine, to be found by whoever came back first.

The return was delayed, and Zayna remained withdrawn like a guest who feels awkward and embarrassed for having stayed too long. The only time they saw any expression in her eyes was when she looked at the huge radio on top of the abandoned heater. She would snap to attention when she heard the news-broadcast theme song. She and Mubarka would sit together taking in reports on the battles after Salama stopped bringing the newspaper to the mansion.

He'd been in the habit of bringing an issue of *al-Ahram* with him whenever he came back from a trip to this city or that, and Mubarka would leaf through it in search of anything that might set her mind at rest about Salem until it fell apart in her hands. She wouldn't leave it alone until he'd provided her with a new issue. However, when reports started coming in about the siege of the Egyptian army in Fallujah, he stopped bringing the newspaper to the mansion, and Mubarka was forced to rely on the radio broadcast. The radio didn't provide as much information as the newspaper, but it did start broadcasting reports on the Arab armies' retreat and the flight of growing numbers of refugees in all directions.

Consequently, Mubarka began waiting for her son's return. As for Zayna, she was waiting for more than a return to her son: she was waiting for the chance to avenge his father. At dawn on the day of his departure she'd kissed his feet, begging him to stay. He'd bent over her head and kissed her, then removed her determinedly from his path, and at noon he'd returned to her as a corpse. Insisting on seeing him naked, she licked the congealed blood from the hole with seared edges on the left side of his chest. She didn't shrink from the spot where the bullet had penetrated his heart, and didn't cry until she had placed her lips on his and made certain from their dryness that he had died thirsty.

Zayna hadn't believed all that was being said about the establishment of a Jewish state in keeping with some heavenly or earthly promise. Rather, she was convinced that these white men had only left their homelands—which were, after all, more beautiful than Palestine—and come to her homeland in order to deprive her of Ghassan. When she told Mubarka this, she saw a look of incredulity in her eyes and, afraid she might think she was crazy, added her final proof, saying, "You don't know what Ghassan meant to me, or what kind of a man he was."

Mubarka had been staring at her, not in doubt over her sanity, but in an attempt to discover what it was that connected her to this dark-skinned woman with the olive-green eyes, beyond the fact that they both had a son missing. She realized that this slender young woman, who seemed like a cunning angel that had stolen Satan's powers of allurement when the Creator was looking the other way, also resembled her with respect to her fortunes in life, since each of them had found the man who was worth living a lifetime with, and had lost him.

When the Arab armies withdrew and the United Nations resolution dividing Palestine into two states, one for the Palestinians and one for the Jews, was issued, Zayna beat her breast.

"What! So which state is Majdal in? In ours, or in theirs?" she asked her cousins, who assured her that the Arabs had rejected the partition and that the Arab armies would liberate all of Palestine and bring her family back to her. But when the wait became too protracted, she began asking them to help her find her brother Ziyad so that she could go be with her son.

They tried to explain to her that Syria was such a big place that they wouldn't be able to track him down. But she wouldn't listen. She would simply dictate her demands, then burst into tears that rained down her cheeks, saying she would leave on her own to look for her son.

After the sentinels had brought her back at night more than once, Salama put a huge lock on the gate. However, she figured out how to jump over the wall, so they began keeping a close watch on her. She would climb the big mulberry tree and threaten to jump the wall from on top of it, and no one but Mubarka could persuade her to come down. Then Mubarka would take Zayna into her arms and let her sob herself to sleep.

Mubarka stood on the veranda eyeing the raucous children with a satisfaction that encased a smoldering ember of sorrow. For, although her surviving children may have taken revenge on death for her, the new children hadn't erased the pain she felt over those who had passed away. In fact, she could hardly distinguish in her grief between her own children and those of Mas'ada and Tafida, who had spent more of their lives with her in Zagazig than they had with their own mothers.

It had become clear that Salama's belated discovery of the pleasure of marriage wasn't going to yield any more children after Adel. Blessed with his mother's petite green eyes, Adel himself had come along in an untimely fashion, like a mango out of season, and a smitten Salama carried him around wherever he went. Meanwhile, the baby-making contest among the younger couples continued apace, filling the mansion with children and restoring it to its pre-epidemic state.

Mubarka kept watch on the swelling in the young wives' tummies, attended each baby's birth, and named him or her after one of the children that had died. The only exceptions were Adel, whom Salama named himself, and Mahmoud's eldest daughter, whom he insisted on naming Mubarka. Mubarka was the one to name Mahmoud's second child, Nagi, as well as Abd al-Maqsud's children— Ahmad, Yusuf, and Ali—and Kamel's children, Mansur, Mustafa, and Samiha.

Abd al-Maqsud's and Kamel's wives weren't surprised to hear their husbands calling Mubarka "Mother," but all three of the young wives were embarrassed by the way she interfered in their intimate lives.

"All that's left now is for you to grab it with your hands!" quipped Zahra Abu Gamus, Kamel's wife. Zahra's father made it his profession to mate his bull with al-Ish's buffalo cows, and she joked that the only thing Grandma Mubarka hadn't done yet was make the rounds of their bedrooms and position their men on top of them, then grab hold of their organs and insert them manually the way people did when they wanted to help a bull mount a buffalo cow. Mubarka took no offense at the fair-skinned, willowy young woman's teasing. In fact, she started teasing her back by addressing her with the male pronoun, not only because of her manly physique, but because she'd brought a shisha as part of her trousseau when she first came to live in the mansion. On her first morning of marriage she'd gotten up early, left her groom asleep in bed, and come down to the garden, where she lit a fire to make herself a cup of tea and sat there smoking honeyed tobacco. She'd accustomed everyone to this habit of hers, since she found it impossible to get started doing anything without her morning fix.

Mubarka warned her of the effects it might have on her ability to conceive. "Why don't you stay away from it just these two days?" she suggested, in an attempt to get her to avoid smoking on the fertile days right after her period.

She'd memorized their menstrual cycles, and would check on each of them at the same time every month. "Did you get your period, girl?" she would ask one of them. If she said yes, Mubarka would curl her lip in disapproval, and the first chance she got to be alone with the husband, she would scold him for his negligence. On the other hand, whenever any of them showed signs of being pregnant, she would start pampering her, assigning her share of the housework to another woman or doing it herself, and with every new birth she would cross another number off the debt death owed her.

Not content to reclaim the deceased by using their names, Mubarka also started reclaiming their childhoods in the new generation. She expected each of the new children to behave the way his or her namesake had. She was astonished to see how restless and scattered the new Mansur was, whereas her son, by contrast, had only rarely moved around, focusing all his talent on reciting proverbs, and had spoken like an adult. She was offended when a neighbor woman knocked on the mansion door to complain that Ahmad had hit her son, since no one had ever complained that his namesake had been hostile toward another child. Her grandson Yusuf began controlling his bladder before his second birthday, and for a long time she kept running her hands over his bed in amazement at how dry it was. She was bewildered by the stillness in his eyes, which lacked even a hint of the impish gleam that she used to see in the eyes of her son. Even so, she hadn't been deprived of the continuation of her line. The genes the first Yusuf had inherited from Mubarka, he had passed on completely to Atiya, who went on wetting her bed until she reached womanhood. Like her grandmother before her, she combined the wetness of blood with the wetness of water, and by the time she was ten years old, she was being trailed home by a line of mesmerized boys who didn't wake up until they heard the mansion gate clank shut in their faces. When Mubarka saw this, she compared the diffident admiration in the eyes of the young men of her generation with the audacity of the boys of her granddaughter's day, who would follow her all the way home from school and fight openly over her, and she wondered whether she'd been less attractive than Atiya when she was her age, or whether boys had just gotten more brazen.

Atiya's powers of attraction weren't felt only by strangers. They also began causing resentment and hatred among her younger paternal cousins. At the same time, they had no choice but to unite in the face of other boys' insolence, which, in one case, ended in tragedy.

One boy had the audacity to scrawl in huge letters on the mansion wall, "If anybody gets inside this mansion, he's sure to get what he wants." The al-Deeb boys hurriedly removed the words, then went searching for the person who had written them. The boy came and stood outside in the middle of the night, screeching, "I'd die just to ride you once, Atiya!"

Hardly had he gotten the words out of his mouth when her cousins surrounded him. Mansur came up to him and sank a knife into his heart. The boy, who wasn't even sixteen years old, flailed about like a slaughtered chicken until he fell motionless. Salama called the police himself lest the slain boy's family take revenge on his sons.

Soldier-laden trucks came roaring into the village following the district commissioner's car. The district commissioner placed the blame on the mayor, who not only oversaw a village where security had deteriorated, but had a grandson who'd been implicated in a murder. The slain boy was buried under guard by the security forces and Mansur was taken away to the district jail. As for Atiya, who had witnessed the incident from her window, she locked herself in her room for three days. She refused to talk to anyone, and wouldn't open the door to take the food people had left for her. When they finally broke down the door, they found her lying unconscious on a wet bed, her head haphazardly shorn and a fluffy pile of her black hair on the floor. They broke an onion open and waved it in front of her nose until she sneezed. Then they opened her mouth and poured sugar water into it until she cried.

When she had regained her color, she was more captivating than ever in spite of her exposed scalp. She would stand for hours in front of the mirror, eyeing herself with the hatred one reserves for an enemy. And every time she finished looking at herself she would change into clothes that looked worse than the ones she'd been wearing before.

"All that's left now is for you to sew yourself a gunnysack," Mubarka said to her. Seeing that the girl only grew more stunning the harder she tried to conceal her beauty, she tried to encourage her to accept her fate.

For several months security vehicles were stationed in the village, reminding the old-timers of the dromedary riders who'd been similarly stationed during the curfew after the Khedive family's livestock was stolen from their farm in Inshas. Life in al-Ish turned hellish, and people couldn't to go out to water their fields in the evening. Consequently, all the families in the village began demanding an end to the feud, and their leading men intervened by begging and cajoling those concerned to make peace between the two feuding clans. Salama paid a feddan as blood money for the slain boy, and Mansur went back to school after spending a year in a juvenile reformatory.

When the case was over, Salama resumed his post in honor of his half-brother Salem and decided to divide up the family.

"Everybody'll have to fend for themselves from here on out," he said as he ate his supper between Mas'ada and Mubarka. Neither made any comment. The murder had been counted against Salama, who was beginning to show signs of aging. However, the two women were also aware of the financial difficulties that faced him in managing the affairs of a family whose men had developed a taste for being taken care of and, as a result, had remained children. Their stay in Zagazig had deprived them of the chance to learn to weave, and none had the stamina for farm work. Meanwhile, their own children were growing up, and the burden of their schooling was growing steadily heavier.

The factory was going from bad to worse. No sooner had the curse of war been lifted than the markets were glutted with fabric coming out of large factories. However, Salama had kept al-Ish's factory open out of a kind of stubbornness, and began compensating for his losses and covering the families' expenses by selling agricultural land. Then came the Free Officers movement to demonstrate to the Europeans that Egypt was an industrial country and not just a big cotton plantation. The officers were instructed to set up huge textile factories on agricultural land adjacent to cities, which were suddenly transformed into industrial complexes, and small textile factories began faltering. The final blow came with the nationalization of private factories as the government monopolized cotton production and trade, and possession of a single bag of cotton at any time other than the days for gathering in the harvest became a crime on a par with drug trafficking. Salama declined an offer of employment in a government factory, as did all of his workers, choosing instead to trade in cloth, which he bought from suppliers rather than receiving it as a share of the spun cotton. He tore down several meters of the wall that surrounded the mansion and built a small shop in the space. Meanwhile, he closed up the farmhouse and Mubarka's house, where the looms were left to collect spider webs.

He traveled to Cairo to visit Salem for three days, which was enough time for the younger men to open up the two houses again and disassemble the looms. By the time he returned, they'd begun opening the windows and putting up the walls that had been removed when the factory was established. Looking the place over, Salama was overcome with emotion as the laughter and singing of two generations of workers echoed in his ears, along with the sounds of the looms as workers passed the shuttles back and forth through the warp and treadled with the deftness of circus magicians. However, he'd come back from his visit to Salem with another sorrow as well.

Salem's world, like Salama's, was coming apart at the seams. Following the initiation of their movement, which had soon come to be referred to as a "revolution," a conflict had broken out among the officers over how to run the country. Salem had suffered ostracism ever since that time, and he couldn't take it any more. He was in agreement with the officers who believed that the army should go back to its barracks. However, the hardliners had won the day, dismissing the leaders who supported General Muhammad Naguib and leaving Salem and like-minded junior officers in service, yet without allowing them again into their inner circle.

After the modifications were finished, Salama divided the farmhouse between Mahmoud and Abd al-Maqsud, while Kamel went to live in Mubarka's house. It came as a relief to Salama to move the new generation out of the mansion, since this way, each of the younger men would have to take responsibility for his own wife and children. The only people who stayed in the mansion were Salama, Mas'ada and Adel, Mubarka and Atiya, and the hunchback and her daughter Zayna, who were referred to respectively as "the ugly Palestinian" and "the pretty Palestinian," since the cholera epidemic hadn't spared many who remembered Nagiya's departure from al-Ish, and nobody believed the dark-skinned beauty could possibly be the hunchbacked woman's daughter.

Once the three families were gone, things quieted down at the mansion. A forgotten mayor sitting in a fabric shop, Salama began having to struggle to stay awake, especially now that the Free Officers' movement had restored to al-Ish the state of equality and harmony it had known for several centuries. This time, however, it was an equality that reeked of revenge. Al-Ish had never been subject to a feudal system that relegated its farmers to the status of slaves. Even so, its poor residents were given some of the large feudal land holdings that had been expropriated along the borders of the village in keeping with the Agrarian Reform Law. Consequently, there was no longer anyone in the village who didn't have land to farm.

Even though Salama had never behaved like someone with authority, there were plenty of people who took pleasure in seeing the mayor powerless. Still, the honorary post remained reserved for him and his half-brother Mahmoud after him thanks to what remained of Salem's prestige. This protection, derived from the Free Officers Movement, was what had kept him in his post in spite of his grandson's crime. However, it was this same protection that had contributed to his loss of prestige, since there was a belief that the young officer Gamal Abdel Nasser, who had ousted President Naguib, was omnipresent on Egypt's soil, and that he was accessible to virtually anyone—so accessible, in fact, that schoolchildren who wrote to him would receive a picture stamped with his signature. He was also a constant presence in the wagers of people young and old.

"If you're Gamal Abdel Nasser's son, then . . . ," one of them would say before daring somebody to do something, from jumping over an irrigation canal to driving a peg into a grave at night to eating a handful of hot pepper. The only place the neighborhood boys liked to play ball was in front of Salama's shop, and if the ball accidentally hit him in the face and woke him up from his nap, he would blow up at them and confiscate the ball, threatening to rip it apart with a knife.

"If you do, I'll send a message to Gamal Abdel Nasser telling him you called him a bad name!" the owner of the ball would retort defiantly. So he would throw it back to them, and they would snicker at the look of genuine fear on his face.

The more Salama aged, the more he resembled a frightened little boy. When a dispute was brought before him, he would resolve it in favor of the person with the loudest voice, and if anyone came to him to complain about a member of his family, he would apologize and kiss the person's head even before he'd heard the complaint. The boys in the family were uncomfortably aware that the family's reputation was suffering because of him. Adel in particular, who had come to have his mother's proud bearing, was pained by his father's senseless and impolitic concessions. In the end the boys forced him to resign, and the district commissioner opened the door to whoever wanted to apply for the position. However, Mahmoud ended up being appointed in his place.

Every one of the four women still living in the mansion knew what was required of her from the time she woke up in the morning. The family didn't have enough money to hire household help any more. Besides, there was no longer any need to employ other women to help them, since, unlike the past, there were no visiting merchants arriving as guests, nor factory workers to feed.

After finishing their chores they would eat breakfast with Salama before he left for the fabric shop. Then they would sit around mending clothes or spinning wool that had been shorn off the sheep, and Nagiya taught them how to knit mufflers and sweaters for their children. She did her best to involve Zayna in what was going on around her. However, her efforts were in vain, as the young woman continued to isolate herself, and spoke with no one but her absent son.

They were also joined by Zaynab, who came back to the mansion in a huff after Wafiq Asfur brought home a new wife. She looked like the women in the markets who put housewives to sleep by having them sniff henbane, then made off with their jewelry. With a face as long as a donkey's, sunken eyes, and puny breasts that looked like a man's muscles, the woman was the worst possible affront to Zaynab's femininity.

"You could at least have found somebody worth bringing home!" What Zaynab said in exasperation hadn't simply been an angry reaction. She really did wish that Firdous, whom Wafiq affection-ately dubbed "Dousa," was pretty.

"Supposing he'd died," Salama said in an attempt to persuade her to go home again, since she was the children's mother. But she refused, despite the fact that from the time they married, she had never considered Wafiq a real helpmate. In fact, she'd been happy when he settled in Cairo far away from her, since she hadn't been able to feed her children a single piece of meat or fruit as long as he was around. Rather than insist that she go back, her half-brother said her children were welcome at the mansion, although he was still of the opinion that it would provide them with a more dignified existence to be raised in their father's house, and he reminded Zaynab that he'd never wanted her to marry Wafiq.

It hadn't taken her long to see why Salama had opposed her marriage to Wafiq. But, like her half-brother, she feared failure. Consequently, she hadn't spoken about her problems before, deter-mined to succeed in spite of her discovery that her husband was a carbon copy of her father, only worse.

"At least my dad didn't run off at the mouth."

Before their marriage was consummated, she hadn't seen his greed and ingratitude. She'd figured that his insatiable urge to talk and the way he repeated the same story ad nauseam were signs of his love for her and his desire to keep the conversation going when there was nothing in particular to talk about. But she later discov-ered that his voracious appetite for food and his inability either to feel satisfied or to show any consideration for others was the same as his appetite for words without end and his unawareness of hav-ing said the same thing a hundred times before. When someone else was talking he would glare impatiently until the speaker had finished, only to discover that Wafiq hadn't heard a word he'd said.

"And the other things, don't they make up for the food and the talk?" Mas'ada asked her teasingly. But though she had inherited her mother's luscious features, Zaynab was overly serious and refused to get into "empty talk." She'd forgotten everything her mother taught her before her wedding night about how to act in bed. Then she'd forgotten what she learned from her about cooking after living with a gluttonous man who would simply swallow whatever was set before him without savoring a single bite.

He'd frittered away his father's savings on himself and his horse. The money went on barley, meat, hashish, the beer that he was the first person to introduce into al-Ish, and the European clothes he insisted on wearing. When he went to Cairo in a kind of flight, all he left to his four children and his parents was the horse. Abd al-Raziq sold it and used the money to buy a feddan of land. He was happy to have the field even though he wasn't good at farming it, since he felt it was the only thing that tied him to the village and the only justification he had for staying there.

As for Zaynab, she learned how to sew and bought herself a sewing machine, using the income it brought in to support her children and her parents-in-law. After her three older children finished primary school in al-Ish and began commuting to Bilbeis, she didn't have enough to pay for their transportation. So she would come to the mansion early in the morning before they woke up and tap gently on Salama's window, and he would give her whatever she needed.

Salama was impressed by his sister's determination to make her marriage work despite Wafiq's lengthy disappearance. At the same time, he didn't want to pressure her to go on living with a co-wife and put up with the childish things she did with Wafiq. Like a couple of dogs, their favorite place for their obscene flirtations was in front of an audience.

"She giggles all night as if he's tickling her. And in the morning they spread out a mat and sit on it together with her leg draped over his." Zaynab complained ruefully over having had to endure a husband who was a loafer and an ingrate, and she wasn't going to tolerate him along with a co-wife who was as abusive as he was. She would wait until Zaynab had finished cooking, then come into the kitchen to serve herself and him. Then she would bring the dishes back without washing them. She smoked and drank with him, and the two of them would take a bag of empty beer bottles to Bilbeis to exchange them for full ones. He would carry the bag on one arm and slip the other arm through hers. They were criticized by everyone who saw them. However, people were even more critical of Zaynab for staying in the house and putting up with the situation.

Mahmoud insisted that she get a divorce even if the pair showed some manners. However, Salama saw no need for this. Divorce wouldn't serve her children well in the future, and would be especially difficult for the two girls.

"Your sister isn't interested in getting married again, so why should she get a divorce?" Salama asked, hoping Mahmoud would drop the subject. Salama sent for Zaynab's children and her sewing machine, which her father-in-law brought himself, and he and Sakina began coming to check on Zaynab every day. Her father-in-law would leave his wife in the company of the women in the mansion and spend time with Salama in the fabric shop. The two of them would reminisce about the days of conscription and each would tell the other about his business and how things had been before their fortunes declined. They didn't broach the subject of their bygone rivalry, which had never reached the level of out-and-out confrontation or attempts to do each other harm.

Nagiya was delighted by Zaynab's return, since she felt that the presence of a woman closer in age to Zayna might help to bring her out of her silence. She tried to encourage her daughter to teach Zaynab how to embroider red Palestinian dresses with blue lengthwise stripes, or with zigzag stitches sewn with gold thread on the bodice and the ends of the sleeves. These Palestinian dresses were the perfect compromise for the educated girls of al-Ish, who were torn between going back to wearing the long, flowing peasant women's gallabiyas with the pleated bodices, and the citified dresses that peasant women still looked askance at.

"So the girl wants to show off by putting on a dress!" they'd say when a woman had rebelled against the gallabiya, no matter how educated she was or how respectable her profession happened to be. The Palestinian dresses gained such popularity that Zaynab couldn't keep up with the demand for them on her own. And whereas the girls had previously referred to the dresses by their appearance—as being either striped or embroidered—they now referred to them by the names by which they were known in Majdal—Ganna wa Nar ("Heaven and Hell") and Ish al-Bulbul ("Nightingale's Nest").

Zaynab's oldest son Taha didn't feel at home in the mansion in spite of the kind treatment he and his brothers had received from everyone there. He remained withdrawn, feeling like an orphan, and would often comment to his siblings, especially his sister Badi'a, "We're not at home, so don't eat much." The loud girl would laugh, then repeat what Taha had said when everyone was around. The boy, who had inherited his mother's black eyes, would turn red with embarrassment and withdraw even more. His mother would show him the money she was earning, but he couldn't get over feeling like a guest, and nearly wasted away. When he came home from school with his two sisters, his mother would serve him his food alone because she saw how it pained him to sit at the table with the others. Yet even then he would eat very little. After lunch he would study in some corner of the garden and go to bed early, refusing to mix with his cousins. Then he decided to go back to his father, taking his sisters Badi'a and Nagat with him and leaving little Farouk with his mother.

The people at the mansion raised no objection to Taha's decision. However, his mother pleaded with him not to lose contact with her, not to put up with more than he could endure and not to force his sisters to put up with more than they could endure. Taha's face took on more color, and he let the few whiskers that had begun budding on his chin grow out. He started praying regularly, yet without relinquishing his melancholy, and without telling his mother the details of what went on in their house. However, the two girls brought her daily reports, and spent more time with her than Taha did.

After her money ran out, Firdous started picking fights with Wafiq, during which they would call each other every name in the book. His mother, thinking it best to help hasten the departure of the brazen woman who'd made them a laughingstock in al-Ish from the day she arrived, whispered to Zaynab, "Stop being such a softy, and let him and that lazy so-and-so of his take care of the kids themselves!"

However, Zaynab knew it wouldn't make a bit of difference to Wafiq if the children stopped going to school.

"Well, then, get *her* to leave," Sakina told her. "Try not doing their laundry any more, and see what happens."

Taking her mother's advice, Zaynab told her children to stop bringing their dirty clothes to the mansion, and to tell their father about it. The new approach brought results more quickly than either of the two women had expected. When Wafiq asked Firdous to wash his children's clothes, she screamed at him in their presence, "So have they told you I'm a maid, you mama's boy?"

They got into a fistfight and he divorced her on the spot. Then she picked up her things and walked out. Sakina asked Zaynab to go back home again so that her children wouldn't be divided between the two households, and Abd al-Raziq asked Salama to intervene in hopes of getting Zaynab to soften. Zaynab agreed, on one condition.

"God stands between us," she said, insisting that he not go near her room, where she had put her sewing machine. After her children were grown, they asked her to rest. Taha took her on the pilgrimage to Mecca, and after her return she began spending her time on her prayer rug, worshipping and praising God. Years later, when her grandchildren were gathered around her, they asked her if she prayed for their grandfather.

Her eyes flickering with rage, she said, "The only bad thing I've ever done in my life is to call down curses on that dirty old sleazeball." They laughed, pointing out to her that God allows a man to take four wives, whereas their grandfather had only taken one other wife.

"Well, then God got it wrong," she retorted acerbically. "He should have gotten somebody's advice before allowing that sort of thing!"

She shooed them away, telling them not to drag her into more badmouthing. So they went to bed, leaving her to pray and ask God's forgiveness all night long.

When Colonel Salem al-Deeb returned from Yemen wrapped in a flag whose color he'd helped to change from green to the colors of death—black, white, and red—Mubarka, known now as Hagga Mubarka since making the pilgrimage to Mecca, gestured to the military band to stand away from the casket, refusing to allow the soldiers to lower him into the grave.

"You've done your part and killed him. Now leave the burying to us!" she shouted as she blocked the grave. As the commander ordered his soldiers to step back, Mubarka gestured to al-Ish's crippled gravedigger, who was terrified by the shiny stars on the soldiers' shoulders.

"Come down here, Sheikh Mukhtar," she commanded as she stepped aside for him. Dragging his atrophied leg, the elderly man slid down into the grave. Then Mubarka gestured to her sons, who came forward to remove the body from the casket.

The twenty-one shots the soldiers fired into the air in salute to the martyr didn't convince her that she was at a wedding, and after the ceremony, which she endured only grudgingly, she dismissed everyone with a wave of the hand.

"Hurry up now," she said. "Leave me alone with him for a while." The only two people she allowed to stay were Zaynab, Khircellia, and her two little boys Naguib and Gamal. She went on talking to Salem until the sun went down about all the things that had happened while he was gone. She told him everything she hadn't had time to tell him during the hurried, impromptu visits he used to make when, finding himself headed to the Inshas military camp, he would order his driver to turn in the direction of al-Ish. To Salem she released all the tears she'd held back out of pride on previous occasions involving death or absence.

Later, at the wake, she began strewing dust in the faces of the silent women to get them to share in her tears.

"Come on now, you ungrateful wretches, cry over the one who gave you your dignity!"

Sakina sat beside her, her face concealed by a veil that her grandson Taha had imposed on her. He'd also made Zaynab and his two sisters put it on. Sakina began catching Mubarka's tears in her handkerchief, while Badi'a consoled her grandmother from behind her face veil, saying, "Have faith in God, Grandma. The Prophet died, so should we cry for ourselves or for the Prophet?"

The tear in Hagga Mubarka's eye froze and she replied furiously, "The Prophet? Let his family cry over him. I'm crying over my own son, smarty-pants."

The women who'd come to offer their condolences concealed their smiles behind their black mantillas, while some murmured pleas for God's forgiveness and a prayer that God wouldn't hold the grieving woman's words against her. Sakina sat in silence for a few minutes, then patted Mubarka's hands and left. She didn't come back to see her again during the remaining days of the wake.

Mubarka cried her eyes dry, and when they brought her Salem's medals of honor, she refused to let them inside the mansion. "We've got so much copper we don't know what to do with it all!"

In the martyr's honor they decided to provide an all-expenses-paid pilgrimage to Mecca for Mubarka and her son's widow. In response, she said she'd already gone on the pilgrimage with her beloved Salem, who had pampered her there, feeding her things she'd never tasted in her life. So what point was there in her going again? When her grandchildren tried to talk her into it, she shouted, "Why should I go again? Have I chopped down some-body's crops or poisoned somebody's livestock?"

Nor was the widow in need of this honor, and she was surprised that they didn't realize she was a Christian.

When Salem decided to marry Khircellia he'd had only one con-dition: that she be acceptable to Mubarka. When he took her with him to al-Ish, Mubarka had given him a thumbs-up the minute the young woman took her first step inside the mansion gate. She told him in private that she'd seen European women for the first time when she went to Bilbeis to buy her trousseau, and after that in Zag-azig. She confessed that she hadn't been impressed by the ones she'd seen because of their man-like thinness and the hair they left on their bodies. By contrast, she'd been dazzled by the bride he'd cho-sen, with her full figure, her towering height, her intense black irises in brilliantly clear eyes, and her flowing, waist-length raven hair.

"Did you know that her name means 'happy' in Greek? But unfortunately she's a Christian!" he said teasingly, as if to make her stop saying such nice things about her.

"What do you mean 'unfortunately,' you silly goose?" she snapped. "They're all paths to God!"

When he reported to Khircellia what his mother had said, she told him that she too had fallen in love with his mother, and that even if he left her, she wouldn't stop coming to see the Hagga. And in fact, as time went by she visited her more than Salem himself, busy as he was from one war to the next. After she gave birth to her twin boys, she would pile them into the car and head for al-Ish, where she would spend days at a time with Mubarka, and the two of them would exchange one story after another. All Khircellia had left of her mother Litsa were some photographs. As for her father, Marco the Sicilian, all she knew about him was his name, which had remained hidden away and forgotten on a folded-up piece of paper. A boyfriend of her mother's, she had left him for someone else before discovering she was carrying his child. By the time she gave birth to Khircellia, she was with a third man. In the end she

196

found a fried-potato vendor who was willing to register the baby in his name in exchange for one pound, and she never saw him again.

"That's why I like fried potatoes, Hagga, because they smell like Baba!" she said with a laugh when she saw the effect of her story in Mubarka's eyes.

She showed Mubarka her pictures with her mother, a young woman who looked more like a sister to her than a mother, and who was thirty-five years old when Khircellia married Salem. Litsa had gone back to Greece when the Free Officers came to power because she no longer felt at ease in Alexandria after her male friends began leaving the city. She was a poet, or so she used to say, since Khircellia had never been interested in what she wrote. Her mother had noticed that her boyfriends also had little interest in her writing beyond the first days of getting acquainted. Beautiful and frigid, like a bronze icon, she would flit whorishly from one man to another, doing her utmost in the first few days to act the part of the lascivious woman who satisfies the man's expectations, but before long the saintly body she occupied would let her down. The man might speak well of her writing, but she would soon fall prey to melancholy and begin acting like a prim woman who recoiled in disgust at bodily secretions. She would neglect the man and he, in turn, would neglect her, at which point she would drown herself in drink until she set out in search of someone else she could ensnare with the misleading appearance of a restless feline.

"We used to live in a little studio apartment, a tiny bedroom with just a little space outside of it, Hagga. I would hear her sleeping with them, but her screams were screams of pain," said Khircellia in a tone of pity that explained why she'd dreamed of things that ran totally counter to what her mother had been. From the age of nine she'd begun falling in love with any young man she saw, her only condition being that he not be a poet. Her dream was to have a household of her own, and ten children that she devoted herself to with their father. She'd been attracted to Salem when she saw him at the entrance to the cinema in Alexandria's Mahattat al-Raml neighborhood. He'd been standing between a couple of his colleagues, and she was with a girlfriend. She made a note of where he sat, and was so busy tracking him in the darkened theater that she didn't see any of the movie. When the movie was over, she took her time getting ready to leave, and when he was even with the row she was sitting in, she got up just in time to bump into him and drop her purse.

"Typical Egyptian stunts!" Salem would laugh whenever she reminded him of the ruse she'd resorted to to get him to pick up her purse and hand it apologetically back to her. They'd walked out of the theater together, and every time they met thereafter, she felt more and more certain that he was her match.

During their first visit to al-Ish after getting married, Mubarka was gripped with a fear that Khircellia was going to die, since she didn't believe the world could bear such extremes of joy. She observed Khircellia's exuberant warmth toward Salem with a fretful jubilation, pitying her son in advance for the pain he would suffer over the departure of the Greek mare. Little did she know that it was he who would depart from this world in spite of having survived three ambushes: one in Fallujah when Palestine was lost, one in Cairo when they ousted the king, and one in Port Said when Israel allied herself with Britain and France to teach Abdel Nasser a lesson.

"All right, then, so the Jews defeated you, and you drove the king out. Now who are you fighting in Yemen, you idiots?" she muttered to herself. Her mind wandered away with her son's apparition as she thought back on his return from the war in Palestine. He'd snuck in after midnight like an escaped prisoner. He'd let his beard grow out and put on a gilbab, and the only person who could convince him to take a bath and change his clothes was Atiya, who called him "Baba Sa." His mother would send her to his room, and she would come in tripping over the pile of clean clothes she was carrying. She would sit in his lap, hanging onto his neck and begging him to take a bath and put on the clothes she'd brought. When he made no response, she would push him away in disgust, saying, "You stink, Baba Sa!"

He would sniff himself and, discovering that he really did stink to high heaven, would feel embarrassed in front of the little girl. Then he would run after her, grab her, and pick her up. As she tried to wriggle out of his grip he would kiss her by force, then let her go before picking up his clothes and heading for the bathroom.

Salem stayed in al-Ish for several months. Then one day a military vehicle drove up and two officers, both lieutenants like him, got out. They spent some time alone with him in his room. The three of them came out to the garden, where Salem left them to go shave off his beard and put on his uniform. Then they ate lunch and he left with them. From then on his visits home amounted to no more than a few hours every few months. When the radio announced the army's blessed movement, Salem was one of the junior officers who had taken part in it. No one in al-Ish knew how much of a role he'd played in it or how close he was to General Muhammad Naguib. However, his standing became apparent on the practical level through the paving of al-Ish's main road and the construction of a huge service complex on five feddans that had been donated by the family. When the complex was first built, its entrance bore a sign that read "al-Ish Village Complex," but later it was changed to "Martyr Salem al-Deeb Complex." The complex included a middle school, a high school, a hospital, a youth center, a football field, a small building that housed an electrical generator, a post office, and a cistern for clean water.

Electric street lights were installed, and whoever wanted electricity or running water in their home could pay the necessary fees and subscribe to those services. But nobody saw any need for them, since they were content with the traditional street lamps, the public water faucet in the village complex, and the taps that were available at four of al-Ish's mosques. The only two places that ended up with electricity and running water were Asfur's house and the al-Deeb mansion.

Major Gamal Abdel Nasser visited al-Ish for the complex's grand opening, and the picture that showed him exchanging whispers with Salem in the pavilion that had been set up as part of the grand opening celebration was the first and last picture to grace any of the mansion walls. Mubarka had chosen a prominent spot for it in the entranceway, and she hung a black ribbon over one corner of it after Salem's death.

When, some years later, her grandchildren wanted to hang up pictures of themselves receiving prizes for outstanding school performance, she strictly forbade them. She'd come to believe that hanging people's pictures on the wall was bad luck, since, as far as she could tell, it just paved the way for the person's disappearance and set the stage for him or her to turn into nothing but a memory. Her only wish now was for her children to stay in al-Ish and not to travel anywhere even for the sake of their educations. As she saw it, the angel of death in al-Ish was comprehensible, but she had no way of guaranteeing her loved ones' survival in places inhabited by less prudent angels of death, who struck out haphazardly, recklessly taking young men in the prime of life—in a train or automobile accident, for example, or in a war a young man hadn't had any say in. She advised the young fathers, who no longer paid any attention to her, and pleaded with Khircellia when she visited her with her two sons, to stay in al-Ish with their children.

"So, are you having trouble feeding them?" she would ask the fathers when she saw how happy they were about finding work for one of their sons in the Gulf. She hadn't noticed that times were changing, that it wasn't possible any more for the boys to remain jobless, and that what remained of their land wasn't enough to put bread on the table for them. All she knew was that she hadn't gotten her fill of Salem.

Adel never managed to finish high school. He passed all his subjects with the exception of French. What they were asked to learn in the subject was so minimal it was virtually useless, and other students considered it an opportunity to improve their grades. So they laughed at Adel when they heard him say mournfully, "If it weren't for French, high school would be a piece of cake!"

Contenting himself with his middle-school diploma, he applied for work as a mail carrier. But after getting the job he didn't deliver a single letter. Sporting a stylish European gilbab, he would sprawl out on a mound of dirt in front of the post office, alone and silent, or squat with a small group of unemployed friends as they smoothed the ground for the siga board and started playing. They kept moving the board to keep it in the shade until the sun went down. Then they would scatter, and Adel would close up the post office and go home.

If someone came asking about a letter he was expecting, Adel would point to the pile of letters on the post-office table and tell him to go look for it himself. After conducting a number of investigations and imposing a number of penalties because of complaints that he had thrown people's letters in the street, this was the most the postal authority succeeded in getting him to do.

"What's wrong with you, and what's wrong with the world?" This was all he had to say in response to people's objections. He assured them that if they weren't miserable enough already, they would lose their peace of mind and their tolerance if they found out what was going on in the cities, far from the livestock they lived with under one roof. Other people considered him to be the miserable one, saying that if he'd swallowed his pride and delivered the letters to people's houses, he could have made a lot more money thanks to the tips they would have given him. However, they knew that no power on earth could persuade the man living in the al-Deeb mansion to stoop to such a lowly task, even if he was faced with starvation.

Hunger was the last thing that might have motivated Adel. All he cared about were clean clothes and a piece of hashish in his pocket to roll into cigarettes. He would let out a loud whoop whenever he won a round of siga and, in fact, it was thanks to his skill at this game that he got married. He'd been playing one day with Abd al-Sami' al-Gahsh and they were taking turns winning and losing cigarettes, some spiked with hashish and some plain. When the sun was just about to set, they tied, so they agreed on a bigger bet for a final round.

"If you beat me, I'll marry you to the pretty Palestinian, and if I beat you, you'll marry me to your daughter."

Adel won, and went home with Abd al-Sami' al-Gahsh to see his daughter Samira, who hadn't even developed breasts yet. With her honey-colored complexion and green eyes, she looked as though she could be his sister.

The girl was amazed when her mother told her the reason behind the guest's visit. She began looking at herself in search of something she hadn't noticed before. She hadn't thought she was old enough to get married to begin with.

"What's the matter with you?" her father upbraided her. "I mean, did you think you were going to finish high school?"

According to her mother, a suitor from the al-Deeb family would be acceptable even if he showed up stark naked. But her paternal aunt Zakiya was distraught. "That family's mixed up with demons!" she said woefully, trying to enlist her sister-in-law's support in persuading her brother to turn Adel down. She still remembered her bizarre engagement to his uncle Nagi, his lack of interest in her, and his strange disappearance. Little did either of the women know that he'd won the girl in a bet! Two evenings later, Adel came to the house with his uncle Mahmoud to ask for the hand of his friend's daughter, apologizing that his father wasn't feeling well enough to come with them.

Thrilled over the engagement of her youngest child, Mas'ada would come along on his visits to his fiancée, and wouldn't let him go to her house empty-handed. He had to have a gift of some sort: a scarf, a tin of sweets, some fruit, or a piece of fabric.

"A girl's engagement should be the happiest time of her life," she told him when she saw his impatience over the way she delayed him by searching for a present every night. She assured him that later on he and his bride would think back nostalgically on these care-free days. She pampered Samira the way she would have liked to be pampered when she married Ali. When she had married Salama, by contrast, her outings triggered a jealousy that made her smile at first, but that soon turned into a kind of obsession.

"Are you spending the evening with Abd al-Sami' al-Bayez?" He would beleaguer her with questions to the point that she stopped going out altogether, confining herself again to the company of women who ranted on and on about their sorrows over loved ones who had died or gone away. However, the jealousy that had forced her to stay at the mansion evolved into a mad desire. The minute she lay down beside him, he would start undressing with difficulty and ask her to do the same. However, he would have trouble getting to her private parts.

"Lift that leg," he would say. She would lift both her legs, which were still firm and smooth, rather than just one. Trying to shake his foot loose after getting it caught in the blanket, he would retort irritably, "Not your leg. Mine!" When she pleaded with him to let her sleep, he would get angry, turn his back to her, and curl up in a fetal position.

One morning Salama was sitting on his stone bench and, seeing Adel leaving, asked him to stop and have coffee with him. Adel declined, explaining that he was late for work, but Salama pressed him. Taking the cup despite his dislike for coffee, he started sipping it reluctantly as his father launched into a long preamble that led to his saying that he wanted to tell him a secret. He couldn't talk about it with either Tafida's son Abd al-Maqsud or his uncle Ali's son Kamel. Sidling up to him, he whispered, "Your mother's sewn it up."

Adel went red in the face and grinned.

"Come on, now, Baba," he said.

"You don't believe me? All right, then, we'll have Hagga Mubarka examine her."

"No need for that. I'll have a talk with her."

Then they both fell silent. Salama begged him not to breathe a word of it to anyone, and Adel for his part promised to discuss the problem with his mother. Then he left without looking back. He didn't come home until the rooster's crow the next morning, having spent the evening and part of the night with his bride. He crept into his room on tiptoe lest his father hear him.

He started to avoid his father. Every time he was about to get up enough courage to speak to him, he would think better of it. However, his father started watching for a chance to buttonhole him so that he could hear what Mas'ada had said. Consequently, Adel had no choice but to broach the matter with her. He was so embarrassed he practically threw the words in her face. Mortified, she clapped her hands over her chest and cried, "Goodness gracious, the man's gone senile!"

"Humor him for my sake, please!" he whispered imploringly.

"I swear to God, son, he's after me all night long. But he's the one who can't do it any more!"

Adel informed his father of his mother's response, imploring him not to repeat the accusation ever again. It saddened him to hear the reproachful tone he was using with a man who had never treated him with anything but kindness and affection. He consoled himself with the thought that he may have gone overboard on account of the turmoil and sadness he felt over seeing his father turning back into a little boy. After having been a man whose word was like a sword on others' necks, and who never would have said anything in the least out of place or undignified, his father was now like a child who needed someone to scold him for his mistakes and improprieties.

For several days Adel paid special attention to his father in an attempt to repair their relationship. But he was so preoccupied with his bride, who'd begun developing feelings for him, too, that he soon forgot about it.

Samira was pleased at the unforeseen interest in her, incredulous that she'd suddenly become the center of the household. She'd begun warming up to the idea of marriage, happy to have been transformed overnight from a little girl whom people treated dismissively, forbade to sit with adults, and ordered to do her studies, to a little lady whom they respected not only at home, but also at school. Her teachers had stopped dogging her with homework assignments, although their reason for doing so was simply that it wasn't worth their time to bother with a girl who was going to stay home as soon as she finished middle school.

She'd taken a liking to Adel, and found him a sensitive, gentle individual who was nothing like the self-important braggart others thought him to be. He was also unexpectedly different from her father, an irresponsible man who left her and her siblings to their own devices and showed no interest in how her mother managed their affairs. Despite appearing to be a spoiled young man, Adel listened to her and gave her confidence in herself as a mature young woman. He consulted her about everything and talked to her about how many children he dreamed of having with her. He even asked her what she wanted to name their firstborn.

As the days passed, the couple grew more and more attached. He would wait for her outside the school to walk her home, and she would look forward to his after-supper visits, which he began making alone whenever possible instead of letting his mother tag along. The two of them would sit together in the presence of her mother, who would get sleepy after a while. At that point they would start exchanging ardent touches, igniting desires that had been roasting over a slow fire for hours with the help of avid glances and gestures. The exhausted mother would open her eyes to find his hand on her daughter's breasts or her hand between his thighs. Pretending to be asleep, she would close her eyes to give them a chance to compose themselves. They would move away from each other, each struggling to hide the wet spot in his or her gilbab. Meanwhile they would launch into nervous chatter, yet without managing to make the exchange sound coherent or meaningful.

Opening her tired eyes, the mother would ask what time it was, which was Adel's cue to be on his way. He would understand what she meant, but act dumb and answer the question without making a move to leave. Sometimes she would try to join in their conversation, but would get so drowsy she'd doze off in mid-sentence.

"I'm not up to that daughter of yours. She's as bad-mannered as you are!" an exasperated Nadrat would say to her husband the next morning. Unable to stay up chaperoning the girl after a grueling day in the field and in the house, she accused Abd al-Sami' of not caring what happened to his daughter, since he'd gone back to spending his evenings out, leaving Adel unwatched as though he were already a member of the family.

"All right then, we'll sign the marriage contract, and on the last day of examinations they'll have the wedding," replied an equally exasperated Abd al-Sami'. When they asked Adel to set a date for formalizing the marriage he was delighted, since Samira would now be his lawfully wedded wife and he would be free to relate to her however he wished.

However, just days before the date set for the ceremony, Adel was called up for military conscription. He went to sit for the pre-induction examination in Zagazig, but after finishing the examination he didn't come back for the ceremony. Instead, they handed him a knapsack on the very same day and sent him off to the training center.

There were successive reports of Israeli troop buildups on the Syrian border, and a new war appeared to be in the offing following Abdel Nasser's declaration that the attack on Syria was tantamount to an attack on Egypt. After an absence of forty days, Adel came home on a short furlough a changed person: with a barrel chest, taut muscles, and skin as brown as an overbaked clay pot. He also came back dejected, as though some magical force had emptied his eyes of their braggadocio and filled them with a grim modesty.

He spent forty-eight hours torn between his fiancée and his family, all of whom he wanted to see as much of as he could. His father-in-law relented and let Samira accompany him to the mansion, where she helped prepare the lunch with the women of the family while Adel trailed her wherever she went.

Before his departure they received a visit from the family data collector, who took photographs of the father and mother. When Salama asked him the reason, the man replied awkwardly, his head still concealed inside the camera's black hood, "On account of the pension, just in case, you know, God forbid . . ."

"The only thing they're good at preparing for is death," muttered Salama as he fought back a tear that stopped midway down his cheek. Ignoring his comment, the visitor folded up the camera and put it back in his satchel. Then he slipped the tripod under his arm and left to go to another house while Adel had his lunch surrounded by people who were silent as though in a dream. Certain that they were in the presence of a martyr, not one of them brought his hand to his mouth.

After lunch Adel embraced them one by one. Mas'ada and Samira wept, hanging onto his neck, Mubarka wept the way she had when Salem was buried, and Zayna wept as she hadn't done when her half-brother Ziyad tossed her son onto a truck that had gone she knew not where.

The young men returned from university. But as they were drawn one after another to Cairo, life didn't return to the mansion the way it had in summers past.

After her uncle Salem, Atiya was the first person in the al-Deeb family to graduate from high school. However, she finished two years late. In one of the two years she hadn't taken her examinations because of the murder, and in the other she failed them after switching to the home-schooling system. In so doing she left behind the boys in her class, only a few of whom had managed to pass because they were so distracted by her presence that they couldn't hear what the teachers were saying in class, and couldn't see anything but her image in their books when they sat down to study in the evenings. Even so, from the time of the murder, none of them had been able to admit to himself the way he fantasized about her.

When Atiya started her university studies, the oldest of the children born since the cholera epidemic was still a year too young to join her. So that year she lived in the girls' dormitory. When the boys of the family began enrolling in the university it became necessary to rent two apartments, one for the boys and one for the girls. The last family-related task her uncle Salem had performed before leaving for Yemen had been to look for the two apartments, which were located on the second and third floors of a building in Dokki, and to furnish them with whatever they needed. Yusuf's daughter Atiya and Mahmoud's daughter Mubarka lived in the third-floor apartment, where they were joined later by Kamel's daughter Samiha, while the young men lived on the second floor so that they could keep an eye on whoever went up to the girls' apartment.

This living arrangement was burdensome for the family, which had continued to sell what remained of its land, and its younger members were aware of the hardship. In mid-March they would come back and spend two months in al-Ish studying for their examinations, arriving just as the sole remaining orange tree along the mansion wall was beginning to bloom.

They would all come back to the mansion, since those who had moved with their parents to the two clay houses treated them like mere barracks to spend their nights in. Their arrival would create a festive atmosphere and bring life back into the place. As soon as they arrived, they would set about sweeping up what remained of the garden, burning the trash, and getting rid of the bottles and empty tin cans that littered the place. The number of tin cans indicated how much store-bought ghee the women had used. Hagga Mubarka considered it shameful to bring it into the mansion, so whenever Mas'ada went to the grocery store she would instruct her to be circumspect, saying, "If you're going to get some of that Lindane, make sure nobody sees you." She likened the store-bought ghee to the pesticide that was used to get rid of boll weevils, incredulous that people had so lost sight of the blessing of the past that they could actually refer to the foul-smelling stuff as ghee. As for her, she had no compunctions about sniffing the date-stuffed pastries she was served and unapologetically putting them back on the plate, saying, "I don't eat Lindane."

After Adel's induction into the army, the boys' return to al-Ish was delayed until mid-May. They spent two months waiting for the return of Atiya, who had disappeared with a carpenter they had hired to fix some furniture in the two apartments. They didn't know how the carpenter had managed to persuade the medical student to elope with him or how he could have reached an understanding with her, since Mansur and Ali had escorted him step by step as he went about his work in the girls' apartment, after which they had paid him his wages and seen him leave.

A few days after the carpenter's visit, Atiya had left for her lectures as she did every day, but hadn't come back. Mubarka and Samiha searched in every direction, looking for her in the houses of whichever of her classmates they happened to know, but didn't find her. The young men combed the city's hospitals and police stations, but found no corpses of unidentified women, and came across no reports of mysterious crimes. Then Salama happened to glance at her desk, where, next to her neat stacks of books, they found a thick bundle of papers.

It was their love letters to her, written over the course of three years, arranged from the longest to the shortest. At the top were letters from Ahmad Abd al-Maqsud, followed by those of Mansur Kamel, Yusuf Abd al-Maqsud, Mustafa Kamel, Nagi Mahmoud, and Ali Abd al-Maqsud. On top of the stack Atiya had left a brief note informing them that she'd married the carpenter and asking them not to bother to look for her but to go on with their lives, since her heart had chosen. A single reply to all their letters.

They exchanged sheepish glances as they looked at the letters they'd slipped into her lecture notes or inside bags of vegetables she would receive from them before going to cook them with the other girls, or pressed into her hand with the change they'd brought back from the market.

Since lectures were still in session, they decided to wait in hopes that her capricious fling would end and she would come back without anyone in al-Ish learning what had happened. But she didn't come back. Then a decree was issued suspending classes due to the atmosphere caused by the war effort.

People were so preoccupied with those missing in war that they had no time to think about the one missing in love. Everyone's ears were glued to the radio as they counted the types of weapons that had been amassed in Sinai for the decisive final standoff with the enemy. Even her grandmother, Hagga Mubarka, registered no response to the news of her disappearance apart from a change in the rhythm of her drumming fingers. Every time she listened to the news broadcast she would position her fingertips on the table. Every piece of news was tantamount to digging up Salem's grave, his loss made doubly painful for her by her longing for his two young sons, since Khircellia had begun visiting al-Ish less frequently than before.

When the younger Mubarka began telling her grandmother about her cousin's disappearance, she gave her one ear, and with the other ear went on listening to the news. The further the young woman got into the story, the faster the grandmother drummed her fingers, but without uttering a word.

The news broadcaster's stentorian voice shrilled in their ears, announcing that the battles were underway and that two hundred fifty enemy aircraft had been shot down in the early hours of the confrontation. Zayna jumped up and started to dance, Nagiya's face glowed with the hope of going back to Palestine, and Salama took Mas'ada's hand reassuringly, saying, "Adel is fine, Umm Kamel."

Making no comment, Hagga Mubarka kept drumming her fingers until the news broadcast was over and no one was hearing about either advances or retreats. It was as though she felt that the catastrophe was too great for her fingers to convey. In fact, however, neither she nor anyone else could have imagined the true scope of what would come to be known as the Naksa, or the setback. Even when Abdel Nasser delivered his resignation address, stating that he bore responsibility for "everything that happened," no one knew the extent of what had happened. For the first time ever, the mansion residents brought the radio out to the stone bench built into the front wall of the fabric shop that had been closed for years. Transfixed, they listened to Abdel Nasser's speech, which echoed against the other radios amid the silence of the crowds as they listened with bated breath.

The next morning the men began marching out to al-Ish's main road, where they commandeered whatever trucks or tractors happened to be passing through the village. Pushing and shoving their way onto the vehicles, they directed their drivers to Cairo so that they could join the crowds gathered in the streets in rejection of Abdel Nasser's resignation. Supporting himself on his cane, Salama started walking in the direction of the street, and they thought he was going out with the marchers. Instead, however, he stopped breathlessly and sat down at the gate to prevent his grandchildren from leaving.

"Goodbye," he said to the marchers on their way out. "So you think people's lives are just a game?"

As it turned out, he didn't need to lock the gate, since none of his grandchildren came near it, even out of curiosity, and neither did the young people who had come back from Cairo. The defeat turned people's grief over Salem upside down, mingling it with their disappointment in Atiya and their fear for Adel. The younger ones avoided looking their mothers and fathers in the eye, pretending to be looking at books they weren't getting a thing out of.

When all was said and done, Abdel Nasser decided not to resign, and Adel didn't come home from the war. Nor was he the only young man from al-Ish who had disappeared. Four others had left with him, and of these, only one soldier had come back. Emaciated, terror-stricken, and silent, he came back in the same gilbab he'd been wearing when he left al-Ish a day before the war broke out. The minute he woke up, he would go back to sleep again. For days and nights on end, the mothers of the young men who had gone to war pleaded with him to talk in hopes of learning anything they could about their sons.

"Do you all think Sinai is as tiny as al-Ish?" Sa'id al-Gahsh exclaimed irritably. He fell silent for a long time. Then he started talking, though he seemed to be talking to himself more than to his listeners.

"I didn't see anybody," he said. "All I saw was death."

The returned soldier talked about the chaos that had attended the defeat, and that had made it impossible for those who took part in the war to know anything. The young men of al-Ish tried to explain this to Mas'ada who, obsessed with the fate of her youngest child, didn't understand—or didn't want to understand—a thing they said.

She would go with other women whose sons were missing to sit with the returned soldier's mother in front of her house, hoping he would say something new. The soldier's mother would go inside, then come back out again, diffident and apologetic, with nothing new to report. He was always asleep. When at last he responded and came out to join them, they looked into his face and nearly squeezed the words out of him.

"They would spray us like mosquitoes," he said.

The women didn't understand why he was in pain rather than happy to be back. However, encouraged by their attentive listening, he began to get into his story, and explained what it meant for someone to be thrown bound into a river.

He hadn't had a chance to open the knapsack that had been hurriedly placed in his hands. He hadn't even tried on his military uniform or put on the boots they'd given him. The trucks had taken him and thousands of others from the military recruiting centers to Sinai, still dressed in their civilian clothes. Once there, his battalion had been surrounded by a small Israeli force. Speaking with a Bedouin accent, the force's commander had told them to throw down their shotguns, which they hadn't even learned how to shoot yet. So they threw them down. Then he ordered them to take the shovels out of their knapsacks and to throw the remaining contents of their bags on top of the pile of shotguns. After that he instructed them to dig a long trench. By the time they'd finished, they were out of breath.

"I would have died just to be able to get my tongue wet. My mouth was dry as a bone, and they knew it. They started humiliating us by playing with water in front of us. They'd say, 'Who's thirsty?' If somebody raised his hand, they'd give him a drink, then shoot him."

He was in tears, but managed to bring his sobs under control in order to satisfy the anguished women's curiosity.

"They told the ones who were left to line up in a row with their hands clasped over their heads."

His lips quivering, he averted his eyes and took a deep breath before describing how the Israeli officer had ordered his soldiers to come forward one after another and aim at the chests of the even-numbered captives. Then he had the ones who were left drag their buddies' bodies to the trench and fill it in over them. After that he ordered them to get into the truck until it was filled to capacity. The Israelis left the rest behind. However, they fired haphazardly from their Jeep as it followed the captive-laden truck, joking all the way. For forty days Sa'id had lived on whatever insects or plants he could find, until at last he made his way to the mango groves on the outskirts of Suez.

"We never even fought. It's as though the people highest in command had taken a vow to slaughter us," the young man said. Then he left them and went away.

A few weeks later, the absent soldiers' personal effects were returned to the village, so they were considered martyrs and prayed over in absentia after the communal Friday prayer. As for Adel, he was still unaccounted for. Mas'ada would sit with the other women and compare her situation with theirs.

"At least you know what's become of your sons."

"You mean we got to bury them with our own hands? At least you can still hope your son will come home alive!"

Mas'ada sensed that the solidarity the women had experienced based on their shared tragedy had turned into a kind of mutual envy. She withdrew from the mothers of the martyred soldiers, whose families began traveling to the city to claim the compensation due to them. She would sit for hours with the few women who remained in the mansion, and when the younger Mubarka and Samiha commuted to the university, the only person still at her side was Samira, who'd become a member of the family. She hadn't abandoned her sorrowful mother-in-law's quest, and Mas'ada treated her with gratitude. She considered her to be an extension of Adel's own scent, and viewed her ongoing attachment to him as a sign that he would be back. However, no sooner had she begun to calm down than her passion would be rekindled.

"Does this make any sense? Are we just going to sit around like this? What do they mean, 'missing'?" she asked. She paid no attention to his brothers, who considered Adel to have been martyred ever since the beginning of the Six-Day War. She decided to travel to Bilbeis with Samira, where they inquired about the missing man and what had become of him. They received no answer, but they did come back with similar stories from other villages, and with new friendships that now bound them to other missing men's families as they exchanged advice and information.

Adel had begun living imaginary lives through the affirmations of fortunetellers and charlatans who collected their fees in advance, as well as inspirations received by well-meaning people who encouraged Mas'ada to visit saints' tombs and make vows that she would keep once he was back. The stories contradicted each other, and the absent son found himself traveling a variety of paths at the same time. Every one of the various accounts found support in a scene from this or that dream reported by Mas'ada, Samira, or any of the other restive women in the mansion. So now nothing remained but to resort to Khadduga, the blind fortune-teller in Inshas.

"She's the best," asserted Fakiha, the fat woman from Shalshalamun whom Mas'ada found sitting in a sheet-iron cart in front of the police station whenever she went to Bilbeis. The cart was hitched to a donkey eating straw out of a nosebag. Fakiha was sitting cross-legged in the cart, her body filling it so completely that she came right up against its inner walls on both sides. In front of her lay a piece of newspaper heaped with European bread, ta'miya, fried eggplant, and sweet pepper. By the time her husband came out she'd devoured everything in front of her. The man removed the donkey's nosebag and tossed it into the back of the cart. Then he jumped onto the front of the cart, pointed the donkey in the direction of the road, and cracked his whip.

"Those idiots don't know anything. Khadduga will tell you where he's gone."

Taking Fakiha's advice, Mas'ada went alone to see the fortune-teller, taking with her the last gilbab Adel had worn before leaving to be inducted into the army. The woman began cutting pieces out of the gilbab and throwing them onto the fire so that the smoke they produced would mingle with the smoke from the incense. Then she breathed it in deeply. As her index finger traced in the sand the paths he had taken since the beginning of the chaos, she described to Mas'ada the features of the Bedouin man who had hidden him from the Jews. As she tossed another piece of the gilbab into the fire, she saw him in the midst of a group of men.

"It looks like a wedding. Yes, a wedding. But where's the bride?"

She fell silent for a few moments, focusing on the fire. Then she continued: "They're all men? Yes, that's the way their traditions are." She would ask questions and answer them herself.

Mas'ada paid her five pounds and came home clinging to what the blind woman had seen of her son. It was now an established certainty that he was living among the Bedouins with a wife and children. When recalling the story, she didn't focus on the wedding scene for fear of hurting the feelings of Samira, who had continued her studies in order to be able to turn down the suitors who had begun knocking on her door. However, Adel's Bedouin existence was confirmed in Mas'ada's heart with every passing day, and she asked her grandchildren to accompany her on trips to look for him. Kamel pleaded with his sons to obey their grandmother even if she was mistaken. Speaking on her behalf, he said, "Tell those imps that one of them has to come with me!"

In her dreams Adel would be herding sheep and goats. She would see the features of his wife and children, and his wife would speak to him in a strange dialect. Mas'ada would open her eyes, delighted with her dream because she didn't remember ever having heard that dialect in her waking hours. But then she would remember that she'd been hearing the two Palestinian women speak it every day in the mansion for years. Paying no attention to this disheartening realization, she continued to pursue her dream of traveling to the desert and meeting her son face to face.

She wasn't the only mother who'd been living on this type of dream. When Kamel's son Mustafa agreed to go with her, life pulsed anew through her veins, and she took off to see the men and women in Mit Suhayl, al-Balashun, and Qarmala whose sons were also missing. On the day they had agreed upon, they accompanied Mas'ada, escorted by a number of their sons and grandsons, on a journey that ended in the villages of Ismailiya west of the Suez Canal, which was as far as civilians were allowed to go.

They encountered a motley mix of people who were neither peasants nor Bedouins, and who told them heroic tales of how they'd duped Israeli soldiers and provided shelter to fleeing Egyptian soldiers. After listening impatiently to their stories, the listeners produced pictures of their missing loved ones.

"Have you seen this son of mine, sir?" they asked.

"Maybe, Hagga." There were no answers to quench the fire in the questioners' hearts—nothing but recommendations of new trackers and more treks which, once she and her companions had learned the way, wouldn't require them to be escorted by their grandchildren. But every journey left them more confused than they had been on the one before. She didn't stop until her grandson Ali returned legless from the armed clashes that had begun after the Naksa in an attempt to wear down the enemy. She now restricted herself to exchanging visits on holidays and religious occasions with fellow searchers-turned-friends. Like her, they were worn out, and had begun coordinating trips to Mecca for the major or minor pilgrimage in hopes that the fire in their bellies might be quenched by the chance to plead their cause at the tomb of the beloved Prophet.

Not once in his life had Salama chosen the wrong time to do anything. But he did choose the wrong time to die.

He had been lying on his deathbed, propped up by Mas'ada, as his half-brother Mahmoud, Hagga Mubarka, and the hunchback monitored his feeble panting, when suddenly the television interrupted the program that was on and began broadcasting Qur'anic recitations.

He pushed away the glass of lemonade that Mas'ada was holding for him, so she dipped a couple of fingers in the glass and wet his lips. He gestured to those gathered around him and they laid him back down. Then he belched deeply and fell still. Mahmoud closed his eyes, murmuring a prayer, while Mas'ada pulled the blanket up over his face. At that very instant the recitation on the television stopped and a quavering voice rang out, "Fellow citizens, humanity has lost one of the most munificent men who ever lived, one of the most beloved men, one of the most courageous men, one of the most steadfast men: President Gamal Abdel Nasser. . . ."

The voice disappeared beneath a roar that began shaking the windowpanes like the low-flying aircraft that al-Ish had come to know so well. No one stayed inside, despite the darkness that had enveloped the village from the power outage. As Ali flung himself off his wheelchair, his sobs and the wailing of the girls inside the mansion blended with the roar of the shouting in the streets, while the adults who had been attending Salama froze before his lifeless body.

Just as they did when they were waiting for the body of one of their slain sons to arrive from a distant city, people stayed outdoors all night. Elderly men and women occupied the stone benches in the streets and alleyways, and the young people went walking down the road outside al-Ish. They knew, of course, that no hearse would be arriving with a corpse. However, the tragedy had restored the state of solidarity that had disappeared from al-Ish after the summer of the fires, and after floods had become a thing of the past with the construction of the High Dam: the nose ring with which Abdel Nasser had twisted the recalcitrant Nile's neck and reined it in.

The next morning, the drummer passed with difficulty through the weeping crowds, who were surprised at his seemingly unbalanced behavior, since the death of the great leader required no drummer to announce it, and no one listened to him as he cried Salama's name.

When the body was taken to the mosque, all the men of al-Ish prayed over it, but only by coincidence.

The imam broke into sobs as he led the prayer in absentia for the spirit of "the immortal leader Gamal Abdel Nasser," and, in an addition that no one noticed, he said, "and the spirits of any other deceased Muslims present."

Neither the imam nor those repeating after him properly enunciated a single word of their recitation and prayer. When the prayer was over, Salama's son and grandsons gathered to carry his bier, which had become as light as a feather and swung back and forth with ease over the crowd. Noticing that his father was about to fly away, Abd al-Maqsud began crying, "La ilaha illa Allah, There is no god but God!"

"It's a miracle, everybody!" he insisted. "Allahu akbar! God is greatest! God is greatest!"

The pallbearers began swaying rhythmically with the weightless bier, uttering "Allahu akbar, God is greatest!" all the way, and as they approached the cemetery, the crowd began to thin. When they removed the green silk cover, they didn't find the body. Rather, the chest was filled with freshly picked cotton. Mahmoud then realized that his half-brother's coffin had been switched accidentally with the symbolic coffin of the leader. Covering it up again, they went running in all directions in search of the body that was being carried about by sobbing mourners.

There were many people whose memories didn't register Salama's death. When they had a dispute to resolve, whether it was an argument, the distribution of a bequest, or the rights of a divorced woman, one of them might refuse to let Mahmoud rule on it and insist instead on appealing to "the senior mayor." If Mas'ada attended a wake, the women who had gathered to offer their condolences would ask her about the senior mayor's health. And some of his grandchildren would mistakenly write his name as the head of the family when they were filling out conscription forms or applying for a job. Even so, his death weighed heavily on the mansion, bringing poignantly to mind all the deaths that had preceded it.

"He was stolen from us," said his half-brother, who was more convinced than anyone else that Salama had been the village's only true mayor, and that whatever he himself had accomplished in the post had been nothing but assistance in the things Salama hadn't had the strength to do any more. His son Abd al-Maqsud and his grandchildren felt they'd been remiss toward him in his final years. They hadn't appreciated his unspoken grief over Adel, and even though they could see him going steadily downhill, they imagined somehow that he would always be around. They would see him sitting for hours on his bench watching people come in and out, and some wouldn't even bother to greet him. He would get drowsy, spring to attention long enough to brush flies off his face with a calf-tail flyswatter, then doze off again.

The only person who sat with him was his grandson Ali, who would get from the veranda to the garden by wheeling himself with his hands down the ramp they'd installed specially for him along part of the staircase. After speeding down the ramp like someone driving a race car, he screeched to a halt in front of his grandfather, who sat napping on the bench, and who woke in a panic to the sound of its brakes.

"Hope you had a nice nap, Hagg!" Ali hailed him.

Hagg Salama glanced down at the dark-brown stubs beneath Ali's gauze-like gilbab. Seeing the pitying look in his eyes, Ali said playfully, "Thank God part of me got back to you. Isn't that better than nothing?"

The grandfather eyed his grandson in stupefaction, amazed at the determination in his eyes as he talked to him about his basic training and the spirit that had come to life in the army.

"Spirit? They act like a bunch of wimps while people's sons are dying. And you say 'spirit'?" the grandfather shot back.

"All that's changed," Ali replied.

Incredulous, Salama waved his hand dismissively.

"I didn't like that man when he came to al-Ish."

Ali laughed. "You were as excited as all get-out, Grandpa!"

"I had to act that way. After all, one's got to be a good host. Besides, how would you know? How old were you then?"

Ali couldn't get him to budge from his position. When the radio interrupted its broadcast to announce that Lieutenant General Abd al-Mun'im Riyad, Army Chief of Staff, had been martyred at the last point of contact with the enemy, Ali turned impetuously to his grandfather as though he'd won a bet.

"So was he being a wimp too?"

When Ali finished his final year in the Faculty of Engineering, he'd volunteered in the army like his paternal cousins and millions of other young men, dreaming of nothing but revenge. After all, the blow that had left a martyr in every family had to be returned.

After basic training he joined the Army Corps of Engineers and took part in constructing the epic "missile wall," under bombardment by enemy aircraft. They eventually succeeded in establishing the line of defense, which was a major step toward the hoped-for revenge, since it put a stop to Israel's capricious sorties into Egyptian airspace.

Ali wasn't able to talk his grandfather out of his opinions, which he claimed to be the fruit of life experience rather than mere illusions. His industry and his business had both gone downhill under the Free Officers' Movement. He'd lost a brother and a son in wars they'd entered without adequate preparation, one of his grandsons had come home crippled, and he didn't know what had become of the others. Sometimes one of them would come back on a brief furlough or pass through for a few hours, but they weren't enough to assuage his mother's longing, even though she might manage to feed him a home-cooked meal.

Sitting uneasily in his seat like an awkward guest, the young man would say, "The battalion's being transferred, and the commander gave me permission to come say hello." He would look at his watch more than he looked at the people who were talking with him. Then he would get up and start hugging them as if it were their last farewell.

Ali was the only person Salama confided in about his anguish over Adel's absence. He saw no point in Mas'ada's trips. At the same time, he didn't want to compound her grief. Every time she came back from an excursion, he would listen to her stories, envying the gleam of hope in her eyes. He'd come to fear war more than he feared making problems with any of the families in al-Ish.

Little by little with the passing of the days, Salama began losing his spark. However, up to the very end he remained conscious of himself, and it embarrassed him to drool or make an inappropriate gesture. Consequently, he began eating alone, and in all his interactions, even with his grandchildren, he observed proper etiquette. In fact, he had better manners than a lot of other people. Once, for example, he noticed Mahmoud's son Nagi furtively pointing a camera at him, hoping to get a candid shot.

"Are you going to take my picture, Nagi?" he asked, as the young man waved to him, still aiming the camera in his direction. "Well, then," he went on, "aren't you supposed to ask permission?"

Nagi often told his colleagues at the hospital about the failing Salama's comment, stressing that plenty of college graduates weren't aware of the right that his uncle had so astutely defended.

"If I were a poet, I would have written a book of poems about your grandfather as big as *The Arabian Nights*," Mayor Mahmoud said to Ali and the granddaughters after Salama's death, which had turned into something of a surgical operation that had removed his final years of weakness. All they remembered of him now were the years of his triumph: standing at the head of a line of workers, handing out their weekly wages; ruling on thorny legal issues among the region's notables as a judge whose verdict was considered the final word; or coming back from the mansion victorious over the ghosts.

However, the life Salama had planted in the mansion had begun to wither, and the scent of death emanated from every corner: from the neglected garden, from the dark rooms whose windows had been damaged by the sun and the rain, and from the kitchen, which had fallen out of use now that the women had replaced it with a stove they'd built in one corner of the garden, where lizards would hop about, then disappear into the piles of firewood next to the stove and among the cakes of manure the women stored for use as fuel.

Mubarka went back to eulogizing Salem, Mas'ada went back to eulogizing Adel, and Zayna spent her time listening to a radio program that broadcast people's messages to each other: "From Faysal Abu Awwad to his family in Khan Yunis: 'We're all right here. Please let us know how you are!'" She would listen with all her senses, and when she heard names such as al-Ma'zun, al-Bal'awi, Hamduna, and others, she would brighten up, expecting the next message that came on to be one from Ziyad or Riyad. Nobody could convince her that the messages were from refugees who had fled after the Naksa of 1967, not the Nakba of 1948.

"Naksa, Nakba—what difference does it make? The Ma'zuns, the Hijjawis, and the Bal'awis were our neighbors in Majdal!" said Zayna, her eyes tearing up. Mahmoud's daughter Mubarka and Kamel's daughter Samiha, who had both completed their educations without being proposed to by anyone, either from al-Ish or from among their classmates, began rocking Zayna comfortingly. The younger Mubarka had found a job as an accountant at the cotton gin in Minya al-Qamh, happy for the chance to escape for a few hours a day from the mournful women at the mansion, while Samiha worked in al-Ish as a teacher at Martyr Salem School. When Mubarka saw her granddaughter approaching with her tall, willowy figure and the swanlike neck she'd inherited from her mother, she bemoaned the fact that her beauty was beginning to fade. In the moments when she managed to forget her sorrows, she might chide the girl good-naturedly, saying, "So, don't you know how to catch yourself a man?"

"What can I do, Grandma? All the fellows that could see me have been taken away to the army!"

The granddaughter's jocular response to her grandmother was the literal truth. The only people left in al-Ish were women, children, men old enough to be her father, the blind, or young men who'd come back disabled from the war front.

"A girl's lamp only shines for a while. Then it goes out," Grandma Mubarka said. She was the only woman who noticed the two girls wilting, one after the other. However, they were no exception among the girls of al-Ish, including Samira al-Gahsh, who had finished a diploma in commerce and now sat waiting for Adel's return, more certain than ever that he would be back. She'd sparked gossip among the small village's women, who were amazed and bewildered at her determination.

"Maybe he went too far with her before he left."

The girl paid no attention to the women's prattle, persevering in a wait that had been difficult at first, but that had grown easier when the suitors had stopped knocking at her door after all the young men had been conscripted and she was relieved of her mother's pressure. This way she had time to write him a new letter every night. The letters started piling up, but she said they would get to him some day, even if they got there late the way other people's letters had when Adel was the postman.

People in the village received the announcement of the crossing with caution, fearful that it might be a new ruse. The deception they had witnessed in the early days of the Naksa was still fresh in their minds, and the Israeli radio broadcast that could be heard clearly in al-Ish asserted every day that if Egypt risked an attempt to storm the mine-infested land barrier on the eastern bank of the Suez Canal, the canal would turn into a lake of blood filled with Egyptian soldiers' napalm-roasted flesh. However, people heard a ring of truth in the announcements that followed, and no Israeli denials were forthcoming, so they began to celebrate.

Despite his uncertainty as to whether all the family's soldiers would return from the front, al-Ish's last mayor rejoiced in the settling of scores. Enervated from fasting and the noonday heat, he thought at first that what he'd heard was a hallucination heralding the onset of a coma, since he hadn't heeded his doctor's warning not to fast. He didn't get up from the sofa where he lay, and didn't ask anyone if he'd heard right. But when he saw everyone else in a state of elation, he knew for certain that what he'd heard had reached their ears as well, and that he wasn't dreaming or suffering the delirium of death.

"Hopefully we'll be celebrating our boys' homecoming soon," Mayor Mahmoud said to his mother as she sat massaging his cold, heavy limbs. She seemed younger than he did, as time had chosen to hone her body rather than weaken it. She was shrinking, and her bones were becoming more delicate. However, she remained as solid as ever, and wished she could suffer in his place.

"If only He'd accept a substitute," she muttered to herself. Then she fell silent, remembering the loved ones she'd buried and recoiling at the thought of surviving to bury another son along with the grandchildren who'd been lost.

When the war ended, the soldiers began coming home one after another in fleeting visits, after which they would go back to their units to complete their discharge procedures. Whenever one came back, his mother would embrace him as quietly as possible, whether for fear that others would envy her son; out of consideration for the feelings of her sisters-in-law, who still knew nothing about their own sons; or out of respect for the dying grandfather, who no longer woke up for more than a few minutes at a time, and to whom the stir caused by the grandsons' return felt like little more than a dream.

The only one who still hadn't come home was Kamel's son Mustafa. His father began making daily trips to Zagazig, where lists of those martyred or missing were posted as information on the soldiers became available. He would leave right after the dawn prayer so that by eight o'clock he could be waiting in front of the Governorate Administration Building before its doors opened and crowds gathered. Not finding his son's name on either list, he would come back with bags of fruit, telling his wife Zahra that he'd met people who had reassured him that their son was all right. He had to make a huge effort to look happy, since his appearance when he got home determined whether Zahra would hold herself together or fall into an epileptic coma. If she went into a coma, she wouldn't recover until the next day. Then she would be limp as a rag for several days, with a blue tongue that would hurt if she ate anything.

Kamel made a vow that if his son came home safe and sound, he would rebuild the Silent Sheikh's shrine, which had fallen into disrepair, its roof now collapsed on top of the grave. Every day that went by without news of his son robbed Kamel of some of his serenity, and rather than bringing fruit and kunafa, he began bringing coffee beans and sets of porcelain coffee cups.

"Where are you, Mustafa? Answer me!" he would shout into the night, unable to get back to sleep until the morning light had begun stealing in. Then off he would go to Zagazig once more. Meanwhile, the coffee cups were being passed around at the mayor's wake. Befuddled, Kamel stood there receiving the people who'd come to offer their condolences, responding to them exultantly when he remembered that the wake was for his uncle and not his son.

One day several months later, as Kamel was poring over the lists of the names of the missing in Zagazig, a soldier in uniform came knocking. Zahra answered the door with disheveled hair and wearing nothing but a house dress.

"Mustafa Bey sends his greetings, and says to tell you he'll be coming back soon," the soldier announced. Grabbing hold of him, Zahra pinched his arm and his cheeks and ran her hands over him excitedly.

"Are you a human being or a jinni, brother?"

"I'm Mahmoud al-Sayem, madame. Mustafa is my commanding officer, and I swear to God he's fine and on his way home."

With difficulty he extricated himself from her grip before her cry rang out and she fell to the floor, stiff as a board. They learned later that the soldier had been on his way back from the siege of Deversoir, which had dampened the heady effect of the initial victory since the Israelis had managed to take advantage of a gap in the Egyptian offense and encircle the Third Army. The extent of the losses suffered by the besieged army wasn't known precisely, as a result of which the names of its officers and soldiers hadn't been listed among either the martyrs or the missing. After the disengagement talks the survivors were identified and prisoners of war were exchanged. Hence, Mustafa's return was now just a matter of time, since no soldier from al-Ish would ever have joked about such a thing.

Kamel and Zahra went days and nights on end without sleep, unable to rest until they'd seen the whites of his eyes. When they did see him at last, it was with difficulty that they recognized

Mustafa inside the folds of a field uniform with eagles on its broad shoulders, and whose waist, cinched with a leather belt, you could have encircled with the fingers of one hand. When they knew for certain that the skeleton that had hugged them was their son, they could let themselves cry, and they both slept for three days and nights, leaving it to others to put flesh back on Mustafa's bones with three meals a day of meat and fatta.

When Kamel woke up after making up for his long months of fear-induced insomnia, he decided that the first thing he would do was fulfill the vow he had made. The shrine looked like a caved-in mound of dirt amid the red brick and concrete houses that had begun replacing those constructed from unbaked brick and wood. Nor was the sheikh's grave in any better condition. Kamel single-handedly removed the bones he found in the briny soil, which confirmed the stories the people of al-Ish had passed down about the swamp on which the village had been built. After carrying the basket of bones to the farmhouse, he went back to help tear down the old structure and dig the new foundation. A tractor came to help move the gravel, sand, and red brick, and the building began going up. After the building was finished and decorated with green neon lights, the bones were placed back inside the shrine and they held a celebration in which all the popular vocalists in Sharqiya took turns singing. Not long afterward the same singers were back in al-Ish to perform at the returned soldiers' group wedding: a rowdy celebration that made up for the years of doleful silence.

"Marry your relatives, and we can keep everything in the family." This was Hagga Mubarka's point of view, and the returned soldiers complied with her wishes. Each of them chose one of his paternal cousins. Abd al-Maqsud's son Ahmad married his uncle Mahmoud's daughter Mubarka, his son Yusuf married his uncle Kamel's daughter Samiha, Kamel's son Mansur married Wafiq Asfur's daughter Badi'a, and his brother Mustafa married Badi'a's sister Nagat. The only one who married outside the family was Ali, who asked for the hand of a poor illiterate girl. As for Nagi Mahmoud, he persevered in his strike against "entering the prison," even though, being his parents' only son, he'd been exempted from conscription and could have married before any of them. After graduation he'd gone to work as a doctor at the Qasr al-Aini Hospital in Cairo, and, like the other young men in the family, had been absent from al-Ish due to the state of emergency hospitals had witnessed throughout the war of attrition that preceded the victory of October 1973.

After completing a circuit of the village, the wedding procession came to a halt in the courtyard in front of the mansion, and the singers took their places on a farm tractor trailer that had been set up as a stage next to the mansion wall. Beside the stage was a row of chairs for the brides and grooms, and Ali sat next to his bride in his wheelchair. When she approached the carpet under their feet, Ali's bride took off her shoes and carried them. Ali grabbed the shoes and tossed them under her feet, indicating that she should put them on. However, she stayed on the edge of her chair the entire time, awed to find herself seated among the members of his family.

The group wedding was a cause of envy for some, and a source of amusement for others.

"So, we've got a family that rides itself!"

"Well, isn't that better than riding strangers?"

Figuring out how each bride and groom were related to each other became a favorite pastime for people as they spent their evenings on the stone benches outside their houses or next to the waterwheels. Paying no attention to people's comments, the soldiers who had returned with the banners of victory proceeded to conduct themselves in bed with a highly advanced combat doctrine and a reticence their fathers had known nothing about. Things were so quiet that Mubarka would come out at night and press her ear to the bedroom doors, but hear no movement. But, when signs of pregnancy began to appear, she knew things were proceeding normally, and interpreted the silence to mean that war had taught the young men to be circumspect.

"What's wrong with the girls, then?" she wondered. Then she thought about it again, and remembered that she herself had never screamed or shouted. It was her men that had made all the noise. As for Mas'ada's snoring, the only thing that made the people of al-Ish forget about it was her wailing over Adel's absence. In the end Mubarka had to concede that times had changed, and that the poor things had been ruined by schools and wars. However, she abandoned her regrets when, nine months later to the day, the cries of death were banished from the mansion by the cries of life.

They dubbed the newborns "the generation of 1973," and those who had come back from the war carried on with their merry indolence. There would be heated discussions over meals and exchanges of battle stories that went on until bedtime. It was easy to see that none of them had taken the war lightly. Ahmad Abd al-Maqsud swore that at noon on the day of the crossing, he'd been climbing the net that had been spread by the commandos along the Bar Lev Line. He said he'd seen angels next to him, scrambling over the sand without a net, and that it was the angels who had repelled the first shots fired by the Israeli armored cars.

"With my own eyes I saw an angel hugging the main gun of a tank. He was being riddled with bullets, but he kept holding on like a leech."

Seeing Yusuf wink in disbelief, Ahmad swore angrily that when the Israelis saw the sight, they'd been terrified, since the entity that was holding on to their tank's main gun was deflecting the bullets without bleeding a drop and without falling off, even though they kept spinning the gun around violently. Then they opened the turret and fled.

Yusuf said to Mustafa, "Well, I didn't see anything. Did you see any angels, Mr. Major?"

"When we were crossing I didn't have time to look. After we were surrounded, I had time, but it's ridiculous to think that the angels would have been surrounded like us!" Mustafa quipped.

Muttering a prayer for God's forgiveness, Ahmad looked at his watch, then withdrew to go to the mosque. As if to reinforce the difference between them, he started letting his beard grow out and avoided mixed company. Then he asked his wife Mubarka to cover up and not to mix with the other men in the family.

"Covering up I can understand," she said. "But these are my brothers and my brothers' children."

"A brother is one thing and a cousin is another. And you'd be allowed to marry one of your cousins." Others in the family condemned his attitude. At the same time, they were aware of the fact that the ties between them were beginning to weaken. But this wasn't the only reason they'd begun trickling one by one out of al-Ish. Over the course of three years, the mansion and the two other houses had been filled with children who all looked alike as though they'd come off a single factory production line. After all, they were the product of what Nagi, likening their intermarriage to single-cell division, jokingly referred to as "self-mating."

They didn't have anything left to sell in order to feed this many mouths, so they began looking for jobs, and letters of appointment in schools, universities, and companies began coming in.

After renting apartments in Cairo and Zagazig, each of the young men took his family and the furniture he'd bought when he got married and moved them to his own apartment. They agreed that they would gather in al-Ish on the weekends. However, their visits started tapering off until they only came twice a year: on Eid al-Fitr and Eid al-Adha.

No one from the generation of those who'd come back from the war was left in al-Ish except Ali, who went on living in the mansion. Having decided to reopen the little store that had been built into the mansion wall, he swept it out and cleared the cobwebs off the shelves his grandfather Salama had installed in his fabric shop. All he needed was to replace the yardstick with a scale in order to start up business in his store, which sold a combination of grocery items and animal feed. But he soon went bankrupt. He restocked the store, and went bankrupt a second time. So he closed it up and went back to being unemployed and depressed until Nagi volunteered to get it up and running again.

The merchandise sold well, but the income brought in by the little grocery store wasn't enough to make up for what was consumed by his wife Hanem, whose mouth was in constant motion. She would eat anything. The third time around he started to avoid stocking the store with tempting items such as sugar, tahiniya, hard candy, and other sweets, even though they were the things that sold best in all the grocery stores. But as far as Hanem was concerned, anything and everything was edible. She would munch on things like legumes, broad beans, and green beans in the same way she munched on roasted watermelon seeds, pumpkin seeds, and peanuts.

"She puts the seed in her mouth and lets the shell come out her nose," Ali said, likening her way of eating nonstop, even when she was conversing with a customer, to the way a winnowing machine works. Meanwhile, he continued to live through periods of bankruptcy from which he would be rescued by his brothers and cousins. When one of them visited al-Ish, he would offer to revive the store out of his own pocket or with help from his brothers, knowing full well that in a few months' time it would run out of money all over again.

S adat walked down the airplane steps after his return from Jerusalem, behind him ten prisoners of war who'd been listed among the missing. The camera began panning over them. Mas'ada gasped and sank to the floor when she saw Adel's face filling the television screen in front of her.

The president was proud of his trip, feeling that he'd achieved a new victory by going to the Knesset and challenging the Israelis to pursue peace. So as not to arrive empty-handed, he'd taken with him an Israeli prisoner he'd pardoned, and the Israelis had responded with a gift of their own: they'd released ten out of the hundreds of prisoners of war whose existence they'd refused to acknowledge for an entire decade.

When Adel arrived in al-Ish, they didn't want to upset him with the news of his father's death. However, he didn't give them the satisfaction of pitying him. He seemed already to know of Salama's and Mahmoud's deaths, and the first thing he did before resting was visit their graves.

Nor was he surprised by the effects of time on all the other people he'd known. He wasn't amazed to find that the girl he'd left a mere fifteen-year-old was still waiting for him. In fact, in the presence of the family members gathered around him, he asked her for his letters.

"I'll read one every day, just the way you wrote them."

As he sniffed the bundle of letters, whose number he knew precisely, she wondered how he could possibly have known. He also knew exactly how Samira's body would be when he saw her again. He knew that her nipples, which had been a couple of pointed bumps that might have belonged to a boy or a girl, were now the size of a couple of broad beans. The only thing he hadn't been expecting was the delicately braided pubic hair that made him shriek with delight, while at the same time leaving him with the pained sense of having been duped like a professional gambler whose expectations hadn't played out.

The Israelis, who had discovered as soon as they captured him that he was just an untrained private, hadn't persisted in interrogating him about the war. They hadn't pulled out his fingernails the way they had with officers whose status they knew despite the fact that their field uniforms were devoid of any stripes that might give away their ranks. However, they had resorted to all manner of both harshness and leniency in hopes of discovering the secret behind his peculiar behavior. They questioned him and had him examined by prison physicians, professors of psychology, and American medical missions. He wasn't aware of the presence of anyone around him, whether he was resting, in an inspection line, having a meal, being checked for personal hygiene, or in any other situation. He carried out instructions like a robot, his feelings somewhere else. He would be quiet, then suddenly start laughing and applauding. Then he would shake an invisible hand in the air and dust off his clothes. He might laugh while a buddy of his was being tortured before his very eyes. Or he might look annoyed, knitting his brow furiously or shaking his finger while others were singing at a recreational gathering. He might fall asleep under gushing water or while they were spraying him for lice. The guards would listen in as he engaged in polite conversation with the air and look on as his trousers swelled between his thighs until one of them, enraged by his eccentricity, would give him a swift kick.

He remained a riddle because, unbeknownst to his captors, he would start his day by setting up an imaginary siga board, then spend the whole day playing against an imaginary opponent. If he won a round he would clap, and if he lost, he would start to rave nonsensically, rejecting the outcome with his usual obscenities. When it was time to close the post office in al-Ish, he would shake his opponent's hand and walk back to the mansion to eat and rest a bit. After joking for a while with his mother and father, he would head eagerly for Samira's house, certain that she would be there waiting for him every night. He would pour the sweetest, lewdest words he could think of into her ears, causing her body to soften and turning its curves into putty in his hands. The wait was pouring more warm clay into her body, leaving him with the task of slimming down her waist, scraping a bit off her back and thighs and applying it to her buttocks, then removing some from her abdomen and adding it to her breasts. He would do this until he developed blisters on his fingertips that swelled up and burst, though the doctors at the Israeli prison couldn't find any cause for them.

Neither Adel nor Samira needed the week that Nadrat had requested in order to get ready for her only daughter's wedding celebration. Samira refused to let anyone lay a hand on her to remove the hair on her body. Her mother, surprised at her daughter's sudden bashfulness, prepared a sticky paste of lemon, sugar, and water and begged her to let her remove her hair for her.

"If you'd only let me do your arms and your legs."

Samira curled her lip in refusal.

"All right, then. Do it yourself!"

She brought the neighbor women and female relatives to talk to her, but the bride wouldn't give in. She wanted the groom to see the effect the wait had had on her body. However, after ten years of contemplation he'd arrived at a knowledge of everything, and could perceive all the things he hadn't been able to see. Even the feel of her skin under his fingers was no different from what he had expected. He leaned over and sniffed between her thighs to see whether the aroma was the same intoxicating blend of lavender and fermented fruit that used to fill his nostrils during the nights when he would conjure images of her in his cell. The delicate braids hindered his ability to sail with his nose down the brook that lay camouflaged between her thighs. She laughed, aroused by the pain of having his nose stumble through the braids she had tied together into a chastity belt, leaving him the task of unfastening it with his teeth.

She'd gotten the idea from a picture of an African girl's head that she'd seen in a magazine. Impressed with the delicacy of the tiny braids that Egyptian girls knew nothing about, she'd taken to braiding her own hair in her body's most hidden region. She'd done the braids in horizontal rows from the place where the pubic hair begins at the top and down to the upper edge of the vagina, and in two lengthwise rows along the two "riverbanks." She'd also gathered the hair that grew along the insides of her upper thighs into the braids that extended along and across the two banks.

He pulled the braids back on both sides, revealing the defiant rosy nub that now butted up against his nose. The moment he touched it, a fountain of liquid gushed out and drenched his face. It wet the braids and streams flowed down over her thighs. He began licking up the viscous liquid, sucking it out of the braids with his teeth and his lips. This copious outpouring granted her the divinity he had already recognized, and which had robbed him of his freedom even before he fell captive to the Israelis.

During their courtship a wet spot had been obvious the minute the two of them began their fondling and caressing, holding their breath lest they rouse her sleepy mother. When Samira had to stand up to see him off, she would back out of the room or gather her gilbab between her legs. However, it had never occurred to him that she would hold on to the coarse hair whose tufts he had run his hands over when they were still nothing but a bit of soft fluff.

"I was tiding myself over till you came back," she said simply as he snipped off a braid with his teeth. He grasped it between his index finger and thumb and held it up to look at it. She showed him how she could undo the braids, comb the hair, then braid it again without looking at her hands.

They spent the time exchanging the innovations they'd collected in their heads over the course of ten years until they went limp, arms and legs intertwined, like a pile of ashes in which nothing was visible but two pairs of blinking, cat-like eyes.

She reached under the pillow and brought out a silver necklace, which she swung back and forth in the air the way he'd done with her braid. One side of it consisted of intertwining letters engraved on a metallic surface, while the other bore a picture of him enclosed in glass. She'd usually worn it with its metallic face showing. When a suitor came calling, she would greet him with a welcoming smile as her mother had instructed her to. However, as she approached him with the cup of tea, she would flip the necklace over in such a way that the suitor alone could see Adel's picture on the other side. As she withdrew, she would stealthily turn the necklace over again. This brief glimpse of her true love would be sufficient to send the suitor to some other girl. By the time all the potential suitors had come around and she'd sent them away by wearing the necklace with Adel's picture showing, her wait had come to an end without her having taken it off even to bathe.

With their riotous displays of affection, Adel and Samira brought back memories for Mas'ada of her times with Adel's uncle Ali. With the winds of deprivation still whistling in their ears, they would do it anywhere, any time. Adel began urging her to make up for his long absence by working to catch up with his nephews, who had followed the generation of victory (the generation of 1973) with a second batch of newborns.

"We'll outdo them with the generation of peace!" he said jokingly as he pressed his ear to her tummy after she told him her period had stopped coming. And in fact, Samira not only caught up with them, but surpassed them. She used no birth control, happy with the kittens she was bringing into the world. With green eyes like hers and Adel's, they looked like a family of settlers who'd been left behind accidentally by some foreign colony that had established itself in al-Ish, then gone its way.

He went back to his job at the post office as supervisor to three employees who had been appointed in his absence. They'd expanded the office's scope of activity so that it was no longer just a place to send and receive letters, but was, in addition, a cashier's office that disbursed retirement pay and pensions for martyrs' families. However, he didn't go into the office, but resumed his custom of sitting outside with his remaining old friends, including his father-in-law, who had been forced to give up smoking after suffering a stroke that had left his mobility impaired.

Adel changed nothing in his daily routine, and when his signature was required, the employees would bring the papers outside for him to sign. After a number of investigations and penalties for negligence in relation to a contractual obligation he knew nothing about, he left the Postal Service, spitting on the investigators who didn't believe what he said even though the Israelis themselves had believed him when he denied knowledge of anything connected to the war.

Mansur intervened and got him a job as a conductor on a public bus. However, he only held the job for a few months, since the company couldn't tolerate the confusion and losses that he caused on every line assigned to him. He revealed a talent for forming friendships in villages he'd never seen before, and his new friends would ask him to put in a word for them with the driver to convince him to stop longer than he was supposed to at this or that station.

"Just long enough for the boy to have a bite to eat," someone would say, asking him to wait until the duck his wife had slaughtered for her conscripted son had finished roasting in the oven, since she wouldn't let him go until he'd eaten some of her cooking. He might help someone get on the bus with a sheep that would bleat and urinate in the aisle. A coffee shop owner along the way would invite him for a cup of tea and a drag of opium, and if one of the passengers objected, he would shout, "What are you so hot and bothered about? Have you got an appointment to keep at the ministry?"

He wrought such havoc with the bus schedule that nobody knew any more when the bus would come or leave. And as if that weren't enough, he would occupy the first seat like a VIP and sit there making fun of apprehensive passengers, some of whom were riding the bus for the first time in their lives. If someone vomited from motion sickness he would curse and spit, and when passengers called him to collect their fare, he would put them off again and again, until finally he would bellow, "So is your money burning a hole in your pockets?"

After a period of going back and forth free of charge, transportation company officials started to think people weren't riding on that line. Then the inspector boarded the bus and, finding it filled to capacity, discovered that the problem lay in the lazy, disgruntled conductor. They docked him several days' pay and transferred him to another line, where he put on the very same act. And things went on this way until a decision was made to fire him.

Sensing Samira's exasperation, Adel had no choice but to learn an occupation that represented the cruelest possible insult to his good looks and elegance. He learned to repair kerosene heaters, and applied himself to his work with remarkable discipline. Clad in an apron, he would spend hours in front of heaters that blackened his complexion with kerosene smoke, then come home to Samira at the end of the day. Time had done nothing to diminish Samira's beauty. But it had buried Adel beneath a layer of distress thicker than the layer of soot on his face.

He gave up his evenings out and began struggling with the pittance he earned to keep his children looking respectable. This time, however, the life he had opposed so stubbornly for so long decided to oppose him with the same stubbornness, flooding the markets with Chinese-made wick heaters that quickly replaced the heaters that required users to pump air into them.

Then one day Samira woke up and didn't find him next to her. They looked for him, but he was nowhere to be found. People who traveled to various cities would come back with stories. Someone might swear he'd seen him working as a porter in the vegetable market, but no sooner had his nephews gone to the market to look for him than someone else would swear he'd seen him selling combs, needles, and greeting-card envelopes on a bus, and that when their eyes met, Adel had been so embarrassed he'd jumped off the bus while it was still moving.

Month after month and year after year she waited for him to come back, all the while having to endure the reproach of her mother and her aunt, who prided herself on her foresight.

"This is just plain irresponsibility. The war was a different situation," said her mother. Unable to go on receiving charity from the family when the rising cost of living was crushing everyone, Samira asked for an administrative divorce after he'd been gone for five years. But on the very day she remarried, he showed up in al-Ish to cry outside her window.

The new husband's complaints to Adel's nephews didn't stop him from circling his house all night long. Consequently, the man ended up having to divorce her and go back to his barren wife, giving up the dream of having children, which was why he'd married Samira. However, over the course of the six months they'd spent together, he'd grown attached to her children. So now it was his turn to circle the mansion in order to see them, and to wait for them when they were on their way to and from school.

For the second time Adel placed his hand in that of Abd al-Sami' al-Gahsh as they recited the Fatiha and repeated after the ma'zun. Nothing in the marriage contract had changed but Samira's status, since she was no longer "a virgin of legal age," but "a previously married woman." After the ma'zun had left, Adel accompanied her back to the room that had witnessed their delirious ravings. It was the same room down to the last detail. However, neither of them found the person he or she had known before.

She didn't take off all her clothes the way she had done in the past so as to set him on fire all at once. She only took off her gilbab, revealing a red nightgown. Feeling the anguished, bitter

240

agitation that he might have experienced with a prostitute, he turned out the light and didn't look again at the nightgown, which framed details he didn't need his eyes to see. She lay down beside him, spreading her legs with the elegant politeness of a woman who knows the rules of hospitality. He reached down and touched the softness of the hair-free spot, thinking back ruefully on the happy surprise of the braids on their first wedding night. He took off his clothes and tore her nightgown with a feeling of vindictiveness more than anything else, then flung himself on top of her. He quickly went limp, drowning in her wetness, and collapsed at her side. He didn't know how to get her to talk about her marriage to the short man who was twenty years his senior, and thirty years her senior. He wished she would lie to him and tell him he hadn't touched her. He wished she would call him names, and make fun of his shortness or the bald spot that lay hidden under a turban that was half as long as he was tall. She knew what he wanted without his saying a word. However, she saw no need to speak ill of a man who had never done anything to hurt her.

Jealousy and the desire to spy retroactively on her nights with her former husband began to intensify, pouring fuel on his flames to the point where he went back to seducing her wherever they were: in secluded corners of the house, in the bedroom, in the mansion's dusty courtyard. It looked as though they were getting back into sync with each other. But it was a fire devoid of pleasure, which flared up quickly and went out just as quickly, leaving nothing in its wake but the taste of sorrow. Then he began questioning her directly. However, she never mentioned the man's name with anything but the most profound respect, doing her utmost to avoid revealing any of their intimate secrets. She would talk about Hagg Sulayman's goodness, the way he used to play with her children, and how kind he'd been to them. She would allude to ordinary health problems he'd suffered from, but without saying enough for Adel to gather anything about his prowess in bed.

Adel's face registered an escalating rage.

"What do you want to know?" she asked, choking on her tears. She cried, and he cried with her, with the pity, disgust, and distress of someone whose wife has suffered the ordeal of being raped. At the same time, he remained as furious as ever with the woman about whom he had known every little thing when he was away in an Israeli prison, but whose six months with Hagg Sulayman al-Nuss remained shrouded in tomblike darkness.

Weary of the way Adel was constantly catching fire, then cooling off within moments, she began avoiding being alone with him anywhere. She tried to get him to think of looking for a new job rather than staying at the mansion and living off charity from his cousins and their sons. Once when Mansur, who'd become mayor of Minya al-Qamh, was visiting al-Ish, Samira placed a copy of her diploma in his hand and asked him for a job: "Anything that'll give me a few hours of rest from your uncle."

He got her a job at Minya al-Qamh's telephone exchange. She started commuting back and forth every day. She would come home exhausted, dying to see her children, and occupy herself with their needs. She also put on the headscarf and started praying regularly. When she finished her share of the housework, she would pick up the Qur'an and start reading aloud. Mubarka would correct her mistakes until finally, her patience running out, she would shoo her away, saying, "Get up, Little Miss Potty, and go see to your kids!"

After Hagg Mahmoud's death, al-Ish went back to being mayorless. It didn't revert to being unknown the way it had been before it was discovered by Muhammad Ali's mission in the early nineteenth century, but the government no longer saw any need to concern itself with the villages. Nor did al-Ish enjoy the state of equality it had experienced before the khedive established its place on the map. On the contrary, money earned by those who had gone to work in Saudi Arabia and the Gulf Emirates began pouring into the village during the summer vacations, one outcome of which was that the village's clay houses were leveled and digging was begun so that houses of red brick and concrete could be built in their places. When the Gulf states found themselves on the verge of bankruptcy after financing Iraq's war on Iran, then America's war on Iraq, the path to the east was closed. However, the path to the more generous Europe in the north opened up. With it came an increasingly fierce competition in which every new traveler had to outdo his predecessors in the height of the buildings he constructed. The new apartment buildings ranged from five to seven stories in height. Young men would lay their foundations, leave again to pump more money into them until they were finished, then come back and occupy one or two floors with their families. The windows of the upper stories would be left exposed to sun and rain and birds would nest in their balconies, which were so close to the ones across from them that they nearly touched.

When the village's remaining farmers sat outside on the stone benches, chatting after the midafternoon prayer, their conversations no longer revolved around seeds, harvests, or the best way to deal with a blight that had afflicted one of their crops. Instead they would talk about the prices of iron and cement and the circumferences of the pillars around which an escalating competition revolved. Engineers from al-Ish would come up with building designs, and contractors would implement them. In the process, they were never surprised by their clients' requests.

"I want you to put in twenty-two pillars," someone might say, and the engineer would know that the person simply wanted to have more pillars than his neighbor did, regardless of the area or height of the building, and regardless of the size of the pillars involved. And he would have no choice but to carry out the request; if he didn't, the client would go running to some other engineer.

A stroll down the streets of al-Ish would tell you which forlorn houses had no male children to tear them down and rebuild them or whose residents had emigrated to the city. Houses like these looked like shanties now engulfed by the neighborhoods that had gone up around them and the mounds of debris that had resulted from the razing of neighboring buildings. Reference to "the mansion" provoked ridicule of the yellow structure now hemmed in on all sides by high-rise apartment buildings. Its wall was in a state of collapse, and cats and dogs passed over it freely, rummaging about in search of something to eat amid piles of chicken feathers and the plastic bags that were constantly being dropped out the windows of the adjacent apartment buildings.

The old house, which still clung to the grandeur of the name "mansion," was the butt of the apartment dwellers' ridicule, not only because of its tumbledown state, but also because of the strangeness of the people who lived there. Among them were elderly women—the oldest of whom had sprouted new teeth as she stood on the threshold of her second century—and two men, one an invalid, the other crippled by a lack of resourcefulness. As for their children, poverty was visible in both their faces and their clothes.

After the grocery store went bankrupt for the last time and no one volunteered to get it started again, Adel and Ali grew closer than ever. They began spending their time together, each trying to approach the other's world. They learned how to play chess instead of siga, and Adel began looking at the books Ali kept on hand. He felt as though he was as handicapped as his nephew, who never once had been bitter or resentful over the loss of his legs and being deprived of the chance to work as an engineer. Rather, what pained Ali was his marriage to Hanem, which he considered the worst insult life could have dealt him. He felt ashamed when he saw the difference between his sons' appearance and way of conversing, and those of their uncles, Adel's sons. He was certain that it was due to the difference between the two mothers.

He'd despaired of improving their behavior or appearance, and when people criticized him for losing patience with them, he would say, "God says wealth and children are the adornment of this life, but my kids would be lousy adornment even for an orphanage!" Everything he taught them ended up being sabotaged by the ignorant woman he described as being "as tall as a black year is long." And if people teased him, telling him that he must love her, since otherwise he could divorce her, he would ask bitterly, "How's that? She's like an acacia tree that you can't get close to with all those thorns that come out from the bottom up!"

His antagonistic words also reflected a change in the equation between them. She'd abandoned the timidity with which she'd related to him at the beginning of their marriage, and instead of addressing him as "Bey" and "Bashmuhandis," she'd started calling him by his name. Then she got to the point where she would insult him directly and make fun of his handicap.

He started focusing on himself, working on making himself stylish and cultured. He would iron his clothes and ask his nephews to bring him books: novels, poetry collections, and books on politics and science. He would read about everything imaginable, not so much out of enjoyment as out of a desire to put Hanem down by reinforcing their differences. He began making attempts at short stories, poetry, and reflective essays that he would read to Adel. He would accost his cousins with them when they came on visits from Cairo, and hoped that they could help him find a way to publish them. He started writing to newspaper editors and reading the newspaper every day until finally he gave up hope and settled on composing satirical poems in which he lampooned Hanem. He would recite them to people he met, while she received them with a mixture of contempt and obliviousness to their insulting contents, though sometimes she reacted with pride for having become the subject of someone's poetry.

When Adel saw her tummy swelling with a new pregnancy, he would ask Ali how they managed to have sex in spite of their mutual loathing.

"The call of necessity, once a year," he would reply with convincing spontaneity, as though he himself had thought about this irony before. Meanwhile, he continued his downward spiral in relation to both her and his sons, who, like her, had the brains of a mule. Their lack of intelligence manifested itself in their poor school performance and their rudeness toward their teachers. However, Hanem no longer gave them a chance to make fun of his sayings, which had earned the status of proverbs in al-Ish. He'd dubbed her "Lady Shit Stick" and issued a "fatwa" to the effect that she wouldn't enter hellfire as a human being, but would be melted down and made into shoes for the infidel women who went there.

"So is that the only thing he's good at?" she would snap, then go on consolidating the foundations of her empire by having more sons. She would sleep late and leave them with their grandmothers, Mas'ada and Mubarka, who would feed them any old thing before they went to school, since sometimes all they had on hand was some bread, tea, and goat's milk. When the two grandmothers saw the invalid grandson dwindling away under the burden of five sons, Mubarka whispered to her, "Now that's enough kids, don't you think? Do you want to kill the guy?"

"I want a girl, and I'm going to have one. And if he's not up to it, well, it'll be easy enough to find somebody else to do the job!"

The two aging women concluded that Hanem was a problem without a solution. After seeing Ali's and Adel's children off to school, the two of them would sit together on the veranda's sagging floor. As though the two women had traded personalities, Mas'ada would stare wordlessly out at the meager space before her, trying to penetrate the tall apartment buildings and picture the horizon beyond them, while Mubarka sat talking to herself about all the things she hadn't talked about before. Replaying the tape of her life from the beginning, she would spend hours talking to her mother, reminiscing about Muntasir and Aunt Hamida, and commenting on scenes that no one but she had witnessed.

"He said, 'Could we find anybody better than you?' Why? Was I blind or crippled, you stupid man!"

She knew Ali's and Adel's sons by sight without remembering a single one's name. Even so, she never stopped asking about the boys and the young men who came back on visits with their fathers. If one replied that he was Yusuf Ahmad or Salama Mansur, she didn't seem to recall who they were talking about. In fact, she didn't even seem to hear their answers. After a few moments of silence she would ask the young man, "Haven't you seen your cousins Naguib and Gamal?"

"You mean my grandfather's sons, Hagga. They send you their greetings."

The young man would have learned from his older male relatives about his grandfather Salem's twins, who had migrated to Canada with Khircellia and her second husband.

Mubarka would hang on to the young man, who would bend down toward her so that she could kiss him. Then she would go back to her conversations with the dead. Suddenly becoming aware of the woman sitting next to her, her lips pursed in empathy, she asked suspiciously, "Who are you?"

"I'm Mas'ada, Hagga."

"Mas'ada? So why are you so quiet? Don't you snore any more, you loudmouth?"

"Weren't you a loudmouth yourself? Or am I the only one who screamed and hollered when it felt good down there?"

Knowing that Mubarka was about to start reminding her of her noisy lovemaking with Ali, she headed her off at the pass by saying suddenly, "It's almost time for the midafternoon prayer. Have you prayed the noon prayer, Hagga?"

"I've prayed till I'm blue in the face, honey!"

Mas'ada got up and took Mubarka by the hand to busy her with her ablutions and keep her from saying anything irreverent. Mubarka withdrew her hand from Mas'ada's and, patting her chest in apology, called out, "Zayna!"

Then she went in to wake the woman who had been silent for months.

After her mother's death Zayna had withdrawn completely, considering herself a stranger to the family and all of al-Ish. However, she would come back to sit with the two elderly women, grateful for their insistence on bringing her out of her isolation. She had worked diligently to establish ties with a generation of the family that knew nothing about "the pretty Palestinian," as they had always called her. However, from the time she learned of Riyad's martyrdom, she had stopped getting out of bed unless Mubarka came in to get her up. She would go to sleep clutching a tattered newspaper showing a picture of her son, known to others as "Abu'l Yusr." He had been a leading figure in the Palestinian organization al-Jihad al-Islami, and had been assassinated in Cyprus.

When she heard the news on the radio, her son's code name had meant nothing to her. However, the newspapers had published an account of his life, together with his real name. Nagi, who had brought the newspaper, hadn't meant anything by it when he set it down it unthinkingly in front of her.

The newspaper gave his real name—Riyad Abu Sharkh—and the story of his life from the time he'd been displaced as a young child and gone with his maternal uncle to Syria. It described how he had received his schooling in Homs, Syria before coming to Egypt, where he had enrolled in the Zagazig Medical School and established a jihad cell. The Egyptian security apparatus had overlooked the cell's existence in the beginning. But when Egyptian students began joining it in growing numbers, a deportation order was issued against him.

A fourth-year medical student at the time, he had left again for Syria, where he lived back and forth between Damascus and Beirut under the code name Abu'l Yusr. Eventually, however, he'd been found murdered in a hotel room in Cyprus, which he had entered with a Libyan passport under the assumed name Abd al-Salam al-Asfar.

When she finished reading the article, Zayna let out a single shriek, after which she didn't utter another word. They hadn't even succeeded in getting her to cry. Instead, she maintained a silence that she broke only to speak to him as if he were with her.

"What kind of a heart is this that couldn't sense it when you were right here beside me!"

The pain of the lost opportunity to hold him in her arms for the five years he'd spent in Zagazig overshadowed not only the pain of having had to part with him when Ziyad threw him onto the truck, but even the news of his death itself.

"None of those other things were under my control. But Zagazig..?!"

As far as she was concerned, all the other coincidences had been normal occurrences that might be expected to happen. But for her son to be so close without her heart perceiving it even in a dream—this was her own fault, and it was this that had struck her dumb and frozen the tears in her eyes.

Those fleeing from the mansion's sorrow were no less vulnerable to collapse as they fought for their lives, barely making ends meet in the face of the rising cost of living. In spite of their good jobs, they aspired in vain to imitate coworkers whose fathers were businessmen and highly paid professionals and those who, with the money they'd earned abroad, were driving fancy cars, wearing international clothing brands, and spending like maniacs.

"The man wasn't lying when he said the October War would be the last war with Israel," Mustafa said, commenting on the infamous statement made by Sadat, who had led the crossing of the Suez Canal and signed the peace treaty. He'd then devoted himself to growing a big dark spot on his forehead from all the prostrating he did in prayer and nurtured Islamist groups in the universities, opening the way for internecine wars that began after his body was riddled with bullets during the victory parade.

Distress crept into the voice of the man who had returned from the siege determined to love life. Mustafa Kamel, who had resisted illness to the best of his ability, couldn't help but note the irony that while the border war had ended, another, surfeit-induced war on his body had begun in the form of renal and liver failure, which had turned into a personal issue that he wasn't able to resolve. After rising to the rank of judicial advisor and becoming court president, Mustafa had developed a potbelly and his legs had filled with fluid that seeped down from his liver. As a man of the judiciary, it pained him to think that his imminent demise would be the result of a crime committed by some unidentified entity by means of contaminated food or water.

He renewed his ties to al-Ish, and every weekend the driver would take him there to spend two days away from his arguments with his wife and sons. They constantly criticized him for his eating habits given the deterioration in his liver from a hepatitis C infection. However, his purpose in coming to the village wasn't simply to get away from his family. He'd also started spending hours at the cemetery. He would wander up and down the rows of graves, getting to know his future neighbors, and would recite the Fatiha over their graves before resting in front of the family vault at sunset.

"I want to get used to the place," he said with a smile whenever they saw him come panting back, shaking the dust from his huge gilbab. He began renovating and repainting the family vault. He planted a mulberry tree, which he watered every week, and it started growing a handspan a day as though a devil were sleeping among its roots.

He would sit down with Ali for a tête-à-tête and start reminiscing nonstop about his conscription years—years when he'd done his most enjoyable reading—and about his passion for Umm Kulthum, Abd al-Wahhab, and Fayruz. As for the experience of the siege, it had taught him not to take life so seriously, but to treat it as though it were a scene from a movie or a play. His wife and cousin, Nagat, exhibited a motherly tolerance for the stories he told about pretty girls, the nature of his relationships with whom she didn't know for certain, because of the genuine delight that appeared on his face whenever he talked about any of them.

Even his sons loved his approach to life. He saw the essence of humanity in femininity, and the essence of justice in beauty. They would laugh when he described a pretty girl as "the nicest thing in the world," with good food ranking a close second. He was a master salad maker, having arrived by trial and error at the steps for their preparation, and he was constantly surprising them with the types of vegetables he would put in them. He'd figured out how to rescue his children from the lure of TV commercials for French fries and soft drinks, and had trained their taste buds to appreciate home-made foods with innovative blends of vegetables, meat, and fruit that he would pop into the oven in earthenware casserole dishes.

"These are no simple concoctions!" he would say to them in describing the culinary inventions that captured their childlike imaginations.

There came a time when he couldn't stand up in the kitchen any more, and for his sake, his children started to avoid asking for any kind of rich food. Like their mother, they wanted him to enjoy all the things he loved with the exception of the foods that would send him straight to the hospital, since that was where he always ended up if he stopped eating fat-free cheese and the like.

He chuckled as he told Ali about how he'd hit his son Magdi, to whom he referred affectionately as "the rascal," when, wanting to prevent him from going into a coma, he'd conspired with Nagat to put a lock on the refrigerator. But he didn't care about the refrigerator any more as long as there were restaurants that did home deliveries.

"Whenever I'm by myself, I order half a kilo of shish kebab. I eat the whole thing, then go to the hospital and turn myself in."

Anticipating a coma whenever he disobeyed the doctor's orders, he would walk to his room in the hospital before he had to be taken there on a stretcher. He also knew that sooner or later he would go into a coma and not come out again. One day he handed his Uncle Adel a marble slab inside a closed box, instructing him to affix it to the tomb when they opened the vault to put him inside. On it he had engraved a statement in which he addressed those who had come to bid him farewell: "Life is a miracle. Let me sleep now and go your way rejoicing, since your miracle is still happening."

Atiya heard a knock on the door, but when she got up to open it, no one was there.

"Who's there?" she called.

"Yusuf," someone answered. "Get up and go bury your grandmother."

Then she heard the sound of feet going down the stairs.

When she woke up the next morning she remembered clearly what had happened, but didn't know whether it had been real or a dream. And the person she'd heard speaking—had it been her father, whom she'd never seen? Or was it Yusuf Abd al-Maqsud? In any case, she responded to the summons, hoping that the person who had called her was the one who, of all the young men in the family, had been the most madly in love with her. If it was, that would mean enough time had passed for forgiveness to be possible.

She dressed in black, packed a small bag, got in her car, and drove to al-Ish. Despite her surprise at seeing that the village had doubled in size and that its houses had turned into multi-story buildings with unpainted brick walls like the ones in Cairo's slums, she knew her way to the tumbledown mansion. The car's loud rumble as it pulled up in front of the outer wall prompted Hagga Mubarka to look out toward the gate.

Seeing the woman standing before her with a small suitcase in her hand, she said, "So you've come back, you lioness?"

She asked the question in a tone that sounded more like a characterization of a distant past than an insult or rebuke, since the woman, who was nearly sixty years old by this time, had only the subtlest vestiges of her former allure, and only a finely tuned intuition would have enabled one to recognize what she'd looked like in her youth. She bore a distinct resemblance to Mubarka herself at the time when, after her sojourn in Zagazig, she had brought her back as an infant in her half-sister's arms.

When she walked into the mansion, she didn't smell the stench of death—the stench of the vomit and feces she'd crawled through during the cholera epidemic. She didn't smell the mingled fragrances of rumi cheese, sesame halawa, oil, and ghee that used to waft out of the pantry. Nor was she overwhelmed by the aromas of savory foods and vanilla pudding that had once filled the mansion before they loaded them onto a horse-drawn cart with a loaf of round flat bread and a jug of water for the factory workers' lunch.

The only smell left was that of three women's old bones, which reminded her of the smell of babies' diapers.

Even the smell of filth that Hanem had given off in Atiya's absence wasn't there any more, now that Ali and Adel had left. Their sons had gone to Italy, then come back and built apartment buildings on al-Ish's main road that were filled with so many grandchildren that people had lost count of them. No one was left in the mansion now but Mubarka, Mas'ada, and Zayna, who all looked the same age despite the fact that one of them was nearly as old as the other two put together. As Atiya looked at the three women, it occurred to her that there must be an age beyond which time can't leave any new fingerprints on a person's body.

"Well, are you just going to go on standing there?" Mas'ada asked her. With the hem of her gilbab she dusted off a place next to them on the bench, whose legs had sunk into the ground. Atiya sat down and set her suitcase between her feet.

"Will you have some coffee?" Zayna asked to break a silence that had gone on too long. Without waiting for an answer, she got

254

up and brought a tray holding the coffeepot, the alcohol burner, and three cups, the sight of which made Atiya catch her breath. They were the cone-shaped, handleless cups that weren't made any more—the same cups her grandfather Salama had used. Zayna lit the alcohol burner and set the coffeepot on top of it, and the same silence returned. She felt as though she were in a contest with the other three women to see who could hold out the longest. She wanted them to talk, and they wanted to hear what she had to say.

Finally, Mubarka said to her, "Aren't you going to change your clothes?"

Feeling as though her grandmother had thrown her a lifeline, she picked up her suitcase and went inside. The three women followed her, and Mas'ada indicated that she could choose whichever room she wanted, since all the rooms on the first floor were empty, and all three women slept in the same bed in Mubarka's room.

"That way we can watch out for each other," Zayna explained. However, Atiya decided to sleep in her own room on the second floor. The moment she put one foot over the threshold, she sneezed violently from the smell of the dirt and moths in the abandoned room. She stood there filled with a strange feeling when she saw the same bed, the wardrobe where she'd hidden so many secrets among her clothes, and the crisscross lines—as crisscrossed as the trajectory of her life—that she'd drawn on the windowsill as she stood amusing herself with the sight of the young men roaming about below. It took her a long time to find a way to describe the mixture of excitement, fear, bliss, curiosity, and angst that came over her at that moment. But at last she found the right analogy.

"It was like being trapped inside a falling elevator."

She wasn't sure whether her listeners knew what it would mean to be in an elevator hurtling dizzyingly to the ground. However, this was the closest she could come to expressing the feeling she'd experienced when she found herself face to face with her girlhood. She began studying the drawings and lines that had been added to her own on the windowsill, the doors of the wardrobe, and the walls, trying to gather something about the genders and ages of those who had occupied the room after her. The most important hint left by the passage of time was the pages torn out of magazines, which confirmed that the room's last occupant had been a boy, not a girl, since glossy photos of Haifa Wehbe, Nancy Ajram, and Ruby had replaced her idols—Abd al-Halim Hafez, Ahmad Ramzi, and Omar Sharif, with their faded colors on matte paper. She spent that night cleaning the room as though she were trying to reinforce an inward urge to stay. After all, it wouldn't have made any sense for her to make all that effort for the sake of just a day or two.

Yusuf was the first person who came to see her, two days after her arrival. She was taken aback at his unexpected obesity, which made him look older than her. However, even being poised on the brink of old age hadn't made his voice any more confident. He began stammering the way he'd always done whenever he was alone with her somewhere, and he exhibited the same nervousness that had shown up in his handwriting and in the breathless pace of the sentences in his incoherent epistles.

She listened to him like someone in a hypnotic trance. He was delighted by her distractedness, imagining that she'd finally come to realize how attached he had been to her and had begun to reciprocate his feelings. However, she'd simply been listening to his voice, startled by how perfectly it matched the voice she'd heard in her dream. She started to ask him about that night's visit, then thought better of it, and told him instead about how she wanted to stay in al-Ish. She asked him to help her bring her furniture from the apartment where she'd lived alone since her husband's passing.

"Abd al-Fattah?" Yusuf asked in disbelief, as if amazed that death had gotten the better of the carpenter. It didn't surprise Atiya that he remembered his name after all that time.

"No, my second husband," she said sadly, as though to apologize for the escapade that had changed the course of her life. The carpenter had taken her to Bulaq al-Dakrur, where she found herself imprisoned at the top of a building that housed his workshop on the first floor and, on the second floor, the apartment where his wife and children lived. The third floor consisted of two rooms at one end of the roof. Outside the rooms was an open area that he hosed down at the end of the day before spreading out a mat where he received his friends at night. She'd lived for two years in those two unpainted rooms, which he referred to as the "feel-good apartment."

When she asked for a divorce, he hadn't objected, as if he'd been expecting it, and they separated like a couple of strangers who'd met at a crossroads. She'd found a job as a cosmetics marketing representative and decided to complete her education. It would have been impossible for her to resume her studies at the Faculty of Medicine, so she withdrew her papers and registered as a first-year student in the Faculty of Commerce. When she graduated, she hadn't needed her university degree as anything but a souvenir. She made her way up the ranks in the private company, and married an accountant who worked there. But they'd had no children.

"The problem was with me," she said. "But Misbah wouldn't leave me."

He had lived with her until his death ten years earlier. She had applied for early retirement, which, together with the pension she received through her husband, was enough to meet her simple needs. She had lived alone and only left her apartment every few days, since there were no longer any sidewalks good enough to walk on. She would buy what she needed for the next several days and come home with a headache from the exhaust fumes, which irritated her sinuses.

The men of the family began flocking to the mansion to see the returned aunt, who didn't feel the kind of distress she'd experienced during her stay with them in Dokki, where they had camouflaged their physical desires for her beneath hypocritical expressions of romantic interest. Instead, she recaptured the hazy, enjoyable feeling she'd had in the beginning of their adolescent years in al-Ish, when she hadn't been able to tell whether their interest in her was simply male admiration, or brotherly love and the desire to protect her as a member of the family. As for them, they couldn't pinpoint exactly why they were so exhilarated by her presence: Was it the old infatuation? Or were they just happy to be reopening a chapter of their earlier lives? Either way, their visits began restoring vitality to the mansion. Sometimes they would leave their grandchildren with "Grandma Atiya," who would entertain herself with them on the computers their fathers had sent from Italy. They would log on to the Internet, and Hagga Mubarka would look with them in fascination at the abundance of pictures and words. They wowed her with a map of the Earth, which they began enlarging until Egypt took up the entire screen. Then they kept on enlarging it so that they could zoom in on Sharqiya. When they located al-Ish for her and enlarged it until the mansion came clearly into view, she murmured a prayer for God's forgiveness, as though this kind of bird's-eye view was an encroachment on God's prerogatives. They showed her their email and opened letters for her from Canadian, German, and Japanese friends whom they'd never met.

Clapping her hands, she exclaimed, "There's nothing a person can't find out any more!"

Her mind wandered for a few moments as she thought back on the amazement she'd felt the first time she listened to a radio and saw the images on a television screen.

"Do you know how to send God a message on that thing?" she asked.

Then they knew she was going to start complaining about the way death kept passing her by, while at the same time wearing her out with the loss of children and grandchildren.

Hagga Mubarka was sitting on the bench in front of the mansion wall in the timid March sun, when suddenly there wafted in her direction a breeze laden with a scent that had nested in her memory for she didn't know how many years.

As she sniffed the air, the intensifying waves left her no room for doubt. Then she saw someone approaching with a small backpack slung over his shoulder. She felt blood gushing through her lifeless veins. Her hands trembled so violently that they started knocking against each other in front of her chest, and she let out a faint gasp.

"Muntasir!"

Her voice was muffled, not because of weakness, but out of fear for her dignity since, having endured the indignity of losing her mobility, she wasn't prepared to tolerate the indignity of sounding like a senile old woman. As the figure continued his approach, she uttered a prayer for God's protection. Astonishment raised her sagging eyelids as high as they would go. When at last he stood in front of her, his scent closed in on her so entirely that no doubt remained in her mind.

She narrowed her eyes and looked hard at him: He had the same stocky build, the same barrel chest, the same horse's neck, the same round, dark face with a dimple on either side, and the same eyes with their deep black irises and their whites as white as snow. It was Muntasir himself, only he'd gone back to being a young man, just

259

the way he had been when he left. He leaned over and kissed the trembling hands as she babbled in a voice that was barely audible.

"Muntasir? Muntasir? No! No!"

Her fingers fluttering, she took hold of his face and ran her hands over it with tremulous strokes. Not noticing how long his head had been in her hands, she pushed him gently away, saying, "Protect me, Lord . . . protect me from the Devil!"

"But I *am* Muntasir," said the young man, squatting before her. "I'm his grandson. His grandson, Grandmother!"

The tremors in her hands stopped and, although she kept up her murmuring, her eyes glistened with renewed vitality. She didn't believe what she had just heard, doubtful of Nature's ability to produce such a perfect replica. She began scrutinizing him again in search of some mark, however subtle, that time might have left on him, still convinced that he was Muntasir in the flesh and that all that time he'd been hiding somewhere inaccessible to the moths that had eaten away at her own body.

She smoothed out a place beside her and gestured to him to sit down. The scent surrounded her again, and she resumed her dazed contemplation of his face. Could two people be so much alike that even their sweat smelled the same? It was the same scent she hadn't been able to find a description for the first time she'd inhaled it, and which she'd referred to as a "manly smell." Later she'd detected it in Nagi as well, and she'd realized that it resembled the smell of the pollen of a male palm tree.

She gestured again to Muntasir, who grasped her under her arms and lifted her up. She began hopping about in front of him like a lame duck on top of the neglected pieces of paper and plastic bags that filled the street. Supporting herself on the mansion gate, she opened it, and Muntasir helped her up onto the threshold while continuing to support her back. She collapsed onto the bench inside the wall and he sat down beside her, happily sniffing the goose and rabbit droppings and gazing thoughtfully at the house, which looked like a sunlit clearing amid the towering buildings that encircled it.

The women gathered around the guest, listening to him without understanding what connection he had to the family, since even the oldest of them hadn't been born yet when Muntasir senior migrated from al-Ish. However, the glimmer in Mubarka's eyes told them how dear the visitor was to her. Mas'ada made him coffee while Atiya went off to get a room ready for him, and for the first time since Nagiya's passing, they tasted food prepared by the sorrowful "pretty Palestinian," who picked up something of the scent of Palestine in Muntasir. She felt certain that if Riyad had lived a normal life like other people, she would have been preparing this meal for her own grandson.

He was flooded with a sense of strength and stability that confirmed the impression he'd had the moment he got out of the minibus that had brought him to al-Ish: that he'd arrived at last in the place where he belonged. At the same time, he began looking for opportunities to be alone so that he could open up the photo album he always kept close at hand. He wanted to feast his eyes on the picture of his wife Nazek as she threw their little girl Maysa into the air and caught her in her arms on Kuwait's corniche in a moment of happiness they both had expected to last. When he knew he was alone, he would burst into silent tears, relieved that he hadn't found himself obliged to offer any explanations for how he'd ended up in al-Ish, since he'd learned from previous experience that talking about his woes might create misery for others without relieving his own.

He was haunted by images of their deaths after a week of wandering lost in the desert. During that time the jerrican of water and the meager provisions they had brought ran out. He'd been consumed with grief as he watched the baby girl wasting away. He would leave her with her mother in the shade of the car that stood immersed in the sand and walk around in search of some sign of human life. After going just a few steps, he would come back exhausted from wading through the deep blazing dunes. He would come back to find Nazek holding Maysa against her chest. Her skin hanging loose over her delicate bones, the poor baby girl struggled to open her eyelids, now wrinkled like those of an old woman, to look up at her parents with questioning eyes.

When she died, Nazek closed her withered jaws. Muntasir dug a hole, placed her inside it, and began strewing the sand gently over her as though he were tucking her blanket tightly around her in her crib as he was used to doing on cold nights. Taking the dark-skinned doll that Maysa had loved and never parted with, Nazek buried it in an upright position with its head above ground so that they could locate the grave and take their daughter's body back with them if they were rescued.

They were so weakened and wasted they couldn't even cry. Once their saliva had dried up, their tear ducts had done the same. Nazek sat mutely beside the hole while Muntasir shuffled around the car, watching and waiting for any movement, whether on the ground or in the sky. He had his shirt ready to wave as a flag, but no one appeared for two more days.

The blueness of the sky and the yellowness of the earth blended in the distance as their lips cracked and their skin began to hang loosely on their bodies. There wasn't an edible insect in sight, nor a bird in the sky to bear glad tidings of life nearby. No longer able to exchange words of comfort as they had done in the first few days, they began instead to communicate through feeble signals. He tried to talk her into the idea of drinking their sparse urine. She refused.

"I don't suppose there's much point in living after this kind of degradation," she said, and closed her eyes. He didn't even have the strength to bury her.

He remembered, as though it had been a dream, the helicopter that had landed like a hawk and carried him away in the restful numbness of coma. He'd woken on a bed that stood in a long row, with a glucose solution being fed into his veins through a tube that hung down to his wrist. From the hospital ward's rectangular sky, Nazek's parched face peered down at him with eyes whose whites had turned into an eerie abyss.

As Muntasir began adjusting to the family, he would go to visit Ali, who lived independently on the ground floor of his son's house. He would listen to Ali's political analyses and opinions, which, with Muntasir's return, had broadened to include all Arabs.

"People are gullible, you know—their brains are mushy as crap—but I smell a rat here," Ali pontificated, his words bringing more of a smile to Muntasir's lips than pain to his heart. His flight from the US invasion of Iraq hadn't been his first flight, but he hoped it would be his last.

Muntasir had never seen his mother, and had left Jordan for Iraq when he was a little boy. All he could remember of his life in Amman was the moment of flight, when his father woke him on a stiflingly hot night, then picked him up, still groggy, and placed him in a car that sped off. Morning broke for them in Basra, which was the only city he had truly known. When he fell in love with Nazek, his father had agreed to their marriage only grudgingly, since he had lived twenty years on pins and needles like a guest getting ready to go home. All that time he'd wanted nothing more than to go back to Khan Yunis so that he could die there after marrying his son to a Palestinian girl who could understand him, and whom he could understand.

When the war with Iran dragged on interminably, having consumed as many of Iraq's young men as it could, resident Palestinians and Egyptians came in for harassment in attempts to get them to volunteer in the army. Nazek wrote to her uncle, an engineer in Kuwait, asking him to arrange work for Muntasir. But they had only been there a couple of years when the Iraqi army entered the little emirate, and back they went to Basra. By that time, however, the Americans had laid another plan.

When phosphorus bombs lit up Basra's sky, Muntasir opened the amulet he'd received from his father with the key to the house in Palestine.

"Open it only as a last resort." Those instructions, which Murid had received from his father Muntasir, he had passed on to his son Magid, who had passed them on in turn to his son Muntasir before dying from an asthma attack. When Muntasir opened the amulet, he found that it wasn't actually an amulet, as he'd expected it to be. All he found inside was a piece of paper wrapped in a lock of black hair. The paper contained instructions on how to get to al-Ish, Mubarka's name, and the story of the aborted engagement. Her eyes began to glisten when Muntasir placed the lock of hair in her hand.

A week after his arrival in al-Ish, Muntasir began making regular trips to Cairo. He would photocopy papers and submit the documents he'd brought back with him to the Kuwaiti and Iraqi embassies, claiming his right to compensation for the property he'd lost and for unpaid wages in the two countries. He persisted in his trips to the city, and when he returned, he always found the elderly woman who was supposed to be his grandmother waiting for him.

Hagga Mubarka began testing her legs' ability to carry her, and by leaning on Muntasir she finally managed to stand on her feet. She also went back to issuing orders.

She gave instructions for the mansion to be cleaned, especially the second floor, which had descended into chaos. The wind and rain had wrought havoc on its windows, whose cracked paint looked like fish scales on wood that had taken on the putrid odor of old boats. She also issued orders for her spacious northerly room to be given to Muntasir.

She personally oversaw the workers who repainted the walls and the distinctive blue windows, and the process of laying the floor with traditional cement tiles decorated with branches and flowers—tiles that weren't produced anywhere any more but in a particular factory in Bilbeis. Once the renovations were complete, the garden was replanted with trees after being cleared of piles of trash, bird coops, and abandoned stoves that the women had set up before taking their families to the new houses.

Hagga Mubarka sat on the veranda gazing thoughtfully at the mansion, which had easily shed thirty or forty years and regained its youth, though no one, of course, could restore to it the voices of those who had left. From inside she could hear the voice of Sheikh

Mustafa Ismail that she so loved chanting Surat Yusuf, the twelfth chapter of the Qur'an. When the recitation came to the part where Potiphar's wife says to a gathering of women, "This, then, is he about whom you have been blaming me! And, indeed, I did try to make him yield himself unto me, but he remained chaste. Now, however, if he does not do what I bid him, he shall most certainly be imprisoned, and shall most certainly find himself among the despised!" she muttered, "You idiot, who asked you for an explanation or confession?"

She only became aware of Muntasir's presence when she heard him laughing.

Addressing herself to him, she said, "The stupid woman brought shame on herself, and I'll bet she never lived it down!"

"Grandma," he said, "how much did you love my grandpa?" It wasn't a serious question—he just wanted to make sure she was still alive, since he saw in her face the same pallor he'd seen the moment he arrived in al-Ish.

Her hands trembling more and more violently, she cried, "God damn my father, wherever he ended up!"

Then she withdrew into silence as her eyes caught a glimmer of a chapter of her life that the passing of the days had never succeeded in closing.

GLOSSARY

Arak: A colorless, anise-flavored distilled alcoholic drink.

Asaliya: A sweet made by boiling molasses until it becomes a dark syrup, then letting it cool and solidify enough to be molded into various shapes. It can also be sprinkled with ground peanuts or roasted sesame seeds.

Asida: A thick porridge, similar to polenta, often eaten with molasses.

At the foot of the pyramid: A reference to the Battle of Imbaba, also known as the Battle of the Pyramids, fought between Napoleon's army in Egypt and forces led by local Mamluk rulers on July 21, 1798. Napoleon named it the Battle of the Pyramids due to the fact that the pyramids were visible on the horizon from the spot where the battle took place.

Bashmuhandis: "Chief engineer," used as a term of respect.

Bilbeis: A small, densely populated ancient fortress city on the eastern edge of Egypt's southern Nile Delta.

Burqa: The eastern part of present-day Libya.

"Cover me up and wail over me": An old saying referring to a trick employed to avoid taxes. When the tax collector came around, the man of the household would lie down and his wife would cover him up and begin wailing over him as if he were dead. Later, the saying came to be applied to other situations. If, for example, someone tried to get an older man who'd been widowed to marry again but he feared he might not be able to have sex, he might say, "What? Shall I tell her to cover me up and wail over me?"

The crossing: This refers to the massive crossing of the Suez Canal by Egyptian forces on October 6, 1973 that initiated what has come to be known as the Yom Kippur War.

al-Deeb: The name al-Deeb literally means "the wolf."

Dhikr: Literally, 'mentioning' or 'remembering,' the term *dhikr* refers to the repetition of words and phrases as a means of holding God in remembrance. It also refers to a gathering in which such words or phrases are repeated, along with singing, chanting, and, at times, dancing as a form of worship and spiritual ecstasy.

"Fast every Monday and Thursday": The practice of fasting on Mondays and Thursdays is seen by Muslims as a way of emulating the Prophet Muhammad. Its relevance to Mubarka's attempts to avoid physical intimacy with Mugahid is due to the fact that fasting within an Islamic context includes abstention from sexual activity.

Fatta: A dish made of dry bread with rice, in a garlicky broth.

Feddan: A feddan is equal to 4,200 m², 0.42 hectares, or 1.038 acres.

Gallabiya: A long, flowing garment with billowing sleeves, a collarless neck, and slit that extends approximately six inches down the front.

Ibrahim Bey (1735–1817): Born in eastern Georgia and converted to Islam after being captured by Ottoman slave raiders who then sold him in Egypt, Ibrahim Bey became an influential Mamluk commander who shared de facto rule of Egypt for a time with his fellow Georgian Murad Bey. He died in obscurity after his reign was effectively brought to an end by his defeat at the hands of the French.

Gilbab: A long, flowing robe with long, billowing sleeves that opens at the front.

Kayla: A dry measure equal to 16.72 liters.

Keddah: Arabic *qadah*, a keddah is a dry measure equal to approximately one liter.

Kunafa: Vermicelli baked with sugar, melted butter, and honey.

"Leave the bathwater in the tub until midmorning . . .": Hafiza wanted to ensure that others saw that she and her husband had bathed earlier in the morning, since Islam requires a ritual bath to be taken by anyone who has had sexual intercourse due to the state of ritual impurity it brings about, and she was anxious for others to know of her husband's renewed interest in her.

Ma'zun: An official authorized by an Islamic court to perform civil marriages.

Mansur: The name Mansur means "granted victory," while the name Muntasir means "victorious."

Maybe you grabbed a cat's tail: This statement, made by Mubarka's father, reflects a popular belief that grabbing hold of a cat's tail will afflict the person with a curse that causes him or her to drop things. This, in turn, is based on superstitions claiming that cats are possessed by jinn.

Muhammad Farid: A member of Egypt's land-owning aristocracy, Muhammad Farid (1868–1919) was an influential politician and lawyer of Turkish ancestry who provided political and financial support to Mustafa Kamel, founder of Egypt's National Party. Following Kamel's untimely death in 1908, Farid took over the party leadership, which he maintained until his death. Farid called for the withdrawal of Britain's occupation army and advocated wide-ranging social, economic, and educational reforms in Egypt.

Mulid: Annual public celebrations held on the occasion of the birth of the Prophet Muhammad or local Muslim saints.

Mulukhiya: "Jews' mallow," a green leafy vegetable that is made into a thick soup and often served with chicken and rice.

Murad Bey: Of Georgian origin, Murad Bey (1750–1801) was a Mamluk chieftain and cavalry commander who ruled Egypt jointly with Ibrahim Bey. After being defeated by the French at the Battle of the Pyramids on July 21, 1798, Murad Bey fled to Upper Egypt, where he launched a guerrilla campaign to stave off French forces. He died of bubonic plague while on his way to Cairo after making peace with Jean-Baptiste Kléber.

Mustafa Kamel: Mustafa Kamel (1874–1908) was an Egyptian lawyer, journalist, and nationalist. He passionately supported Egypt's khedive, Abbas Hilmi II, who opposed Britain's occupation of Egypt and Sudan. He founded Egypt's National Party in December 1907, only two months before his death

Nakba: Meaning "catastrophe," the Arabic word 'nakba' is widely used to refer to the mass dispossession, displacement, and dispersal of the Palestinian people following the establishment of the state of Israel in May 1948.

Naksa: Meaning "setback," the Arabic word 'naksa' is used to refer to the defeat of the Egyptian-Jordanian-Syrian allied forces in the Six-Day War of 1967.

Qibla: The qibla is the direction in which a Muslim is expected to pray, that is, facing Mecca.

Recite the Fatiha: When families have agreed that a marriage will take place between two of their members, the initial formality is to recite the Fatiha, which is the opening chapter of the Qur'an.

Saad Zaghlul: An Egyptian revolutionary and statesman, Saad Zaghlul (1859–1927) was known for his active opposition to Britain's occupation of Egypt and Sudan. His exile to Malta and the Seychelles sparked the Egyptian Revolution of 1919. Zaghlul was the founder of Egypt's Wafd party, as head of which he served as Egypt's prime minister from January 26, 1924 to November 24, 1924.

Salep: *Sahlab* in Arabic, salep is a sweet, creamy drink made from a flour derived from the tubers of the orchid genus Orchis.

Shubra Khit: The Battle of Shubra Khit took place between Napoleon's forces and Mamluk forces on July 13, 1798.

Siga: A simplified form of chess.

Sultan Hussein Kamel: Hussein Kamel (1853–1917) was sultan of Egypt from 1914 to 1917. Hussein Kamel was the son of Khedive Isma'il Pasha, who ruled Egypt from 1863 to 1879. In November 1914, the British forces deposed Hussein Kamel's nephew,

Khedive Abbas Hilmi II, and declared Hussein Kamel sultan of Egypt a month later. The newly created Sultanate of Egypt was then declared a British protectorate, thereby bringing an end to more than a century of de jure Ottoman rule.

Surat Yusuf: The verse quoted from Surat Yusuf on page 265 is Qur'an 12:32, taken from Muhammad Asad, *The Message of the Qur'an* (Gibraltar: Dar al-Andalus, 1984), p. 341.

Ta'miya: The Egyptian word for falafel.

Tasbih: Meaning "praise," tasbih involves repeating certain phrases such as "Glory be to God!" (subhan Allah), "Praise be to God!" (al-hamdu lillah), and "God is greatest!" (Allahu akbar), particularly after finishing one of the five Islamic daily prayers.

Zagazig: A town located in the eastern part of the Nile Delta and capital of the Governorate of Sharqiya. Zagazig is a center of Egypt's cotton and grain trade.

Modern Arabic Literature

The American University in Cairo Press is the world's leading publisher of Arabic literature in translation.

For a full list of available titles, please go to:

mal.aucpress.com